the strange children

BOOKS BY CAROLINE GORDON

ALECK MAURY, SPORTSMAN
THE GARDEN OF ADONIS
GREEN CENTURIES
NONE SHALL LOOK BACK
OLD RED AND OTHER STORIES
PENHALLY
THE STRANGE CHILDREN
THE WOMEN ON THE PORCH

Reissued by Cooper Square Publishers, Inc.

CAROLINE GORDON

the strange children

Cooper Square Publishers, Inc.
New York
1971

Originally Published 1951

Reprinted by Permission of Charles Scribner's Sons
Published 1971 by Cooper Square Publishers, Inc.
59 Fourth Avenue, New York, N. Y. 10003
International Standard Book No. 0-8154-0394-1
Library of Congress Catalog Card No. 71-164525

Printed in the United States of America, by
Noble Offset Printers, Inc. New York, N.Y. 10003

TO

MARY MERIWETHER FERGUSON GORDON

AND

MORRIS MERIWETHER GORDON

"Rid me, and deliver me from the hand of strange children, whose mouth speaketh vanity . . ."

PSALM 144

the strange children

I

AT three o'clock in the afternoon the house became so quiet that you imagined that you could hear the river lapping softly at the foot of the green hill. Lucy Lewis was sitting in the window seat in the dining room, reading "Undine." She looked up, disturbed by the unusual stillness. At this hour of the day, Jenny, the cook, was usually moving about in the kitchen, washing the luncheon dishes, but Jenny had said that she had a toothache and had gone to her cabin right after lunch, without washing a dish. "Don't touch a dish, Jenny!" Lucy's mother had said before she went upstairs to take a nap. (*She* took a nap every day after lunch. It was the only way she could stand life, she said.) Lucy glanced about the room again uneasily. From over the mantel, Stonewall Jackson, blue-eyed, black-bearded, his uniform without stain or wrinkle, stared past her unseeingly. They said that he had been killed when he was young, but he looked like an old man.

She thrust her hand down among the pillows of the window seat. When she had started reading an hour ago something warm and silky had rested its comfortable weight against her leg, but now the pillows were cool to the touch. Borcke, the dachshund, had got restless and had padded upstairs to her mother's room; nothing he liked better than a nap on the foot of somebody's bed. Her mother had said that she would not sleep long. In fact, she could not: somebody was coming, somebody who had telephoned while they were at lunch to say that he was on the road. Her father had said, "Well, I'll be damned!" when her mother gave him the news. Her mother, too, had seemed excited. Lucy, herself, had been busy concealing her book under the cloth—she was not allowed to read at the table—and had not heard the visitor's name.

She thought now that it did not make any difference who it was. It was always the same when they had guests, particularly guests who came from far away. They would get out on the upper gallery with their drinks and then discover that they didn't have enough ice or cigarettes or gin or something, and keep her running up and downstairs till her legs dropped off. She stretched her legs out in front of her and looking down at them wished that they were plumper. "*Your* legs are so *thi . . . in*!" her friend, Lois Taylor, had said, lying on her back in the middle of the bed, extending her leg high in the air and then bending it a little so that the dimple in the knee showed. Lois was ten years old, almost a year older than Lucy. She had light hair, which she wore long, like Lucy, but where Lucy's eyes were grey, hers were brown. There was a heifer down in the lot with eyes exactly the color of Lois', "only more spiritual looking," Lucy's mother said.

Lucy got up and went to the window and looked towards Gloversville. The heat that shimmered over the cornfields made it seem very far away. She could hardly make out the clock tower of the courthouse and the cross on the Catholic church seemed no larger than a bent pin. Her eyes went to a dark green blot west of the church: the wooded hill on which Lois lived. It was hard to believe that yesterday at this time she had been there, sitting with Lois in the swing on the latticed back porch. Ellen, Lois' older sister, had made banana ice cream in the two-gallon freezer and had called Lois and Lucy in from the yard to lick the dasher. Mrs. Taylor, Lois' mother, had left her sewing and had drawn a rocker up beside the swing to eat a few spoonfuls of the ice cream that fell off the dasher. Mrs. Taylor weighed nearly two hundred pounds and was always sewing something for one of the girls. She had not wanted Lucy to come home today, but Lucy's mother had said that a visit had to end some time: "She can't *live* with you all, Mrs. Taylor!" Lucy, staring into Stonewall Jackson's implacable eyes, thought that she might enjoy going to live with the Taylors. There were enough of *them* to fill a house: Ellen, Margery, Fred, Tom, Lois and Mr. and Mrs. Taylor. One could not imagine their house ever being quiet. If you waked in the middle of the night there you heard some car passing by or the courthouse clock striking the hour. But in this house, brick-walled, high-ceilinged, cool, there were rooms where nobody ever went, or only rarely. Her father stayed in his study most of the day. If he walked about in the yard it was to think about General Lee or Stonewall Jackson and you mustn't disturb him. (If you disturbed a person while he was thinking about his book his idea might get away from him and he might be as much as a month getting it back.) Her mother was in her bedroom, painting or reading or taking a nap—when she wasn't doing the housework. Jenny, their cook, was always telling them that her grandmother was sick and going off with her beau, Mr. Stamper. "Is it the *malade imaginaire* again?" her father had asked at lunch. Her mother had made him hush so Jenny wouldn't hear him. "It's toothache this time," she said, "her own tooth." Jenny had piled the luncheon dishes in the sink and had gone down to the cabin "to sleep it off," she said. If Jenny hadn't had the toothache she and Lucy might have gone for a walk in the woods; they often walked there at this time of day.

The house was built into the side of a hill. On the east side tall columns supported double galleries that looked out over the river, but on the west side the dining room windows were level with the ground. Lucy went now to the west window and kneeling on the long window seat looked out on the lawn. The ground in front of the house was planted with old-fashioned shrubs: crape myrtle, althea, lilac, some of them so old that they had grown as tall as trees. Beyond them a drive ran between scraggly cedars, to the foot of the long slope. Jenny's cabin stood there. It was shaded only by the trumpet vines which Jenny herself had planted about it, but outside the gate, on the other side of the road, the shade was dense—under "the Holy Roller tree," as her mother and father called the big maple that shaded "the Holy Roller Rock." The Holy Rock was as big as Jenny's cabin. Painted on it in white letters a foot high were the words: PREPARE TO MEET THY GOD! When they had first come here to live her mother had said, every time they drove through the gate, that it made her nervous to see those words there on the rock. She had wanted her husband to ask their tenant, Mr. MacDonough, who was an elder in the Holy Roller church, to have the letters removed, but he said that they did not own the land on that side of the road; the rock was none of their business. Sarah Lewis had planted some sprigs of ivy at the base of the rock. When the MacDonough children played there with Lucy they sometimes pointed out how the ivy grew all over the rock but never grew over the letters. None of those children were Sanctified yet, but they all acted as if they were.

It occurred to Lucy that they would be coming home from school soon, or if they were kept in, as often happened, Jenny might have waked from her nap and might be persuaded to take a walk. She got up, walked softly out of the dining room and around the corner of the house on to the graveled drive. The book she had been holding under her arm fell to the gravel with a light clatter. She stooped and, picking it up, looked with affection at the blue cover that had silver waves curving over it. In the hollow of the tallest wave, foam breaking all over it, was a little scroll with the letters UNDINE. It was her mother's copy that they had got out of the old walnut bookcase in her great-grandmother's parlor, the last time they were at Merry Point. Her mother had not allowed her to take the book with her to town. "I don't want you losing my 'Undine'," she had said.

Lucy went with a brisker step down the long driveway and paused before Jenny's cabin. The door was shut, the blinds drawn down. Lucy waited a few minutes. There was no sound. She passed through the gate and crossing the road, approached the big rock. Ivy grew all about its base, thick enough and dark enough to make a home for snakes. She set her foot on the lowest ledge and sprang up without touching a leaf. The rock was old and worn here and there in great hollows. The letters went across the rock zigzag. She looked at them, asking herself which letter she would sit down on. Once when she and Jenny and Lois were sitting here, waiting for the mailman, Lois, laughing, had insisted on sitting on the "A" in PREPARE. But Jenny shook her head and did not laugh. "Nice little girls don't talk like that," she said. Lois had never liked Jenny much after that, and Lucy, herself, had been embarrassed about sitting on the letters since then. She sat down now in the crook of the great R and opened her book.

It fell open at the place where she had left off. The aged, pious fisherman, sitting beside his nets in the cool of the evening, about to sing a holy psalm "with clear throat and upright heart," heard "in the darkness of the forest the rustling sound as of a man on horseback. . . ."

Looking down at the words, she felt a sense of secret power. A long time ago, when she had first begun to read, she had marked her place with a blade of grass, a turned down page, a strand of her own light brown hair, but nowadays she did not need to do that. Her book always fell open at the right place. She read on:

> A handsome knight, richly adorned . . . came riding on horseback toward the cottage through the shadows of the trees. A mantle of scarlet hung down over his violet-blue doublet, embroidered with gold; out of his gold-colored cap sprang plumes of red and violet blue; in his golden baldric blazed an extremely beautiful and richly damasked sword. The white charger which carried the knight was slighter of build than is common among steeds of war, and stepped so lightly over the greensward that his hoofs seemed to leave no impression on the delicate verdure. . . .

There was a breeze from the north. The shadows of the maple leaves wavered to and fro across her page, light, aqueous; she might have been sitting to read in the bed of a running brook. Dreamily, she raised her eyes. The house was still there, on top of the hill: an old brick house, whitewashed but so long ago that here and there a brick showed rosy through the wash. You could not see the galleries from here, but you could see the west side and the ell. The north wall of the ell was unbroken except for two tiny windows just under the eaves. Those windows and the bare wall had always reminded Lucy of eyes squinting in a blank face, a face that stayed blank so that you would not know what was going on behind it. *Nothing ever happens, Nothing will ever happen,* she thought, and her eyes left the house and went to the bridge that spanned the river. Its rails and girders shone in the fierce afternoon sunlight as if they had been molten. Where the long shadow of the bridge fell the water was almost the color of copper, in other places olive-green. Something glinted on the other side of the water; a car had just rolled up on to the bridge. The man in the car drove slowly, resting his left arm on the side of the car and looking down into the yellowish-green water. The river looked yellow because it was Dog Days, the time of year when it was too hot to swim, her mother said. . . . She herself would like to live at the bottom of a brook or lake. Her hut would be built of reeds. She would wear a crown of water lilies on her hair and busy herself all day long with her housekeeping: stringing little parti-colored shells on wisps of water grass, or plaiting, perhaps out of osiers, a little cage in which she would keep a seahorse for a pet. . . . A lock of her long, light brown hair had fallen over her forehead. She shook it back and opened her eyes wider. The car had not proceeded along the river road as she had taken for granted that it would. It had left the highway and even at this moment was halting beside the rock: a dark green convertible, with its top lowered. A big, curly-headed man sat at the wheel. His coffee-colored suit was splashed here and there, as if he had driven through the river instead of over it. He sat and looked at her. His eyes were brown and shone. He said:

"Sabrina fair! Listen where thou art sitting!"

Lucy stared at him and said nothing.

He shook his head. He looked up at the old brick house,

crouched on the hill, and then back at her. He said: "This is the place, all right. Signs and wonders do attest it. . . ."

He was out of the car and up on the rock beside her. He had seized her in his long arms and was swinging her up over his head.

A thin scream burst from Lucy, then, horrorstruck, she compressed her lips and looked stoically into his upturned face. A few golden hairs were mingled with the glossy brown hairs of his eyebrows. The eyes themselves gleamed, the way a chestnut gleams when the burr first falls away from it. To look into them was, for her, like falling into tumbling water. She shut her own eyes and did not open them until she felt herself being set down gently on the rock.

He was kneeling beside her. He put his hand out and gave her shoulder a quick pressure. His green-brown eyes darted merry gleams at her. He said:

"Two . . . weeks ago . . . today . . . *where* . . . do you suppose . . . I was?"

She resisted the impulse to draw away from him. "I don't know," she said faintly.

"At Rumpelmeyer's," he said.

She did not answer.

"At *Rumpelmeyer's*," he repeated. "There was a fat man in a fez sitting at our table. What do you suppose that old devil was doing?"

She lowered her gaze from his face to a clump of grass that grew in a fissure in the rock. "I don't know," she said again.

He released her, and straightening himself to his full height, shook his head slowly from side to side. *"A Monte Carlo,"* he said. "I'm damned if he wasn't eating a Monte Carlo! As I went by I just up-ended it. 'Sir,' I said 'do you mind if I turn down this empty glass?' "

She did not answer him. He put his arm about her shoulders

and drew her to him in a quick embrace. "You haven't forgotten *Uncle Tubby*?" he asked.

Lucy murmured something and stood with her eyes downcast. The blades of grass were airier than feathers and had a rosy tint in the sun. One of the fragile blades was bending double under the weight of a butterfly that had just alighted on it. The butterfly's body was blue-black, its wings yellow, ornamented with purple dots. Her father knew the names of butterflies. He had pursued them with a net when he was a boy. "He might make a good botanist," her mother said with a laugh, "but never a good gardener. . . ." She, Lucy, had accompanied her father and mother when they traveled in Europe. A lot of people came and went. In bedrooms, mostly, that were not at all like the ones they had here at home. *Pensions* they called them. For a second there, when he had said "Uncle Tubby," she had almost remembered, but it was gone now.

His arm fell from about her shoulders. He said: "What are they doing up at the house?"

"They're all asleep," she said, and added: "Mama's asleep. Daddy *might* be up, working on his map."

"Aha!" he said. "The old *siesta*. We'll break that up."

He was down off the rock and around at the other side of the car, holding the door open for her. She climbed in. The leather seat was unbearably hot. The horn was tooting madly. They raced up the drive and stopped under the willow tree, so suddenly that she would have fallen against the windshield if he had not stopped her with the flat of his hand against her stomach. He lifted her up and set her on the ground with almost the same gesture, just as Borcke charged down the front steps, barking. Her father and mother rushed after him. Her father was dressed, but her mother's dark hair hung over her shoulders in two long braids and she wore only a thin green robe over her nightgown. She shrieked and stood on tiptoe to throw her arms about the visitor's neck.

"Tubby . . ." she said, "Tubby. . . . It's so div*ine*!"

As she stepped aside to let the two men shake hands—only Tubby put his arm around Daddy's neck and hugged him—Sarah Lewis bent on Lucy the candid, radiant smile she usually reserved for adults.

"Isn't it *divine* that Uncle Tubby's here?" she asked.

Lucy did not answer. The four of them went up the steps. As they were about to enter the house Sarah drew back, looking down at Tubby's wet trousers. "You didn't *swim*?" she said.

"There was a big river," he said. "Behaved quite decently. And then a vicious little brute of a stream. Kept winding all around me. Finally bounced right up in the car. . . ."

"Ashland Creek," Sarah said. "You came the Ashland Creek road!"

"A most desolate way," he said. "Signs every now and then said 'Ford.' But not a habitation, much less a garage, for the last thirty miles."

Sarah was laughing so hard that she had to lean against the door frame. "*Tubby!*" she gasped, "my poor Tubby!" She straightened up, wiping her eyes on the back of her hand. "We're so glad you've come!" she said and stepped before them into the hall, which at this time of day was darkened for the sake of coolness.

The visitor held his head high and took long steps. It seemed to Lucy that he might stride right through the hall over the gallery and off the hill before he came to a stop. But when her father opened the east door and they went out on to the gallery he stood and gazed at the yellow river and then at the far meadow and the corn fields. "Say!" he said. "You didn't tell me you were in the money!"

Stephen Lewis' lean face flushed. "Not exactly," he said.

His wife went quickly up to him and hung on his arm, swaying a little and laughing. "But we're 'way above our raising!" she said.

Uncle Tubby looked at Lucy. "*That's* why she's so cold to me! An heiress, hunh?" He bent his shaggy head over her. "Je demande une *lawlee pawp!*" he uttered in finicking tones. "You may laugh off Rumpelmeyer's, but what about that *tabac* on the Place de l'Odéon? Remember there were witnesses! We were seen entering it practically every Thursday—when Madame Combet went to confession. I suppose next thing you'll be telling me is that you don't remember *her*?"

"I don't remember her very much," Lucy said in a stilted tone.

He made with his big, outstretched hand a gesture that indicated that he had heard enough. "A *belle dame sans merci!*" he said.

Sarah Lewis let go of her husband's arm and slipping her arm about Lucy's shoulders drew her toward her. "The poor child's been dragged around so, from pillar to post. . . . And you know they forget it on the boat. Really, they do."

Uncle Tubby was looking at the columns made of rose-colored brick that supported the gallery. "Damn creditable pillars," he said. "What a pleasure—to me, who was with you in the ships at Mylae! to see you provided with an establishment suited to persons of your quality. . . ." He broke off, shouting, "Pompey! You black rascal!"

"It was Steve's rich brother," Sarah said, "gave us the house and a hundred acres of land. Wasn't it darling of him?"

"I long to know that fellow," Uncle Tubby said. "I long to shake him by the hand. Everybody ought to have a brother like that."

Her father laughed. "Well, you've got one now. Brother Warren B. Zaalberg."

Uncle Tubby laughed, too, and threw his head back so sharply that a tendril of trumpet vine was jarred from its place on the pillar. The green spray, curving back upon itself, the first and last leaves actually intertwined, gave Lucy, for a second, the impression of a wreath set upon his coarse, clotted curls that were the exact color and consistency of the hairs in the tails of her great-grandmother's buggy horse. He *was* more the color of a horse than a man. Chestnut, a real chestnut. Wreaths were put upon horses' necks when they won a race. You could imagine him winning all the races, the Derby, even. . . . He was still laughing about Mr. Warren B. Zaalberg. . . .

"I've given him of my blood and he's given me a modicum of his'n. But I can't look on him as a blood brother. Still, we'll drink to him. . . ."

"We'll get your bags first," her father said and had started through the door when Uncle Tubby roared, "Pompey!" again and, pushing past Stephen Lewis, ran through the hall and down the front steps to where his car was parked.

"I've got to get something on," Sarah Lewis said and went into her bedroom and shut the door. She opened it immediately to say: "Lucy, will you tell Uncle Tubby where to go?"

"Well, *where?*" Lucy demanded.

"The third floor," her mother said and shut her door again.

Lucy stood in the hall and watched Uncle Tubby coming up the steps, carrying a big pigskin bag easily in each hand. Her father had disappeared down the steep flight of stairs that led to the lower floor. She could hear the refrigerator door slam and the sound of water running over the ice cubes that her father would by this time have taken out of the refrigerator. Uncle Tubby came abreast of her. She motioned to him to ascend the stairs to the third floor. He thanked her with a low bow, while with a wave of one of the bags he dismissed his imaginary companion: "Be off, sir. To the quarters."

Lucy could see the colored man—he was not more than eighteen years old and wore a blue coat with brass buttons, over pink and white striped trousers—running down the stairs. Involuntarily she pressed back against the wall while a ripple of laughter went through her. Uncle Tubby, halfway up the stairs, heard the minute sound and turned and smiled at her.

"Where'd you get him?" she asked before she realized what she was doing.

He had come to the landing. He set both bags down and grasped the brown railing with both hands. For a moment he looked as if he might vault over it and land in the hall beside her, but he only leaned far over, to say in a hoarse whisper:

"I *won* him. In a poker game. From General Nathan Bedford Forrest."

"General Forrest!" she said scornfully. "He don't ever play no cards."

He leaned still farther over, to look through the open door to where, beyond the river, on the white highway the cars kept spinning all day long.

"You never saw him in Paris," he said. "In the *spring*. You'd be surprised."

Her mother came out of her room, in blue jeans, but with her face made up and her hair freshly braided. "Don't you want to go downstairs and help Daddy?" she asked.

"No, I don't," Lucy said and walked out on to the gallery and sat down in the swing. The dachshund sleeping there in a nest of pillows groaned softly and rolled over on his back, all four paws extended in the air. She bent and laid her face against his warm muzzle and said in a high, thin voice: "Borcke . . . Borcke . . . *Borcke Dog!*", thinking how when she got her pony and rode him along the lanes he could run beside them. . . . But they couldn't buy the pony till another check came in, Daddy said. . . . If they bought it then. . . . *Couldn't you wait till next summer? You've got Borcke and the cats. Couldn't you just wait till next summer? You'll be nine years old then. . . . Yes, if I'm not dead, with y'all's goings on. . . .*

Her father came through the door, holding a tray full of bottles and glasses. Her mother came after him, bearing a bowl full of ice. "Lucy," she said crisply, "will you run downstairs and get me some limes—half a dozen limes—out of the refrigerator?"

When Lucy came back with the limes Sarah was lying in the hammock and the visitor was sitting in the swing beside Borcke, a glass in his hand. He had taken off his coat. His shirt, which was almost the same color as his hair, was open at the throat. He said to her father, "Where are you operating now?"

Her father looked off over the fields for a moment before he answered. "In the Wilderness . . . Grant is just making his first move by the left flank. Toward Spottsylvania. . . ."

"And Longstreet has just rolled up his left flank?" Uncle Tubby said. "If Lee hadn't waited to re-form his troops he might have routed Grant. I make something of that in the poem."

"I don't know," Stephen Lewis said. "There weren't sufficient reserves, as a matter of fact. The half of Grant's army that he had left was as big as Lee's whole army. . . ."

Sarah Lewis swayed forward in the hammock, fixing the visitor's face with her dark eyes. "But where would *If It Takes All Summer* be if Lee had won?" she asked. "Honest, Tubby, did they really pay you fifty thousand for that poem?"

"Did it really take you all summer to write it?" Lucy asked and then bit her lip as she realized that she was speaking at the same time as her mother.

Sarah clapped her hand over her mouth. Her eyes suddenly

brightened. Lines in her cheek went taut, then smoothed out again. She took her hand away from her face. "It took him all winter, too," she said severely. "You don't just dash off a poem of five thousand lines, Lucy. . . . Tubby, how much *did* you make?"

"They paid twenty-five thousand just for the title," Tubby said. "Zaalberg didn't want to leave any Civil War properties lying around after *'Gone With the Wind.'* Then Bill Wimscott got him to read it. The contract provides another twenty-five when they start shooting. . . . I'm going back out there in January. . . ."

They were all silent a moment, then Sarah said, "Is Anne still in Mexico?"

He shook his head. "She's back in New York. Just taken an apartment in the sixties."

"I thought she was going to get that same little house that she liked so much. In Cuernavaca."

"She got it, all right, but it didn't work out. Cigar factory had moved in next door, or something. . . . She was lucky to get this place in New York. It's right around the corner from where her sister lives."

"Oh . . ." Sarah said. "It's too bad, in a way, that she went to Mexico, isn't it?"

"Why?" Stephen Lewis asked. "It seems to me it's as pleasant a place as one could go for a divorce."

"But she always liked it so much. . . ."

". . . and now she won't want to go there again?" Tubby asked. "Sally, that's a pathetic fallacy. . . . Mexico was fine for her this winter. She's better off in New York now."

"Is she going to get a job?"

"Oh, she's going to look around. But in a leisurely way. I believe she has a translating job on hand."

He bent his head and stared at his clasped hands for a second, then he looked up at Mama and smiled. "It was tough while it lasted," he said, "but that's all over now. I must say it was a godsend, having enough money to go on with, while Anne was in Mexico and all. I just signed up with *Now* for another little job. That'll help."

"Civil War stuff?" Stephen Lewis asked.

"Not exactly. They're going to call 'em AMERICAN LANDSCAPES. Twelve towns, oh, say, like Chillicothe, Ohio. I haven't picked them all yet. I'm to do a brief history of the town, from the first trading post up till the present time. I've already run into some pretty interesting stuff."

Stephen Lewis said: "It'll be a lot of work!"

Tubby laughed. "Oh, there are ways of covering the ground. I don't intend to give my life to a study of Chillicothe, Ohio."

"But why do it at all?" Sarah asked, "now that you're rolling in money?"

"Well, not exactly rolling. When it comes down to it, it's not easy to wallow in the stuff. Slips out from under you."

She nodded. "I know," she said mournfully. "We spend half our lives waiting on checks, then when they come in . . . bing!" She spread her hands wide. "But, Tubby, I'm disappointed in *you*. Really, I am. I thought: 'Now there's one person won't need to even *think* about money, oh, for ages!' You know, you could make fifty thousand go a long way."

He grinned. "I'll get by," he said. "This stuff for *Now* won't take me more than three months. I can settle down as soon as I've finished that. I've already got a start on a new long poem."

"A new poem!" Stephen Lewis said.

"It's about the Conspiracy of Pontiac. Nobody's ever done anything on Pontiac."

"I didn't know that you were interested in Indians," Stephen Lewis said.

"I wasn't till I got to reading Parkman." He grinned again. "Good old Parkman! He's done a lot of the work for me."

"Why don't you settle down here?" Sarah asked. "You could have the top floor. Really, it's an awfully good place to work, Tubby."

"When the fause thieves let it be," her husband said.

"Well, we don't have much company in the *winter*," she said. "You know that, Steve. . . . Will you fix me a drink?"

Her husband got up and went over to the table. "Let's drink to *If It Takes,*" he said.

"Don't put any sugar in mine," Sarah said. "Tubby, we thought you were going to stay in India a year. I said, 'When Tubby gets back he can tell me all about sacred cows,' and the next thing we knew you were in Paris. . . . What made you come back so soon?"

He glanced at Lucy before he spoke. "There was a damsel in distress," he said. "All General Forrest's fault, really."

"His fault that the damsel was in distress?"

"No, but you know how chivalrous the general is. Nothing would do him but we should go over and rescue her."

"And did you?"

"Well, it's quite a business, rescuing these damsels in distress. Takes longer than you'd think."

"Not than *I'd* think," Sarah said. "But there were two months after that. All during March and April we didn't hear a word from you. Where were you?"

"At Toulon. With the Reardons."

"At *Toulon!* Oh, we did hear they'd moved there. What in the world for?"

"That's a long story. . . . But Isabel felt that there ought to be somebody in the house besides just the two of them."

"The two of them! They usually have about four dozen people staying in the house besides the two of them."

"They don't entertain much any more," he said.

She stared at him. "They *don't*? Well, what *do* they do, then?"

"They live very quietly. It suited me fine. I stayed two months. That was where I started the new poem."

"You mean you wrote *poetry* while you were staying with the Reardons? Oh, come now, Tubby!"

"Eight hundred lines," he said. "Worked till noon every day. Then I'd have a swim. Then we'd all meet for lunch. After lunch we'd take a *siesta*. Then it'd be time for *None*. Isabel and Kev always went, but I'd cut *None* and take another dip. I usually dropped in at Vespers, though."

Sarah said: "Tubby, darling, have you gone quite nuts?"

He shook his head. "That's the way it went at the *Villa Marthe*. Rather different from St. Tropez."

"St. Tropez!" Sarah said. "Last time we were there it was harvest time. They had a big party. There was a Papal countess made passes at Steve and a fairy with Prussian moustachioes and three or four of the Fentress girls. The trees were hung with lanterns and they had huge vats full of grapes and we all got in and trampled them with our bare feet. . . ."

"I didn't," Steve said.

"I did. I wasn't going to miss the only chance I'd probably ever get to trample grapes with my bare feet. It was wonderful, but awful slippery. Betty Blair fell down and Jim Blair kept hanging over the edge, saying 'None of this vintage for me!' But Kev Reardon fished her out, red as blood all over. And that little engine they crush the grapes in was tooting and grinding all the time. . . . Some people drank the *marc* raw just as it came out. . . ."

"Is Isabel writing any poetry these days?" Steve asked.

"She's started a few things," Tubby said, "but nothing ever

seems to come off. She says she doesn't think she'll ever write anything again."

"Why should she?" Sarah asked.

"Because she's a damned good poet."

"I dote on Isabel," Sarah said. "At least, I adore being with her, but I could never think of her as a poet. Her poetry always struck me as just an extension of her personality."

"Isn't everybody's?"

"Yes, but with Isabel it's more like a third arm. Awfully well shaped, you know, but you wonder why it's there. At her best, her poetry is just Millay gone metaphysical, isn't it?"

"Oh, I don't know," her husband said. "More like a female Hart Crane. That image in 'The Water-Bearer'—'the Cranes of Ibycus.' "

"She thinks *you* hung the moon," Tubby said.

"She ought to," Sarah said. "He loosed her on a waiting world."

Steve laughed. "That's right. Her first poem appeared in 'The Triad.' . . . when Bob Prescott was on his vacation. He was fit to be tied when he got back and found that I had taken on a lady poetess from Minnesota."

"It's hard for me to associate Isabel with Minnesota," Sarah said.

"*Minnesota*," Lucy thought, "Laughing Something, a place where Minnehaha might have lived, only if you asked them they would say she lived somewhere else." Her mother wasn't talking about a place, anyhow, but about that lady. Even at the moment of uttering the name her lips drew a little away from it. That meant that she didn't like the lady. But she wouldn't come out and say so. She and the others would talk around and around her—she was this way and that way and they wondered why she wasn't some other way. None of their friends ever quite suited them. You would think they were crazy about a person but the minute he turned his back they were on him, tearing him to pieces. Somehow he never looked the same afterwards. She closed her eyes in order to see more clearly the green sward that surrounded the house littered with the dismembered bodies of visitors: a head tossed into the honeysuckle vines, an arm draped on a stalk of yucca, a pair of legs that had collapsed on the path that went down to the river. Sometimes after they had spent hours taking a person to pieces they would turn around and put him together again, but some of the people they just left lying there. Why, they were all over the lawn!

". . . Born in the country outside St. Paul," her father said. "Her name was Ilse Rauschenkampf and she was the eldest of seven children. Used to walk three miles a day to school, seems to me she told me, in the early days of our friendship."

"She used to write to Steve at least once a day," Mama said. "Wanted to know whether she should come East for the publication of the sonnet. It *was* a sonnet, wasn't it?"

"On the moon," Daddy said. "An amazing poem for a seventeen-year-old girl to write."

"Did she write it before she came East?" Tubby asked.

"She wrote it in high school. She got a scholarship to Vassar that fall. She was the brightest kid in her high school. Won all the prizes."

"If she hadn't won that scholarship she couldn't have gone to Vassar," Tubby said.

Steve said: "And if she hadn't gone to Vassar she wouldn't have met Laura Grover and if she hadn't gone home at Christmas time with Laura she wouldn't have married Tommy Grover. . . ."

"And if Tommy Grover hadn't been shot down over France

she wouldn't have married Kevin Reardon," Sarah said. "But she married somebody in between. I always forget his name."

"Fellow named Edwards," Tubby said. "That was a mistake. She told me that she wouldn't have done it if she hadn't been so desperately lonely after Tommy was killed."

"What became of Edwards?"

"Locked up somewhere. In this country, I think. Do you know, his family wouldn't give her a cent of alimony? He was a mother's boy and his mother was a regular old Back Bay bitch. Maintained that he and Isabel could have a happy home if Isabel would only do her part. God, the poor girl! The last three years they were married they had to stop going out at all. He'd sit up to the table, wearing a bib and drooling. Used to cry if Isabel got the biggest pear when they passed the fruit."

Mama threw her head back and laughed out loud. Lucy looked at her and wished that she would not open her mouth so wide when she laughed. Mama's mouth was too big, anyhow. It had been the same size when she was a little girl, Mammy said. There was a verse that Mammy said they used to say to Mama when she was Lucy's age: *And when she oped her mouth to grin, a troop of horse might enter in.* They thought it was funny when Mammy recited those lines but if she, Lucy, were to recite them now they would say that she was being rude and make her go into the house.

She continued to study her mother's face as she sat there, swaying back and forth in the hammock. Mama was not exactly homely, but she certainly wasn't very pretty, either. Having such dark eyes made her look cross at times when she really wasn't cross—though the Lord knew she was cross often enough. And she was thin in the wrong places. There were two bones in her neck that you could see clear across a room when she wore an evening dress. That painter that was painting a portrait of Mama last summer said those bones were "full of character" and he put them in the portrait he was painting but Lucy thought that the picture would have been prettier if he had given Mama a nice, smooth neck.

". . . We used to stay with them at St. Tropez," Mama said, "but somehow we never saw much of them in Paris. I must say it wasn't Isabel's fault. She was always telephoning and trying to make dates. . . ."

They were still talking about that strange lady, the one who wrote poems about a "water-bearer" and had a villa on the Riviera all hung about with magic lanterns.

Lucy could see the villa quite plainly. It stood on a high hill, with lemon and orange trees making a green shade all around it—Mama said that all over the Riviera trees were growing with lemons and oranges hanging on them. The villa was pink —Mama had visited in a house once that was pink all over— there were terraces in front of it going down to the sea. Flowers grew all over the terraces. On one of them there was a big pool, like the pool at Monte Carlo that Mama told about. The water in the pool was green because it came out of the sea and every morning the lady went down to bathe in it. It seemed to Lucy that she could see the lady now, running barefooted over the soft grass, in a filmy white dress, her long golden hair streaming behind her, holding in her hand a green scarf that streamed backward, too. . . .

". . . But when we got together it wasn't much good," Mama said. "They didn't seem to be able to put their minds on us. Like Bobby Sampson, you know, that time we came back from Paris and he was living in that weird place in Tudor City and had us and one of those young men who do exagminations of James Joyce the same evening and he kept us downstairs and the exagminator up in a little balcony, only he got confused, running up and down the stairs, and Steve got mad as the Devil when Bobby talked to him like *he* was doing an exagmination. . . . You know how it is. The Reardons were always having to go on to some other place, or else they were putting on an act. . . . I always thought that was more Isabel's doing than Kev's. But then I'm partial to Kev. I feel at home with him. Isabel's always been a conundrum to me."

"I think she has a very direct approach to life," Tubby said.

"It's too direct for me," Mama said. "I mean—well, life's pretty darn complicated, when you get down to it, and Isabel —I never could understand how she just sailed through man after man. Oh, hell, I suppose all I'm saying is that I can't understand being so beautiful that every other man you meet falls for you. I must say, though, that Isabel's always been ethical about that. I never heard of her as much as laying a finger on another woman's man. I'd trust Steve on a desert island with her."

"I don't like her hands," Daddy said.

"What's the matter with them?"

"They ought to be longer."

"Well, the body's long enough. When she walks toward you it's like something swaying over the ocean floor. . . . Does she still keep her marvellous figure, Tubby?"

"Yes."

"They were the first people we ever knew to have a bar in their house," Mama said. "Remember that place they had on the *Ile de la Cité?* The first time we went there it was awful. Steve said afterwards that he knew that there was something funny about the place but he couldn't figure out what it was. And I was so mean I wouldn't say a word. I don't know why it is, but it simply *enrages* me for people to have bars in their houses. . . . When we met in restaurants it wasn't much better. They were so awfully rich and we were so awfully poor.

We used to compromise on the *Pré aux Clercs*. You know, that place down near the *Deux Magots?* There was a cat there, big as a bear. Named *Tout Petit*."

"No, he wasn't," Lucy said. "*Tout Petit* was in the garden at the villa."

"Lucy," Mama said, "there has been more than one cat named *Tout Petit* in my life. . . . Do you suppose it's Isabel's humble origins that give her that fairy tale quality? I always feel that the ordinary canons don't apply to her. Like that time she danced with the man on the Rue de Lappe."

"Odd place for you to go dancing," Uncle Tubby said.

"I know. We were standing there, gaping at those poor souls and a man stepped up and asked Isabel to dance. He had lots of black hair and smelled horribly of depilatory but she went right off with him."

"Did he behave all right?"

"Oh yes. When he brought her back he bowed to Kev and told him that he was a fortunate man. And he went off, looking rather thoughtful. I imagine that the poor fellow was thinking that he might have been converted if he'd ever got hold of anything like Isabel."

"How did Kev take it?"

"Calmly. Just thanked the man and said that he thought he was lucky, too."

"Kev wouldn't mind a thing like that," Tubby said. "In some ways he and Isabel are alike."

"They certainly don't look alike," Mama said. "She's so tall and blonde and he's so short and dark. Well, no, he's not so dark—his hair isn't really darker than yours, Steve—but he has such dark eyes. Like a deer, I always thought. . . . But I see what you mean. Isabel'd think up the crazy things to do and he'd do them. In the quietest way."

"I suppose that's the bond between them," Daddy said.

"You mean he's grateful to her for keeping him from being bored?"

"Well, a man as rich as Kev has to put up with a lot of boredom."

"I liked Kev better before he married Isabel," Mama said. "After that he changed, somehow. I used to get sort of impatient with him. I remember one evening at the *Boeuf sur le Toit*. Isabel wasn't with us, for some reason. A gigolo came over and asked me to dance and when I said no, Kev told me not to hesitate to have the man called back if I wanted to dance—that Isabel often danced with them. The *Boeuf sur le Toit* was a crazy place for us to have gone that night, anyhow. All he and Steve wanted to do was talk, which was all right with me, but I was damned if I was going to *hire* men to dance with me. I know I'm getting along, but I haven't got to that point yet. Four years ago, too."

"And you were just as lissome and lovely then as you are now," Tubby said.

Mama made a face at him.

"Well, Kev's quite a catch," Daddy said.

"Yes," Mama said, "but Isabel's had lots of rich men in love with her."

"Isabel doesn't care anything about money," Tubby said.

"No, but I can't imagine her without it."

"Her father used to raise minks for a living," Tubby said.

"That's what I mean. Everything about her is extraordinary. Even her childhood. She wasn't hauled around from third-rate hotel to third-rate hotel, the way Steve was when he was a child. Or her father didn't crash in the stock market, the way your father did."

"He crashed on the pavement," Tubby said. "Twelve storeys."

"Oh, Tubby," she said, "I'm sorry!"

"Hell," he said, "it happened, didn't it? As a matter of fact, there were seven suicides on our street that year."

"But that's what I mean," Mama said. "Her people weren't genteel poor, like ours, or didn't go bankrupt, like yours. They raised *minks*! How many people do you know whose fathers raised minks?"

"She's the only one."

"That's what I mean," Mama said again. "She's out of this world. Everything about her is out of this world. . . . Tubby, what's the place at Toulon like?"

"A bit on the grim side."

"Why in the world did they move *there?*"

"I told you it was a long story."

"I suppose it's all that money. Makes 'em restless. And then, if you have two or three places it gives you something to do. . . .

Nobody spoke for several minutes, then Daddy said: "Tubby, remember when you got your Rhodes Scholarship?"

"I sure do," Tubby said.

"That was when I felt sorry for Kev. He didn't exactly envy you, but he was mighty low after you left."

"Not as low as I'd have been if I hadn't got it."

"It was a starter for you, but it was sort of *fini* for Kev," Daddy said. "Lathrop wanted him to go to the American School at Athens. Lathrop always said that Kev would have made a good archaeologist. You know, the fellow still reads Greek. . . ."

"But he doesn't do anything with it," Mama said. "I never thought about it before, but I've always felt sorry for Kev. And it isn't because he's insignificant looking, either. It's because he never seemed to have anything to *do*. He could have gone on over to Oxford with Tubby. Why didn't he?"

"The war came along," Daddy said. "I suppose we're all more shaped by our circumstances than we realize."

"I'd like to be shaped by a few of his circumstances," Tubby said. "Still, I see what you mean. According to that line of reasoning, my old man did a lot for me when he jumped out of the window."

"Like Robert E. Lee," Mama said. "Who knows whether he would ever have amounted to anything if Lighthorse Harry hadn't got in jail for debt."

"That's what they say is the matter with Kev now," Tubby said.

"You mean too much money instead of too little?"

"The psychiatrists say that he has no father-image to pattern himself by. That's why he's moved back into his father's villa at Toulon. Even got his father's old butler back. Opened up the chapel that's on the place. Has what amounts to a resident chaplain, for he's hand in glove with the local *curé*. I must say the fellow's interesting. One of the foremost Patrologists in France, but one can get enough of his society. Kev has Mass said in his chapel every morning, and they sing the offices, too."

"How old world of him!" Mama said. "Do you think he's really trying to get back to his father?"

"Seems obsessed with the idea of following in his footsteps. Has had his father's library catalogued and stays up till two or three every night, reading, and studies with the *curé* in between *Tierce* and *Sexte* and *None*. . . ."

"Has he joined the Catholic Church?"

"Oh yes. Over a year ago. Isabel didn't mind that. But this other stuff is pretty hard to take. She's been pretty worried about him. Finally got him to a psychiatrist."

"What did he say?"

"Well, he thinks it's a pretty puzzling case. There's evidently some trauma. May be latent homosexuality. . . ."

"I don't believe that," Daddy said, looking at Tubby.

"Kev's father wasn't always religious, was he?" Mamma asked.

"Made a fortune in grain. One of the sharpest operators on Wall Street till he was forty-five years old. Turned pious then and spent the rest of his life praying. But he'd had a shock. When his wife left him. . . . Kev's had a shock, too. I tell Isabel I think it's that lick on the head."

"Did he get a lick on his head?"

"Didn't you hear? They were driving back to Paris at night and thought they'd stop off at Tarascon. You remember that road that goes off sharp to the right? Just after you cross the bridge? Kev overshot it and backed into a man. Killed the fellow outright and the woman who was with him died twenty-four hours later. Isabel and Kev were flung free, but they lay out in the woods all night long."

"We did hear they'd had an accident," Mama said, "but we didn't know it was that bad."

"They fell on a pile of rocks. You know how those rocks are all over the *Crau*? Isabel got a bad concussion. Fell on top of a big pile of them. Kev landed at the bottom of the heap with a broken collar bone and a broken ankle. He was out a lot of the time but he'd come to, off and on, during the night. Found a spring and he'd crawl to it and get water in his tobacco pouch and then crawl up and pour it over Isabel. . . ."

"I call that heroic," Mama said.

"Oh, he's got nerve. I never knew any fellow had more nerve than Kev Reardon. After all, he got his *Croix de Guerre* for drawing enemy fire."

"I'd clean forgot he had the *Croix de Guerre*," Mama said. "Tubby, do you truly think there's something wrong with Kev?"

"Well, he's done some pretty strange things lately."

"What kind of things?"

"I'll tell you about them some time," Uncle Tubby said. He looked at Lucy. "How's Lady Souse?" he asked. "How's Stutts Watts, the poet?"

"I don't know," she said. "I don't know anything about those old people," and it was true that they were to her now nothing but names, imaginary companions, who, her father and mother told her, had traveled all over France with them. But she had been four or five years old then. Uncle Tubby was thirty-two and still had General Forrest and Pompey. Perhaps it took boys longer to grow up than girls.

She leaned back in her deep chair and thought of all the far places Uncle Tubby had been in. To Hollywood, to see about his long poem that was being made into a movie, and after that to India, to interview the Mahatma Gandhi for a magazine he worked on called *Now*, and then from India he had gone to Paris. In an aeroplane. Because that damsel wanted him to come over there in a hurry.

He was not talking about the damsel now but about what he and she, Lucy, had done in Paris. Every morning, he said, he had walked with her and her nurse, Madame Combet, in the Luxembourg Gardens. On their way they had stopped at the Church of Saint-Sulpice for Mass. He said that he still had callouses on his knees—he would show them to her as soon as he got into shorts—from kneeling on those cold stone floors. He was surprised when she said that she did not remember Monsieur l'Abbé. He well remembered being introduced to that worthy by Lucy herself, at the corner of Ferou and Vaugirard, right under the windows, it happened, of Monsieur l'Abbé's parishioner, Monsieur Hemingway. After that, under Lucy's direction, he had saved all his stamps for Monsieur l'Abbé, until Lucy bestowed her favors elsewhere, on one

Ramon, the *patron's* son, after which he had stopped saving stamps for Monsieur l'Abbé and had even given him the cut direct when they met in the formerly sacred purlieus.

The "purlieus" were the streets around the church of Saint-Sulpice. Every time he said *"Saint-Sulpice"* it was as if a great bell started tolling somewhere and she was moving, with many other people into a vast, chill place where candlelight flickered on stone. But she could not really remember the church or even call Madame Combet to mind, though she had been told often how much the old lady had loved her, and there was in her room at this moment a little New Testament in French, with a book mark, a picture, showing Jesus on one end of a cross-cut saw and a little boy on the other, with the motto *"Tout est facile quand Jésus aide,"* that Madame Combet had said that she must keep always. She would look at it and say to herself: "Madame Combet . . . Madame Combet . . ." but nothing came back, except running fast on the street to keep hold of a warm, dry hand, or stopping sometimes beside something black that was higher than her head, while a hand, yellowish, mottled with brown spots, disappeared into a black bag and came up holding something—the stamps, probably, for Monsieur l'Abbé. She thought all at once that if it had been winter and Uncle Tubby wearing a heavy woolen suit and she sitting beside him on a sofa she might have remembered better. For she had sat on a sofa, in front of a fire, close up against somebody who bent over her, to read from a book that lay open on her knee:

> So now you know why Henry sleeps
> And why his mourning mother weeps
> And why his weeping mother mourns
> He was not kind to unicorns. . . .

A unicorn was an animal you read about in books, white, usually, with a horn in the middle of its forehead. . . . A little horse. . . . If they would only quit talking and drinking, for the more they drank the more they talked, there would still be time to drive out to Mr. Warfleet's and look at the pony that he had said would do nicely for her. . . . *You got only one child? Then I'd advise against a Shetland. Rather bite than eat. . . . Now this pony is part Morgan and part Arabian. See the deer look to her head?*

Her father was trying to catch her eye. He wanted her to go downstairs and get some more ice. She stared past him. He sighed and fished three slim ice cubes out of the water and dropped them into Uncle Tubby's third drink. Uncle Tubby pretended that Pompey had handed it to him and with a "Thank you, my lad," rose and began pacing up and down the gallery, telling them about people they had known in Paris. . . .

. . . Thirteen hands high. Brown, with white spots. A star on the forehead, a white stocking and one white splotch on the barrel. The mane was half white, half brown, but the tail . . . the *tail* was *pure white and rippled!* She opened her mouth too suddenly. Air, rushing into her windpipe, made her gulp. Her mother started and set her glass down on the floor beside the hammock. "Lucy," she said vaguely, "why don't you go and comb your hair?"

"You've got to dress from the skin out," Lucy said.

Her mother looked down at her jeans-clad legs. "Tubby," she said, "how would you like to drive out in the country and look at a pony? We can't buy it yet," she added hastily, "but we could look at it."

"Why, certainly," Uncle Tubby said. He turned to her father. "You know, there's a poem in the Wilderness," he said.

"Think of those two armies, locked in a death-grip, in all that scrub oak!"

Lucy sighed. Her mother heard the sound and looked at her and smiled and made a sign which meant that Lucy must not interrupt the person who was speaking.

"Yes," her father said, "I remember you had that idea at Cassis."

Uncle Tubby laughed. *"Cassis!"* he said. "That was where I had all my good ideas."

Cassis, Lucy thought, and suddenly there was a blue sky and white waves and a shining ribbon of sand was unrolling itself at the foot of the gnarled trees and the gnarled trees danced faster and faster until the black core of the forest melted away and there were only a few transparent trees shining in the sun.

It was at Cassis that Uncle Tubby had written the long poem that was going to be made into a movie. The poem was in a black book on the top shelf of Daddy's desk. Gilt letters went in a column straight up one side of it: *If It Takes All Summer.* Her father had read out loud from a letter that said that Uncle Tubby was going to get fifty thousand dollars for the title of the poem. "That's a hell of a lot of money for a poem," he said. Her mother had frowned and looked out of the window. "Do you suppose he can take it?" she asked. "It doesn't take long to spend fifty thousand dollars these days," her father said. "No, but if you make one fifty thousand you can always make another fifty thousand," her mother said, and her father laughed at that and said, "Well, let's let him spend this fifty thousand first."

II

THEY stopped talking about the Civil War and talked about a picnic they had gone on that summer at Cassis. It had lasted three days. The man who made the *bouillabaisse* sang a different opera all the way through every day. Her father and Uncle Tubby had recited their own poems and an old gentleman named Monsieur L'Hermite had recited Racine. He had walked over the mountains, bringing seven different vintages of wine in a hamper. Four of his hounds had come with him. She had been in Paris then, with her nurse, but when they talked about how after supper they would go out in the bay and, wearing special glasses, dive to look at the flowers that grew on the bottom of the sea, she could see the flowers, too: pink and blue and purple, star-shaped, some of them, others round, like little Banksia roses.

The town clock struck four. It was coming across all those fields and the water that made the sound so mellow. She got up and leaning on the rail, looked out over the valley. Patterson's barn, which all afternoon had glowed silvery in the hot sun, turned lavender as ragged clouds drifted over it. The sumac bushes that fringed the lawn were shaking. Two heads appeared, surrounded by foliage of a lighter green than the sumac leaves.

"Hey, look; Birnam Wood *is* coming to Dunsinane," Uncle Tubby said and came and stood beside her.

"Mr. MacDonough has got Mr. Lancaster to help him," she said over her shoulder to her father and mother.

"What are they going to do with those branches?" Uncle Tubby asked.

"It's for the Brush Arbor meeting," she told him.

Her father had come over and was standing beside them. "The Holy Roller meeting," he said, "starts tonight."

Uncle Tubby's glass swung out in an arc so wide that a few bright drops fell in the wake of the men passing just then beneath the gallery. "Why do these holy men gather in your back yard?" he asked in a whisper, and added, smiling at Lucy, "Is it your fame—or your impiety that attracts them?"

His eyes, when he smiled, were as full of light as any eye she had ever seen in a human head. She looked away from him to her father. *His* eyes were clear, too, and as yet no little veins showed in his lean cheeks. It was when he spoke that you realized that he had had three or four Tom Collinses since lunch time. He said, "They've been here longer than I have," and leaned over the rail, shouting, as if Mr. MacDonough were a mile away and not right there under the porch. "Better hurry if you going to start the meeting tonight!"

One of the men stalked on without looking up. The other man turned up a thin face, encircled by a ragged auburn beard. His enormous dark eyes dwelt on each of the three faces, in turn, before he smiled, revealing sharp, stunted teeth that might have belonged to a child. "You come on and help us!" he said and ducking, as if he were afraid of what the sally might bring forth, followed his companion around the corner of the house.

"That's Mr. MacDonough," Lucy said. "He don't eat mutton . . . or lamb."

Uncle Tubby was looking at her father. "She's kidding me."

Stephen Lewis shook his head. *"Agnus Dei, qui tollis peccata mundi.* . . . His life is one long Eucharist."

"His wife and children, too?"

"Aren't any of the children Saved except Ruby," Lucy said, "but Mr. and Mrs. MacDonough are . . ."

"And Sanctified," her mother said from the hammock.

Lucy turned around. Her voice sounded shrill in her own ears after its long disuse. "That's what *you* think! Mrs. MacDonough's Sanctified but Mr. MacDonough isn't."

Sarah Lewis sat up in the hammock. One of her dark braids had slipped from its pins and hung rakishly over her shoulder. She held her hairpins in her mouth and spoke through them thickly. "Lucy, Mr. MacDonough is a great deal more religious than Mrs. MacDonough. Mrs. MacDonough shews tobacco. . . ." She hesitated a moment and added, "And she had a child before she was married."

"She's seen Jesus flying through the air on wings!" Lucy said.

Her mother looked down at the hairpins which she held now in her hand, and said nothing. Uncle Tubby's eyes were bright on Lucy's face. "How do you know, Lucy?" he asked.

"Ruby told me, and so did Mary Magdalene."

The hammock creaked as her mother lay back among the pillows. "If she said she saw Jesus flying through the air on wings, she saw him, as far as I'm concerned. She wouldn't steal a pin."

Uncle Tubby laughed. "Not many people go around stealing pins."

Sarah Lewis turned her head and looked at him reflectively. "I expect they're hard put to it to find a safety pin sometimes. With all those babies."

"Who's the other fellow?" Uncle Tubby asked.

"Mr. Lancaster," Stephen Lewis said. "He's quite a worldly fellow. An agnostic, in fact."

"But he's got a magnificent tenor voice," Sarah said. "He goes to the meetings to sing."

"And never gets religion?"

"It'll be seven times harder for him than anybody else," Lucy said. "He killed his brother. . . ."

"And has never repented of the crime?"

"He didn't mean to kill him," Lucy said. "He thought somebody was stealing his watermelons and he laid down in the patch with his gun till midnight. Then he come up to the house and he saw somebody skulking around in his corn and he thought it was a fellow making up to his wife and he shot his heart out, but it wasn't that Slocombe fellow at all, it was his baby brother."

"You mean he thought a baby was making up to his wife?" Tubby asked.

"No, stupid!" Lucy said and then looked quickly at her mother, but Sarah didn't seem to have noticed that Lucy had called Uncle Tubby stupid. She said: "Albert Lancaster was twenty-two, I believe, but he was the youngest child: the fair-haired boy principle. . . ."

"I see," Uncle Tubby said. "You certainly lead a rich life around here."

"I don't know," Sarah said. "It seems to me that there are just as many murders in the cities."

Lucy wondered why what Uncle Tubby had just said made

her mother angry. She could tell that Sarah was angry by the way the lines in her face all went tight. She had opened her mouth to say something else but Uncle Tubby was turning to Lucy. "Do you go to the meetings?" he asked.

"I am this time," Lucy said. Her eyes followed her mother who just then extended her empty glass to her husband. "That's your third drink," Lucy told her. "If you take three drinks you can't drive. Can she, Daddy?"

But her father was looking past her into the hall. "There's somebody coming," he said.

"Oh, God!" Sarah said. She got up out of the hammock and standing on one foot shook down first one and then the other pants leg. "Go peep and see who it is," she said to Lucy.

Lucy tiptoed through the hall and sliding behind the half open front door peered out on the driveway. A car had been parked on the other side of the lilac bush. Two women were coming up the brick walk. One was young and wore a green flowered print dress and a big hat and walked slowly, supporting a smaller, older woman, dressed all in grey. Lucy ran back to the porch.

"It's club women," she said.

Stephen Lewis picked up a tray from the table and beckoning to Uncle Tubby, silently retreated through the hall and down the back stairs. Sarah, too, ran through the hall. Lucy was left alone on the porch. She heard quick footsteps and then the sound of a dresser drawer opening. Her mother would be putting on fresh lipstick or perhaps changing from the jeans to a dress. But she couldn't do anything about the way she smelled. She looked down at the skirt of her dark blue gingham. There was a grass stain on the hem. She had wanted to change her dress right after lunch, but her mother had told her to wait until they went out to Mr. Warfleet's. If these ladies stayed a long time it would be too late to go to Mr. Warfleet's. . . .

The knocker sounded. Lucy advanced slowly to the door. Her mother was ushering two ladies into the hall. She hadn't changed to a dress, after all, and she couldn't have had time to braid her hair, either, but it was pinned up neatly and her sunburned skin glowed smooth through fresh makeup.

The young lady had eyes almost as dark as Mama's. The eye shadow she used made her lids shine. She looked around the square hall, then at the Confederate flag draped over the mirror, and out at the river and the purple-green fields framed in the doorway. "I just love this house," she said. "Miss Grace, did you know that Jim and I almost bought this house?"

The old lady was smiling at Lucy. Sarah drew Lucy forward. The gin smell rose sharply above the mingled fresh odors of powder and the flower perfume that Sarah had brought from France. She ought not to use that perfume when she's drinking, Lucy thought, and was about to curtsey—disregarding her mother's commands, she did it only on impulse—when the young lady put out a hand and gave her a friendly jab on the shoulder. Lucy arrested the bending of her knee and muttering, "How-do?" slipped ahead of them into the parlor and seated herself on the hair-cloth sofa that occupied the center of the room, then, as they entered, was about to get to her feet again when she realized that her mother, sitting forward in her chair, her hands clasped between her denim-clad legs, was giving her whole attention to what the young lady was saying.

". . . We stopped the car on the other side of the river and just sat and looked over here. 'It's up to you,' Jim said. He can make up his mind just like that. . . ." Diamonds to the size of your thumb were clustered on the young lady's ring finger; her wedding ring was platinum, inset with diamonds. "I said, 'Jim, you just bring me out here to torture me. . . . No *place* to

put another bedroom . . . without spoiling it, I mea
then Daddy gave us that lot in Englewood. . . ." Her
were as softly grained as rose petals. Her hat was
brown straw, looped with narrow black velvet ribbon.
delicate gloom of its brim her face took on a flowery pallor. Her lips opened wider until her whole face swayed at you, like a flower on its stalk. "I told Daddy he did it just for meanness. . . ."

"Only room for a shower upstairs," Sarah said, "and as for the lower floor, they were using that one for a hen house. A roost going up to it from outside and a row of nests along the wall. A setting of eggs in one of them. I sort of hated to disturb it."

"Did you put any on this floor?"

"Eggs? . . . Oh, no, you always have to go upstairs or downstairs to the bathroom. You were right. It's an *impossible* house. . . . She was looking at the old lady. "You're Mrs. *Merritt*!" she said. "You live in the house with the iron balconies."

The old lady's laugh was like a breeze in the room. "They've fallen to ruin. I told Tom the other day that we ought to rip them off."

Her hair had a deep, soft wave and shone like silver. Her skin was as fine as tissue paper that somebody had squeezed into a ball and then smoothed out again. She sat down slowly in the red arm chair. Long ruffles were sewed to the sides of her grey voile dress. One of them fell to the floor. She lifted it and folded it carefully across her knee. "Outmoded elegance," she said. "I don't know why people in Gloversville had all that ironwork shipped up here from New Orleans. It served no purpose whatsoever."

The young lady, Mrs. Eglinton, still stood, looking first at the long yellow curtains and then at the white mantel, whose wide shelf and fluted columns had been carved, Lucy knew, by "slave labor." When she heard the phrase she thought of men with sharp profiles, downbent, moving, with half-lifted knees against rays of the setting sun. But this mantel and all the others in the house had been carved by Negroes who happened to be slaves at the time they did the carving. Like Old Aunt Mary who came sometimes to Merry Point, to spend a week with Mammy. She had been a slave at Brackets, when Mammy was a little girl, or as Aunt Mary said, "a chap." When Aunt Mary was at Merry Point she made Lucy sweep the front porch and set the chairs back from the dining table. She said that those had been her jobs at Brackets. Besides sewing. She had to sew the seams on the legs of one pair of pants every day; somebody else put on the waistband. Mammy said that she had always helped Aunt Mary with any work Aunt Mary had to do so they could go out and play sooner, but Aunt Mary said that she didn't remember anything about that.

Mrs. Eglinton was looking at Lucy and winking. She hadn't been in the room any time and she had already winked at Lucy twice. She didn't look as pretty when she was winking. It was as if she stood a little way off and looked at herself and every now and then she realized that you might not like what she was saying and turned her prettiness off so you would have a chance to see that she was nice, too. Her hips were as trim as a quail's under the green silk as she crossed the room to stand before a picture that hung on the north wall. Lucy turned her head and stared too.

There was something in the center of the canvas that was intended, she knew, for a patchwork quilt. A figure lay upon it, arms and legs spread wide, while around it other figures revolved: Daddy, in his big straw hat, mowing the lawn; Lucy and Borcke running ahead of him; Electra, the cook they had

had before Jenny, standing in a blue dress before the block, rolling out biscuits; a young poet swimming in the river, which, in the picture, was blue and not muddy, the way it was this time of year; her hens, Red Lily and Leaf Flower, with the red rooster Mammy had given her; some visitor going down the brick walk with his wife; and she herself and the four MacDonough children crouched beside one of the columns of the gallery. She wondered whether Mrs. Eglinton would know that that rose-colored blob there beside the column was Lucy Lewis. She hadn't recognized herself till they told her who it was, but ever since she had liked to come in here from time to time and seem to see herself walking about in the picture.

Sarah had risen to stand beside the guest. "It's called 'Life at Benfolly,' " she said.

The old lady laughed. "It looks like a merry-go-round."

"It's meant to," Sarah said.

Mrs. Eglinton winked at her. "Did you paint it?"

"No," Sarah said, "it's by a young painter who visited here. I suppose that's the way life here impressed her. It *was* a hectic summer. . . ." She sketched a circle in the air with her thin, nervous hand.

"Do you know Melvin Archambault?" Mrs. Eglinton asked.

Sarah shook her head.

"He's from Chicago, but he had a show last year at Palm Beach. The most livid greens. Jim says, 'Evelyn, you can't possibly like that stuff,' but I said, 'Jim, I really do. . . .' We bought one water color. Miss Grace, I'm going to hang it in that little place between the dining room and the living room. . . . Have you ever made any talks on art?"

"No," Sarah said, "I don't know anything about it."

"She's always painting, though," Lucy said. "But they aren't any good and she has to tear them up."

The old lady smiled at her, folding her hands. They were

swollen at the knuckles, like Mammy's. "When I was twelve years old I used to come out here to take china painting lessons from Miss Clara Swanton. . . . Sarah, does this room still sway when you get enough people dancing in it?"

"We haven't done much dancing," Sarah said. "Really, we don't have much company."

"One night we danced so hard that old Mr. Swanton made us stop," Mrs. Merritt said. "Around four o'clock in the morning, I must say, in justice to him. And the next day he had those iron bars driven through the walls. He said the house might last then till Belle got married. But poor Belle. . . ."

"She was the one went crazy, wasn't she?" Mrs. Eglinton asked. "But Miss Grace, I've always heard that she was so attractive."

"All the Swanton girls were attractive," Mrs. Merritt said. "Sarah, how does your grandmother like your house?"

"She never has seen it," Sarah said. "She stays out there and sometimes six weeks go by and she doesn't see a white face." She laughed. "But she sent one of her niggers over here the other day, with an old bed she was giving me and when he got back she said, 'Morris, how did you like Miss Sally's house?' and he said, 'Lord, Miss Sally, I sure hate to think of Little Miss Sally living in a place like that.' "

"Why, it's a perfectly beautiful house," Mrs. Eglinton said.

"I know, but he didn't look at the house, just saw how poor the land is. The hogs have rooted the foundation out from under Ma's house, but he never has noticed that. . . ."

"It's the roof's the worst," Lucy said. "She has to put spittoons on the stairs when it rains."

"I haven't been out there in years," Mrs. Merritt said. "Twenty-five years."

There was a silence, then Mrs. Eglinton said, "It was the Shanklins built this house, wasn't it, Miss Grace?"

"Lord, no," Mrs. Merritt said. "The Greens built it. Old Captain Green. . . ."

"That one?" Mrs. Eglinton said. "You know I didn't know about him till the other day when Jim told me."

One of the curtains stirred slightly in the breeze. From the slope below the house came the sound of laughter and faint shouts: the MacDonough children must be home from school. Lucy slid half off the sofa, then rested, her bare legs propped against the slippery horse hair.

". . . clubbed to death," Mrs. Eglinton was saying, "right down there at the mail box. When Grant came up the river from Donelson. . . ."

"When he took the town?" Sarah said.

"The old man's body servant had him down at the gate in a wheel chair and when the other Negroes went past he was afraid he'd have to stay with Old Marster so he just clubbed Captain Green to death and went with them." She laughed. "I get all that from Jim. I declare, he knows what every man, woman, and child in this county was doing in 1862. He knows all the battles and what Grant said to Lee and everything. . . ."

"Jim is just like his father," Mrs. Merritt said softly, then straightened up in her chair. "Sally, Evelyn Eglinton here is just as smart as she can be. . . ."

"It's American history this year," Mrs. Eglinton said. "We want Mr. Lewis to talk to us about the Civil War. The first meeting is in September. Will the seventeenth be all right?"

"Steve's just up to his ears," Sarah said, moving her shoulders nervously.

"Well, he can spare one little old afternoon. Do either of you play Contract? There are eight of us. Meet Friday night. But Marie Evans has got to go to Birmingham to live. . . ."

"You wouldn't play with me," Sarah said. "I tell you now

he's not going to do it. He's one of the meanest white men ever lived."

Mrs. Eglinton's flower lips opened. She swayed forward on her green stalk. "Just let me ask him, anyhow."

Sarah's eyes dodged aside, like somebody coming around the corner of the house on something they mustn't look at. She drove them back to Mrs. Eglinton's face. "He's in Nashville," she said. "I'll make him write you a letter. As soon as he gets back I'll make him write you a letter."

Mrs. Eglinton winked bravely. "Or call me up," she said. "Tell him I'd at least like to hear his voice on the phone."

Mrs. Merritt stood up in a flutter of voile. "Evelyn, I told Tom I'd be back by four o'clock." The others stood up, too. Mrs. Merritt came over and laid her hand on Lucy's shoulder. "Sarah, this child isn't a Fayerlee. And she doesn't look like Professor Maury, either. Is she like her father's people?"

"She's got his coloring," Sarah said, "but not his features, or mine, either, thank Heaven. She's sort of a changeling. Aren't you, darling?" Her hand, too, rested on Lucy's shoulder. Lucy could feel the fingers trembling.

They were in the hall. Through the door which had been flung wide open when they came in you could see the willow tree. Under its drooping boughs Daddy and Uncle Tubby stood facing each other. Uncle Tubby had taken off his coat. His shirt sleeves were rolled up; he held a glass in his hand. Daddy still had on his checked shirt and those old blue fisherman's pants that he had brought from Concarneau, and on his bare feet sandals that were held on by two crossed leather thongs. The fisherman's pants had two big patches on them that Lucy had not noticed before.

He heard them coming and turned so that his back was toward them. Uncle Tubby glanced up at the porch and went on talking. He was asking Daddy something. Little points suddenly showed in his eyes, he thrust his face closer to Daddy's. Daddy's back stayed stiff and still. Lucy knew what his eyes would be like if you were around there where you could see into them, the fair brows drawn straight across and the eyes a cold blue, like a pond frozen over in the night.

Uncle Tubby looked at Mrs. Eglinton and bowed as the ladies went past, but Daddy didn't turn around or make any sign. They were past them and at the lilac bush. Mrs. Eglinton helped Mrs. Merritt into the car and then got in herself. She put on fawn-colored gloves. Her face shone pink as a camellia as she tossed her head back under the big hat. Her hands took hold of the wheel. The car began to move. Mrs. Merritt sat hunched in the seat, looking straight ahead until it moved, then she straightened up and smiled and waved her hand.

Sarah took two steps beside the car. "Goodbye . . . Goodbye . . . Miss Grace, I'm so glad y'all came. . . ."

They stood there, waiting, until the car had passed through the gate and was headed back toward town. Sarah drew a deep breath and started up the walk.

Lucy followed her. "You told a lie," she said.

Mama didn't answer. She went on around the corner of the house. Daddy and Uncle Tubby were on the lower gallery. Daddy was sitting on the feed-box and Uncle Tubby was standing in front of him, talking. Mama stood and looked at them and then she fell down on her back on the ground and kicked her legs in the air.

"*My God!*" she said.

Daddy sat where he was on the feed box but Uncle Tubby came and stood and looked down at her. "That was quite a boner we pulled, wasn't it?" he asked.

Mama stopped kicking and sat up. She covered her face with both hands, first, and then she took her hands away from her face and clasped her stomach in, tight. "I make the supreme sacrifice, and you two louts can't even keep out of sight!"

Daddy looked sulky, the way he always looked when anybody said there was anything wrong with him. "They thought I was Mr. MacDonough," he said. "That was why I didn't turn around."

"Mr. MacDonough! Good God!" Mama said, "Mr. MacDonough wouldn't be caught dead in those pants."

Uncle Tubby was looking at Mama. "Did you know those ladies?" he asked.

"I don't know them," Mama said, "but I know who they are and they know who I am. . . ."

"Who are you?" Uncle Tubby asked.

"I'm Professor Maury's daughter, fallen among thieves," she said. "Oh, God, you louts!"

"She had to go to school with the boys. That's what makes her so peculiar," Lucy said, seeing that Uncle Tubby was still staring curiously at Mama and then was afraid that Mama would be angry, but Mama said only: ". . . One of the things." She looked at Daddy. "I didn't care about that Lassiter girl, but Mrs. Merritt is a friend of my mother's"

Daddy still looked sulky. "Old bitches," he said. "I'm not going to have them hounding me."

"Mrs. Merritt is not a bitch," Mama said. "She's a lovely lady of the old school."

"Was Mrs. Lassiter the one who served her face up to you on a platter?" Uncle Tubby asked. "I thought she had a lot of stuff."

"She was born a Lassiter. Married Jim Eglinton," Mama said. "All those Lassiter girls are perfectly beautiful." She looked at Daddy. "It's her husband's going to give you that bird dog. The one that goes in caves that you liked so much. . . . And here she comes out here and you won't even speak to her."

"I never saw the woman before in my life," Daddy said.

"Well, you would have if she hadn't been in Atlanta when we went there to dinner. My God, Jim Eglinton is *connected* with me!"

"How?" Uncle Tubby asked.

"Oh, his mother was a Minor. . . ."

"Coal?" Uncle Tubby asked.

"Virginia, you dope! They're all intermarried with the Fayerlees. . . . My God! Sometimes I feel like we're criminals in hiding, having to skulk through town, scared all the time we'll run into somebody we know."

"You *have* committed a crime," Uncle Tubby said. "Steve's views on the Civil war challenge the existing order."

Daddy grinned. "They'd ride *you* out of town on a rail if they knew you didn't believe in the sanctity of private property."

"I haven't got any immediate designs on their property," Uncle Tubby said. "What do they think of you, really?"

"They think we're nuts," Lucy said and was a little taken aback to hear her voice sound so loud and clear.

"They think we're Nudists," Mama said. "When we bought this place word went round that we were going to found a Nudist colony. . . . Poor things! I suppose they'd been hoping somebody would."

"Had you been guilty of any indecent exposures?" Uncle Tubby asked.

"Not any more than usual. Well, those Greek sandals of Steve's. I heard that Miss Minnie Wellfleet doesn't like them."

"He wears them to town," Lucy said.

"Whereas I go dowdy," Mama said. "And he can't get it into his head where the center of town is. Made a U turn right by the bank the other day, with Mr. Tom Davis standing there looking at him."

"Who's Mr. Tom Davis?"

You would have thought from the way Mama looked at Uncle Tubby that he was the one she was angry with. She said in a rasping voice: "He's a man that the Yankee newspapers are always writing up for being a benefactor of the Southern farmer. . . ."

Daddy walked over and handed her a cigarette. He was still not in a good humor but he was afraid she would say something else about Yankees. She took it without thanking him and stood, holding it in her hand, and looking off over the river. "He's the great-grandson of our old slave trader," she said.

"He's the president of the bank," Daddy said.

Uncle Tubby slapped his thigh. "Gad, that's symbolic!"

"It's going to be mighty symbolic when we have to try to borrow some more money from him," Mama said.

"Well, we've still got four hundred of the advance left. Let's cross that bridge when we get to it," Daddy said.

Lucy went over and stood beside Mama. "Shall I wear my blue linen, Mama?" she asked.

Mama started. *"What?"* she said. Lucy thought that she was talking to her and repeated, "Shall I wear my blue linen?" But Mama was looking past her at Uncle Tubby. "*What* did you say?" she asked.

Uncle Tubby laughed and looked across the river to the long, white road where the cars kept spinning all day long. "I said the Reardons ought to be here pretty soon."

"The *Reardons*!" Mama said.

Uncle Tubby looked embarrassed. "Kev's visiting a friend in this neighborhood so I told them they might as well come on here."

"In *this* neighborhood?"

"Well, it's only a hundred and fifty miles from here. Bardstown."

"Who's he visiting there?"

"Some Trappist monk."

"Trappist monk!" Mama said. "How can you visit a Trappist monk?"

"Seems they had things to say to each other, so they got a dispensation. . . . I told Isabel that as long as they were this far they might drive by here. It's all right, isn't it?"

"Oh, of course," Mama said. She looked as if she might say something else, but Daddy went over and took hold of her arm. "If you're going to Warfleet's you'd better start," he said. "It's nearly five o'clock."

Mama looked at him. *"Warfleet's!"* she said.

Lucy felt the bottom drop out of her stomach. She cried out, "You said you'd go this afternoon. To look at the pony. You *said* . . ." but Mama was not listening. She was walking toward the house.

Daddy looked after her and then he looked at Uncle Tubby. "Tubby, you want a drink?" he said.

"I don't mind," Tubby said and they, too, went toward the house.

III

LUCY stood alone, staring down at the river. You could see the near bank only through the gap in the willows, but on the other bank, where it overflowed every year into Patterson's bottoms, there was a long stretch where there weren't any trees, just a shelf of yellow, blistered mud. Daddy said that copperheads sunned themselves there on the flat rocks. . . . She had known all along. She always knew when they weren't going to do what they had said they would do. She had known when Uncle Tubby stepped out of his car that they would forget all about the pony, but all afternoon, sitting up on the gallery, listening to them drinking and talking, she had kept on hoping. It was no use now.

She walked slowly over the grass and stepped up on to the brick porch. Mr. MacDonough was going through the kitchen door, carrying a bucket of milk. Mama was standing by the stove. Mr. MacDonough did not like to look at Mama when she had her arms and legs bare, but Mama did not know that. He was setting the bucket down in the sink when she came over and standing beside him, looked down at the white, foamy milk. "It's *two* gallons!" she said.

"Nearer three," Mr. MacDonough said, not raising his eyes.

Mama tilted the bucket so that the milk splashed up to the brim. "That Daisy!" she said. "Mr. MacDonough, there was a man came by here the other day and saw her grazing on top of the hill and he stopped his car at the gate and walked up here and said, 'Madam, you're going to have trouble if somebody doesn't attend to that cow's bag. It's as big as a balloon tire.' " She threw her head back, laughing. "I made him go down in the pasture and feel her teats and he said they were healthy, all right, but he never had seen such a bag in his life. . . . He was a Jersey man, too. From over near Trenton."

Mr. MacDonough stared at the wall and smiled. "Daisy's got as pretty a bag as I ever saw," he said. "Gentle, too. She'd let the milk down for David just as good as she does for me."

"Oh, she's a *wonderful* cow!" Mama said. "And you were right about not breeding her last spring. I'm sure she's a better cow for it."

"Yes, ma'am," Mr. MacDonough said. "You breed 'em too young it stunts their growth. On the other hand, you breed 'em just the right time it develops 'em. Why, I've seen a heifer nigh double her size after her first calf. . . ."

Daddy came down the steps and into the kitchen. "Well," he said, "y'all set for the big meeting?"

Mr. MacDonough's eyes brightened. "There's folks coming from as far as Cleveland," he said. "Our overseer, he's coming from Cleveland. . . . And there's three tarriers. . . ."

"Are the tarriers all from this side of the river?" Daddy asked.

"Claude Lancaster's one of 'em," Mr. MacDonough said.

"Claude Lancaster!" Daddy said and let out a whistle. "Mr. MacDonough, Claude Lancaster's going to be a hard nut to crack."

Mr. MacDonough turned his bright, dark gaze full on Daddy's face. "It ain't us that's going to crack him," he said. "It's the Spirit. He holdeth us all in the hollow of his hand. You know that, Mr. Lewis. Claude's told me and he's told several others that he was going to tarry this August. Tarry and see what come of it. Those were his words. Claude's a roisterer and a whoremonger but ain't no man ever said he wasn't good as his word. . . ."

"That's right," Daddy said. He spoke absently and did not look at Mr. MacDonough. That often happened when he and Mr. MacDonough were talking together. They stood looking at each other and talking, Daddy asking Mr. MacDonough questions and Mr. MacDonough answering them as well as he could, but with his full, bright, dark eyes fixed on Daddy's face as if he were studying it for some other purpose, until Daddy suddenly seemed to get more interested in his own thoughts than in what Mr. MacDonough was saying, and Mr. MacDonough realized that he was not paying attention and went away. He took up his bucket and went out now. Mama strained the milk and put it in the refrigerator and began washing the dishes.

Daddy took a tomato from a basket on the table and bit into it. "I wish I had that fellow's gift for imagery," he said.

Mama laughed. "It's terrific," she said. "The Spirit cracking Claude Lancaster the way you'd crack a pecan."

Daddy laughed, too. "We'll have to watch Tubby," he said. "He'll be taking on MacDonough's style."

Mama laughed again. "A long poem on The Spirit!"

"With choruses," Daddy said. "A double spread in *Now.*"

She turned around quickly to look at him. "You think he

won't write any more poetry?" she asked. "I mean real poetry?"

"How in hell do I know?" Daddy asked irritably.

She did not say anything for a moment, then she said, "You know, sometimes I wish you'd left him on the playing fields of Princeton."

"He was twenty years old when I met him. Couldn't have gone on playing football much longer."

She was shaking her head, the way she did sometimes. "It's not your fault, of course. But I've got an idea it's not going to turn out so well. And anyway, it makes me mad. I can't help it. It just makes me mad."

"What makes you mad?"

"Well, for one thing I don't think he ought to have said that about Anne."

"I never heard him make an unbecoming remark about Anne in my life," Daddy said, "and God knows she was trying sometimes. Why, you . . ."

". . . Said she was a beast," Mama murmured.

"A beast?"

"Well, said she was devoid of reason."

"You mean that about the pathetic fallacy?" Daddy began to laugh. "*You* were the one that called her 'The Vassar Girl.' "

"Well, she was. . . . Poor thing. But she was crazy to have a baby."

"Well, she could have. They were married five years."

". . . And feed it on air? Oh, *no*! She believed in his poetry. She didn't want to hang any burdens around his neck. And now just look what he's stepped into! I think Isabel Reardon ought to be ashamed of herself."

"Great God!" Daddy said. "Sometimes I think I ought to take you and have your head examined."

"I don't care," Mama said. "I get tired sometimes, waiting around for you to put your mind on things. Didn't you hear what he said about that damsel in distress?"

"That doesn't necessarily mean that Isabel is the damsel. . . ."

"When he was down in Toulon with them *three months*. . . ."

"He was working on a long poem."

"A long poem!" Mama said. "Ho! Ho! You of all people ought to know that you don't work on a poem long at a time —not more than thirty minutes at a stretch is my observation, for what it is worth. . . . And all that *Tierce* and *None* and *Sexte*! Well, of course it's more convenient for you to keep your eyes closed. Keep 'em closed as long as you can. . . ." She took the dish towel away from him. "Come on. We've got to change Tubby to the ell before they get here."

"What in the name of God for?"

She shut her eyes, the way she did when she thought that the person she was talking to was so dumb that there was no use in trying to explain anything. "Something tells me that I'd better not put Isabel and Kev in the same room," she said.

He looked as if he might burst. "Suppose Tubby *is* having a flirtation with Isabel," he said. "Does that mean that he's got to sleep in the same room with her?"

"It's none of my business, of course," she said.

"It certainly isn't."

"That's why I'm putting him in the ell."

"Without any consideration of how much trouble it makes."

She screwed her face up. "Don't worry me," she said, "for God's sake, don't worry me now! I've got to wash the dishes and get dinner for six people."

"Where's Jenny?"

"I told you she had the toothache." She stopped talking suddenly and stood with her head bent, tracing a spiral on the floor with the toe of her slipper.

"What's the matter now?" Stephen asked.

"I was just trying to remember what he said. . . ."

"What who said?"

"Kev Reardon."

"When?"

"At St. Tropez. That summer. You remember those steps that went down off the terrace and that sort of bosky place at the bottom of them?"

"No," he said, "I never went down there."

"Well, I was standing there with him. Looking at a statue. . . . And he said something. . . ."

"Well what did he say?"

"I can't remember," she said, "but he *meant* it."

"Let's hope so."

"He was trying to tell me something. No, ask me something, something he thought I might know—because of you."

"Now, *really*!" he said.

"I mean he was too shy to ask you, but he thought I might know. . . ."

"Through some process of spiritual osmosis? Listen, why don't you try to remember it after dinner?"

"I will," she said, "if you'll just go on upstairs and get out of the way. . . . Lucy. . . ."

Lucy looked hard at her mother, hoping she would know what she was thinking, but her mother was not even looking at her now, though she had just called to her.

"I knew all along," Lucy said, "I knew all along we wouldn't go."

"Lucy!" Mama said. "I've got to get dinner for six people."

"You needn't get me no damn dinner," Lucy said.

Mama shut her lips so tight that none of the red showed.

"Lucy," she said, "Daddy and I have got to move Uncle Tubby just as soon as I get these dishes washed. Now you take him for a walk or something."

"I'm tired of him," Lucy said.

Daddy set his glass down on the table. "Go on," he said, "I'll come out after a while and we'll look at the stars."

"My God!" Lucy said. "There won't be any for hours."

Daddy took a step toward her. *"What did you say?"*

"I said there wouldn't be any for a long time yet."

"Well, we'll look at them when they do come out. . . . Go on. . . . *You hear me?"*

Lucy walked out of the kitchen and around to the front of the house. Borcke had come out and sat on the top step, slowly slanting his nose this way and that, to catch the wind. She sat down beside him. A faint smell of horse manure came up to her—he *would* roll in it. She pulled him up into her lap. He struggled for a moment, then, when he found that she would not let him go, sank back, but kept turning his head as the breeze shifted.

Uncle Tubby came down the steps. "Where are the slave quarters?" he asked.

Lucy pointed to a plantation of locusts on their left. "They used to be over there, but they blew off the hill. A long time ago."

He sat down on the step below her and took out his pipe. "All wreathed in trumpet vine," he said. "Just like the Big House. I intend that Pompey shall sleep there this night."

Lucy turned and looked at him. He smiled at her and patted her leg.

"Does Pompey sleep in the bed with you?" she asked.

"God forbid. He sleeps on a pallet on the floor. But he snores like the Devil."

"So does Borcke," Lucy said.

He bent his head to sniff Borcke's back. "Horse. . . . You know, the minute I laid eyes on that dog I knew he slept in the bed with you."

"Mama's got to take more care of him when I get the pony," Lucy said.

Uncle Tubby turned around again and clasped her ankle in his big, warm hand and shook it. "Ah, sweet melody of love!" he said. "The exercising, the currying, the deliberation as to whether it ought to be eight ears of corn or six. . . ."

"Four is about right for a pony," Lucy said, "unless they're nubbins. . . . But nubbins," she added dreamily, "are so often wormy. I wouldn't give 'em to *my* horse."

The hollyhocks at the side of the portico shook. The lean greyish cat that had been asleep there uncurled herself, stretched, yawned, and ascending the steps rubbed against Lucy's leg before she sat down and began to wash her face.

"Go on away," Lucy said, "I don't feel like cats."

Uncle Tubby eyed her thoughtfully. "I suppose," he said, "that sometimes you feel like cats and sometimes you feel like dogs."

"I don't hardly ever feel like *her*," Lucy said. "She's a mean old devil-fish." She leaned over, still holding the dog in her lap and lightly twisted the cat's ear. "You know you are!" she said.

"What does she do?"

"Sneaks up into little birds' nests and kills 'em. She killed a little robin once. Jenny beat her with the rake but she killed him before we could get him away from her. And she's just a kitten machine!"

"Perhaps it's incessant parturition that makes her so bloodthirsty," Uncle Tubby said.

"That's what I think," Lucy said. "But she don't eat the birds. She brings 'em in and hollers to the kittens to come and get them. In the spring we have to keep her shut up in the smoke house."

"Doesn't that give her complexes?"

"I expect it does," Lucy said with a sigh, "but it'd give us complexes not to eat. Daddy *has* to get some writing done. He can't think about the Civil War when she's out here yowling." And she imitated several times the cries of a cat bringing food to her young.

He nodded. "I had thought of him as a specialist in carnage but I see your point. You can't have it going on inside and outside at the same time."

Daddy came around the corner of the house. "Tubby, want to take a little walk?" he said.

"Sure," Uncle Tubby said and jumped up.

"Where are you going, Daddy?" Lucy asked.

"Down to the cabin," Daddy said. "Mama thinks Jenny might feel like getting dinner by this time."

"I bet she don't," Lucy said.

"Well, we can ask her," Daddy said irritably.

They started down the hill. Uncle Tubby was talking about somebody they both knew in France, but Daddy did not seem to be listening, walking the way he always walked, his head sunk on his chest, his eyes bent on the ground. They came to the foot of the long slope. Daddy turned toward the cabin but Lucy went through the gate and out on to the road where the mail box stood. "Here's where the man was killed," she said. Uncle Tubby came trotting over, but Daddy stood where he was, frowning.

"How did you know about it, Lucy?" he asked.

"Mrs. Eglinton told me," she said and scuffed up some of the dirt with the toe of her slipper, asking herself if this dirt beside the mail box could be the same dirt that was here then. It was yellow, like that dirt across the river, but drier, and tiny particles of something that wasn't dirt shone in it. Mica, quartz? She had read those names in the Encyclopedia once but she couldn't remember the pictures that had gone with them. A little clump of grass came up by its roots. She mashed it into the ground with her foot. A green stain spread on the side of her slipper. She rubbed the side of her shoe into the ground until the green had changed to yellow-brown.

". . . Body servant. . . ." Uncle Tubby said.

"It's a servant stays by your body, dummy," Lucy said.

Daddy looked at her with hard eyes. "Lucy," he said, "go and tell Jenny that Mama wants her to come and get supper if she's able. Tell her that company has come."

Lucy ran up on the porch and knocked on the door, then stood with her back to the door, looking off into the woods. She liked to stand on the little porch and imagine what it would be like to be Jenny and live in this little house, all covered with vines. Jenny kept the shades down, night and day. It was always dark inside and smelled of carnations, the flower Jenny loved best. There were only two chairs, so you usually sat on the bed. Over in the corner was Jenny's dressing table, covered with blue silk ruffles. On its glass top stood a velvet box that was full of the jewels Jenny's beau, Mr. Stamper, had given her: pearls and diamonds and rubies and garnets and sapphires. Jenny would turn the box on its side so that they all spilled out on the glass, and put the rings on her fingers or drape the necklaces and bracelets over her smooth, dark arm. "I don't know what I'm going to do with that man. He's always showering me with jewels!"

Daddy was yelling. Lucy turned around and knocked harder.

There were slow steps, the sound of a chair being dragged aside, and then a chuckle. Lucy waited. The chuckle came again. There was a brushing sound. Was somebody leaning down to look through the keyhole?

She walked down the steps and over to where Daddy and Uncle Tubby stood waiting. "There's somebody in there with Jenny," she said.

"Nonsense," Daddy said. "You know Jenny wouldn't do that. Right here . . . in the middle of the afternoon. You know she wouldn't. . . ."

"*You* go on up there," Lucy said, but he had already gone up the steps and was knocking at the door, louder than she could ever have knocked. "Jenny," he called, "Miss Sally wants you to come up to the house. She's got company."

There was silence and then the laugh came again. The person inside said something this time. It sounded like "You tell Miss Sally. . . ." Daddy's face had turned a dark red. He stared at the door and then leaned forward with his face close to it, and knocked again. "Jenny, open the door. I want to speak to you."

The door stayed closed. The person inside was talking, breaking off to laugh every now and then. Lucy drew nearer. She could not understand what the person inside was saying, but she knew that it was a woman, from the voice. Daddy and Uncle Tubby were staring at each other. Suddenly Uncle Tubby laughed. "Better let her sleep it off," he said.

Daddy let his hand fall at his side. They stood a few minutes longer, listening silently, then Daddy came down the steps and they walked back to the house. Mama was standing at the top of the drive beside the crape myrtle bush. "Any hope?" she called.

Daddy shook his head.

"Did you tell her to take some aspirin? It looks like she *could* come up and at least peel the potatoes! My God, all the things I do for *her*."

"Let me peel the potatoes," Uncle Tubby said.

Mama looked at him. Lucy knew that she was thinking that

she would see him drop dead before she let him into her kitchen.

"She's drunk," Daddy said.

Mama looked at him as if she thought he was crazy. "Drunk?" she said. "Why, you know she never touches a drop."

"Dead drunk," Daddy said. "That's what comes. . . ."

Mama clapped her hand to her forehead. "My God, it *is* my fault."

"Set her a bad example?" Uncle Tubby asked.

"I gave her a hot toddy," Mamma said. "She was crying with the pain and just before lunch I gave her a hot toddy and I told her to take the bottle down there and fix herself another one if her tooth didn't stop aching."

"I told you. . . ." Daddy said.

"You never told me," Mama said. "You never told me anything and you would have given her a hot toddy yourself if you had thought of it, but you never would have thought of it because you don't think about anybody but yourself, all day long and half the night. . . ." Daddy was looking at her hard. She stopped and shook her head, like a dog coming up out of the water. "*Jenny* drunk!" she said.

Uncle Tubby came over to Lucy. "How long will it be before dinner?" he whispered.

"A long time," she said. "Mama's got to get it."

"What say we take a run in the woods?" he asked in the same low tone.

She looked at her father and mother but they had turned their backs and were walking around the corner of the house. He smiled and held out his hand. She put her own hand in his and let him hold it a moment before she let it drop to her side. She led the way toward the fence that separated the front yard from the MacDonoughs' yard.

The fence was of white oak palings, held together by wire. She unlatched the gate and passed the old brick smoke house which her mother had converted into a hen house. Ranged in front of it were a variety of discarded kitchen utensils: saucepans that had been soldered for the last time, an old iron pot which held no more than a pint of water because of a hole in its side, a broken crock.

Uncle Tubby had stopped and was looking at the iron pot. "Is your father setting up in the junk business?" he asked.

Lucy smothered a laugh. "It's for the chickens," she said, "to drink out of." And she pointed to some rusted pie pans farther down the slope, out of which earlier in the season the newly hatched chickens had drunk.

From the slope below came the hum of voices and the sharp crack of axes. Mr. MacDonough and Mr. Lancaster were chopping up the boughs they had brought and fifteen-year-old Michael MacDonough was nailing them to the uprights that dotted the bare ground around the big hickory. They always had their meetings beside that tree. The tree was dead and its branches gave no shade, so they made an arbor out of boughs and the people sat under it during the three or four weeks that the meeting would continue. They knew when the meeting would begin—this evening after supper—but they didn't know when it would end. They would keep on as long as the Spirit was with them. Mr. MacDonough had heard of a meeting that was so powerfully worked upon by the Spirit that it did not break up till frost came.

They walked on in silence. Uncle Tubby stumbled over an old shoe; the ground was bare, even of weeds, but littered with rusted tin cans, scraps of leather, broken china, old shoes. He was looking at Lucy as if he wondered how the shoe got there. She smothered a laugh. "We've raked and raked," she said, "but we can't get 'em all off. This place had tenants for fifty years before we came."

"Is Mr. MacDonough a tenant or a sharecropper?" Uncle Tubby asked.

"He can't make a crop—he hasn't got any mules. I reckon he's a tenant," she said.

She spoke the last words in a whisper. Ruby and Mary Magdalene had come around the corner of the cabin to sit on the steps. Ruby, who was thirteen and a half and tall for her age, wore a gingham dress that Sarah Lewis had given her last summer. It was so faded by repeated washings that Lucy could not have recognized it as having belonged to her mother, except for a tag of braid that still dangled from one sleeve. Both the girls wore their hair falling to their shoulders. Ruby's was the same color as her father's, Magdalene's was pure gold.

Each of them held a pone of cold corn bread in her hand. Lucy knew that the bread would have a little sugar sprinkled on it, or a light smear of molasses. They sat down on the top step and began to eat slowly. Their hazel eyes stared straight ahead. They did not answer when Lucy said, "Y'all start school today?"

Mrs. MacDonough came out of the house, the baby on her arm, one of her lean breasts hanging free. The baby was crying. She sat down and had put the nipple in his mouth before she saw the newcomers. She held him closer to her with one hand and with the other tried to pull her dress up over her bare breast. "Howdy, Lucy," she said. "Want a piece of bread?"

"I don't believe I care about any right now," Lucy said. She glanced at Uncle Tubby. "This is Mr. MacCollum from New York."

Mrs. MacDonough said nothing. Uncle Tubby was bowing. "We have been admiring your view," he said.

Mrs. MacDonough glanced past him to the far meadows on

the other side of the river. Her face was tanned to the color of leather; she was bent almost in two. You thought that she was old till you saw her eyes. When she looked at them and smiled her eyes were the color of leaves turning in the wind before a rain. "We never have lived in a prettier place," she said. A young Bantam rooster had jumped up beside Ruby and Magdalene and now, with a flutter of wings, was attempting the third step. Mrs. MacDonough thrust out a bare, dirty foot and swept him to the ground. "We can't hardly keep 'em off the porch," she said. "They're so pet. . . . Y'all come up and set awhile!"

Lucy shook her head. "We were just passing," she said. She knew that Mrs. MacDonough did not mean anything by the invitation. It was like "Come on and go home with me." Ruby and Magdalene said that every time they came up to the house to play. Last year she had been green and every time they said that would go and ask Mama if she could go home with them, but now she knew that they said that only to be polite. They had better manners than she herself had, she reflected, only theirs were of another kind than hers. At the table, for instance, if they wanted anything very much they said, "I don't care if I do," instead of "Yes, thank you." Uncle Tubby, the goop, had taken Mrs. MacDonough at her word and was stepping up on the porch!

Mrs. MacDonough's eyes sparkled in her brown face; she held the baby tighter against her breast while with one hand she smoothed her dress down over her stomach. (Mama watched Mrs. MacDonough's stomach all the time; she said she was sure that there was another baby in there now.) Mrs. MacDonough would go straight through anything; you couldn't imagine her giving up. "Ruby," she was saying now, "git some chairs." Lucy realized with horror that they were going to treat her like company, just because Uncle Tubby didn't have the sense God gives a goose. She sat down hurriedly on the top step. "I'd rather sit here, Mrs. MacDonough," she said.

The young rooster had hopped up on the porch again and was making for the cleared space between the two straight chairs in which Mrs. MacDonough and Uncle Tubby now sat. Lucy caught him and held him prisoner, with one hand curved under his breast, while the other stroked the red and green feathers that curved, lyre-shaped, over his narrow back.

She could look through the front room into the lean-to, where the stove sat. The grate was ajar; a few cold ashes spilled down on to the rusty apron, like ashes on an old man's vest. The MacDonoughs must have just finished dinner—they ate at four o'clock in the afternoon. A black iron pot still stood on the top of the stove. She could smell, even out here, the rank odor that always came from the lean-to. It was the dish water they poured out of the back door, she thought, or maybe it was the MacDonoughs themselves. There was no place for them to bathe. The children's faces, in summer, their bare arms and legs, showed always through a light crust of dirt. She glanced at Uncle Tubby. She hoped that he would not tell her mother that when she was playing with the MacDonough children she often ate the same food that they did.

Uncle Tubby was asking Mrs. MacDonough how much eggs sold for a dozen. "I don't rightly know," Mrs. MacDonough said. "Me and Mrs. Lewis ain't had any to sell."

Lucy's eyes went back to the open doorway. The room beyond it was the only one the MacDonoughs had except for the lean-to. The old cabin that had once stood there had burned down long ago. When her father had had the little house built he had expected it to be occupied by one person, the cook, rather than a whole family. But Jenny had liked the little cabin at the gate better and when the MacDonoughs came along her father had let them have it. Her mother had protested that a whole family couldn't live in two and a half rooms. "Well, they've still got all outdoors," her father said. "Maybe they think they're better off with two and a half rooms than with none." (Every Christmas Mr. MacDonough tried to find another place to live, but he didn't have any team or tools so he never could make a trade, and they had to stay on in the cabin.)

Lucy stared at the pine floor. There was a grease spot on it shaped like a man in a top hat and a little way off from it another spot that she always thought of as a rearing horse. Ruby had taken the two chairs out so there was nothing inside to sit on except a stool. A chest of drawers that her mother had given them stood between the two windows and in the far corner, covered by a patchwork quilt, stood the bed on which they all slept at night. She had heard her mother speculate about how they slept. She had never told her that Magdalene one day had explained to her how they managed. Mr. and Mrs. MacDonough slept side by side, in the middle of the bed. Michael slept up against his father. The smallest boy, David Lewis, slept at Michael's feet. On the other side of the bed, Ruby, the oldest girl, lay beside her mother, with Magdalene at her feet. The old baby, Lura Belle, had what was left of the foot of the bed and the new baby always slept in the cradle which was drawn up close beside the big bed, so that Ruby or her mother could put a hand out and rock the cradle if the baby cried in the night.

Sometimes, at night, lying in her own room, hearing her father's and mother's voices on the floor below, not really afraid of the dark but not sleepy as yet and a little afraid that she might be going to be afraid, she thought of the MacDonoughs down the hill, all asleep in one bed, curled, it might be, the one around the other, like rabbits, or kittens, and it seemed to her that that was a better way to sleep than alone, between cool sheets, with only faint voices from the floor below you to tell you that you were not alone in the world.

The rooster squatted suddenly and eased himself of a thin, black mucilaginous trickle. Lucy felt the color rising in her cheeks, but no one was noticing either her or the rooster. She lifted him gently and set him down on the ground.

Uncle Tubby was asking Mrs. MacDonough how much money Mr. MacDonough made a day.

"Seventy-five cents," Mrs. MacDonough said. "Of course some gets a dollar and a dollar and a quarter, but he never asks but seventy-five cents. I tell him he could get a dollar if he asked for it, but Terence, he ain't one to ask."

"A man's got a right to make enough to live on," Uncle Tubby said.

The lids drooped over Mrs. MacDonough's green eyes. "It's the Lord's will," she said. "I reckon it's the Lord's will that some make more than others."

"I've never understood why farm laborers don't organize," Uncle Tubby said. "It's the most basic of all industries." He had set his brown hands on his knees and was leaning forward in his chair, his eyes earnestly fixed on Mrs. MacDonough's face.

"He ought to let her alone," Lucy thought. "She's not like us. He can't *make* her like us!"

A long, snoring gurgle broke from the baby as his lips fell away from the breast. Mrs. MacDonough sat up straighter, beckoned to Ruby. "You take him," she whispered. Ruby tiptoed off with the baby. Mrs. MacDonough, buttoning the faded grey gingham over her breast, kept her eyes on Uncle Tubby's face. "Whereabouts is it you live?" she asked.

"I was born on Long Island," he said, "but I live in New York City now. That is, most of the time."

"Ain't you sorry you're such a long way from home?" she asked, smiling.

He looked at her, smiling, too, and did not say anything.

Lucy stood up. "Uncle Tubby, let's go watch 'em put up the brush."

"Yes," he said. "I'd like to watch that."

They walked down the slope to where the big hickory stood, stark and dead in the middle of the field. A truck had driven out from town a few days ago, to dump a pile of lumber beside it. Seats, made out of the planks, were now ranged in a wide semi-circle about the tree. At the end of each row of seats a forked pole had been driven into the ground. A long pole of the same size was suspended in the two forks. On these poles freckle-faced Mike was hanging the boughs which Mr. MacDonough was chopping up. The boughs were from trees which Daddy had wanted cut down at the edge of the bottom: hackberry and sassafras and nanny wood, but here and there were a few oak boughs and in one place Lucy saw the pale, club-shaped leaves of the tulip tree. She went over and stood beside Mike. "You cut down a tulip tree," she said in a low voice.

He turned around and stuck his tongue out at her. "You want it?" he asked. "Drag it up to the house if you do."

His father, coming up just then with a fresh load of boughs, had heard what they were saying. He looked at Lucy kindly. "One side of it was rotten," he said. "War'n't no hope for it, so we just cut it down."

"I don't care how many trees they cut down," Lucy muttered and moved over to where Uncle Tubby stood gazing at the arbor. He gave her an eager glance. "Isn't it terrific?" he asked.

A man was sitting under the drooping boughs, in the middle of one of the rows. His arms were folded across his chest; a fiddle lay on the seat beside him. He laughed suddenly and rose and came toward them.

"Folks in town have church buildings," he said. "Terence and his crowd, they just have brush."

Uncle Tubby laughed, too. "The woods were God's first temples," he said.

The man looked from one to the other, his face the color of a rooster's comb; his eyes shone like silver. His yellow hair, brushed straight back from his forehead, was stiff with dirt and grizzled at the temples and grizzled, too, in one wide streak over his forehead. He stared at Uncle Tubby and said, "How ya do, Miss Lucy Lewis."

Lucy felt a chill go down her spine. She had seen Claude Lancaster often, driving his team along the big road—once he had worked in their woods for a whole week, cutting down trees—but she had never stood so close to him before. Magdalene and Ruby had stolen up behind her and were standing behind her; she could hear them breathing. Ruby had told her that Claude Lancaster wasn't sorry for what he had done, had said that he would do it over again. All the Lancasters were hard-headed, Ruby said, but Claude was the hard-headedest of the lot. If he hadn't been he wouldn't have killed his brother.

He was not looking at her now. He had shifted his bold gaze to Uncle Tubby's face while he spoke to Mr. MacDonough. "Terence, I been figuring what I'd lead off with tonight. How about 'The Judgment of Paris'?"

"Is that a good hymn?" Uncle Tubby asked.

Mr. Lancaster turned his hard eyes on Mr. MacDonough. "It's one of the best," he said.

There was a light clatter behind Lucy. Lura Belle and David Lewis had been chasing each other over the seats. David Lewis suddenly emerged from one of the rows and running up to Lucy, clasped her about the knees. His upturned face was a delicate oval. His blue eyes shone up at her from under lids the color of bruised morning glories. His hair, as long as a girl's, fell in a gilt shower almost to the ground. "Yuchee! Yuchee!" he panted.

Lucy stooped and flung both arms about him, and as she did so realized that she usually avoided contact with the MacDonough children. The odor of sour vomit came up to her, mixed with earth; the children had been playing in a newly plowed field. "He doesn't know!" she thought and gave him another squeeze before she let him go. "He's so little he doesn't even know!"

Lura Belle had come up and was plucking at his ragged sleeve. The two children ran off. Lucy got to her feet. Uncle Tubby was asking Mr. Lancaster to tell him the names of some of the other songs they sang in meeting and Mr. Lancaster was giving him a lot of jig tunes. Every time he answered Uncle Tubby he looked at Mr. MacDonough. He knew that it was worrying Mr. MacDonough to have Uncle Tubby think that they played reels and jigs in meeting when they never played any instrument at all, because the Bible, they said, was against it.

Mr. MacDonough laid his ax down and straightened up. He looked at the sun dropping behind the woods, and then looked off across the river, to the far fields, which showed now purple, now lavender as the ragged clouds drifted over them.

"Claude," he said, "did you ever think that if it's as pretty up there as it is down here it's a right pretty place?"

Uncle Tubby spat on the ground, pretending that he was chewing tobacco, Lucy thought. "Well," he said, "it strikes me that there's a lot of needless misery down here."

Mr. Lancaster's cold eyes sparkled. "That's what I tell Terence." He pointed across the river. "What about Rob Sansom and his wife? Walking along the road and didn't step over the fence the way they usually done when a truck came by and two trucks piled up on the turn and throwed them over into Patterson's bottom. Dead as a mackerel, both of 'em, when they picked 'em up." He laughed his wild, reckless laugh. Whose fault was that? You mean to tell me them folks got killed because they didn't step over the fence?"

"It was the drivers' fault, evidently," Uncle Tubby said. "At least one of the drivers must have been at fault."

"One of 'em was in the right and the other one said the sun was in his eyes," Mr. Lancaster said. "Testified the sun was in his eyes. Mean to tell me a man has got to go to hell just because the sun was in his eyes?"

Mr. MacDonough was going past them with a fresh load of boughs. He laid them down at the end of the row before he turned and looked at Mr. Lancaster; the way he sometimes looked at Daddy as if there was something he wanted to tell him but didn't know how. He said slowly, "Vengeance is mine, saith the Lord."

Uncle Tubby looked like somebody who had just picked a quarter up in the big road. He had lifted some boughs and was awkwardly hanging them over the poles, but he dropped his bough on the ground and stood in front of Mr. MacDonough. "Mr. Lewis tells me that you are well grounded in the Scriptures," he said. "There's a passage in Revelations that's always bothered me."

Mr. MacDonough was silent, keeping his bright, dark eyes fixed on Uncle Tubby's face.

"It's about the Beast," Uncle Tubby said, "the number of the Beast. Now what does that mean?"

"Here is Wisdom," Mr. MacDonough said in the same slow way. "Let him that hath understanding count the number of the Beast; for it is the number of a man; and his number is Six Hundred and Three-score Six. . . ."

"Now what does that mean?" Uncle Tubby repeated.

Mr. MacDonough's eyes grew brighter. He smiled. "Now don't you know what that means?"

Uncle Tubby shook his head. "No. . . . Upon my word."

"You got one up thar on the hill."

"Got what?"

"Them cars you and Mr. Lewis ride around in," Mr. MacDonough said. "Don't you know they got the mark of the Beast on them? Mr. McCollum, every time you drive that car of yours up to a filling station and tell 'em to put gas in her you're taking bread out of some poor man's mouth. . . . Ain't that serving the Beast?"

Uncle Tubby laughed. "You've been talking to Stephen Lewis," he said.

Mr. MacDonough laughed too. "No, sir. I don't have to talk to him. I was here before he come."

Uncle Tubby had affixed a long sassafras bough to a pole by tying two of its switches into a clumsy knot and he now stepped back to survey his work. The bough hung so low that only a child could have sat under it without having his face tickled by its leaves, but he did not seem to realize that. He did not realize, either, that Mike MacDonough had left his work and was standing immediately behind him, cocking his head every time Uncle Tubby cocked his, and once, when Uncle Tubby stood still, his hands at his sides, leaning over and pretending that he was blowing his nose between thumb and finger.

Ruby and Magdalene had sat down in the front row. They kept their eyes fixed on Uncle Tubby's face and their heads turned with his every gesture. Magdalene looked as she always did, solemn, but Ruby giggled and hid her face on Magdalene's shoulder.

"Uncle Tubby!" Lucy said in a low voice.

As Uncle Tubby turned around, Terence swooped past him, picked a fallen bough from the ground and, swinging it in a wide arc, brought it up to rest, like a monstrous thumb against his nose.

"Yes, Lucy?" Uncle Tubby said.

Ruby was laughing so hard that her father and Mr. Lancaster were looking at her. Magdalene sat straight and stared at the ground. Lucy said steadily: "Uncle Tubby, let's take a walk in the woods."

Uncle Tubby hesitated. "All right." He looked at Mr. MacDonough and then at Mr. Lancaster. "I'll see you both tonight at the meeting."

"That's right," Mr. MacDonough said.

"You be there, too?" Uncle Tubby asked Mr. Lancaster.

"Claude has to come," Mr. MacDonough said gently. "To lead the singing."

They crossed the field and started toward the woods. The sun was right behind the woods now; the trees looked as if they were on fire. Uncle Tubby went first. Lucy walked behind him slowly, savoring a bitterness she had stored up in her mind but until this moment had not had an opportunity to relish. They came to the plum thicket. The glow from the setting sun struck past the black trunks and illuminated the frail plum boughs. *We are walking into a great, red oven,* Lucy thought. *The witch who lives in the woods will roast us in her great, red oven, roast us and tear us limb from limb. But what difference does it make? I am not anybody to save. I am just a changeling. My mother said I was a changeling. . . .*

Uncle Tubby stopped suddenly and threw back his head and laughed. "Strange country," he said. "I never saw such a country! But they do have some good ideas, those MacDonoughs." He walked close to her and catching hold of her hand and swinging it between them as they walked, began to talk French: *"Il y avait un vieil ermite qui s'appellait St. Brendan. Il quitta son pays et traversa l'océan jusqu'en Bretagne. Lorsqu'il y arriva il traîna son bateau sur la plage et il était si fatigué qu'il partit dans les bois et s'étendit par terre. Mais avant de s'endormir il regarda le ciel et il lui sembla qu'il pleuvrait peut-ētre avant le jour. Il prit donc deux arbustes et les lia l'un à l'autre avec un rameau de saule. Alors il considéra son ouvrage et il pensa que la pluie pourrait pénétrer; il inclina deux arbustes de plus, les lia l'un à lautre. . . ."*

Borcke had run on ahead of them, but now he had stopped and was digging in a mole run that crossed the path. Uncle Tubby stopped, too, and picking up a stick drew two intersecting arcs in the fresh dirt that Borcke's hind legs were flinging up. *"Et lorsqu'il se réveilla le lendemain matin, il avait une église! . . . Comprends-tu?"*

"I don't speak it," Lucy said.

"Mais tu le parlais quand tu étais en France. Pourquoi ne veux-tu pas le parler maintenant?"

"I forgot it coming over on the boat," Lucy said.

They had passed through the plum thicket and were in the woods. The crimson glow was just sunlight washing the trunks of the trees. Uncle Tubby was still looking at her. *"Je pense que tu es la plus belle petite fille que j'aie vue depuis longtemps,"* he said.

"Magdalene MacDonough is a heap prettier'n I am," Lucy said.

"She may be pretty, but I bet she hasn't got that look in her eye. . . . That *je ne sais quoi* look. . . . How do you suppose you get it?"

"Tending to my own business," Lucy said.

If he had had long ears he would have looked like Borcke,

his head on one side, his eyes dark in the leafy light and as soft and sad as Borcke's eyes. He smiled and said, "All right, young lady."

It was the first time he had called her "Young Lady." He wouldn't have done it then if she hadn't spoken sharply to him. She told herself that she was not sorry. Grown people didn't expect you to answer what they said to you. Half the time, when they said anything to you, they were just talking to themselves. She had found that out a long time ago.

They came to a place where the ground fell away sharply. The gnarled roots of the trees made a sort of stairway. He turned to give her his hand but she ran nimbly down the roots and was at the foot of the little hill as soon as he. There was a thick carpet of moss at the foot of the root staircase. The path, half hidden in ferns, wound between beeches whose huge boles were roughened by carvings, initials, dates, the inscriptions often enclosed in hearts or winged with arrows. Uncle Tubby walked with his head thrown back, gazing up into the leaves which would not turn yellow for months. Suddenly he stopped, lifted his foot, examined the sole of his shoe and put his foot down again. He did not know that he was walking on top of a stream. Everywhere around here the ground was soggy; a stream flowed under the whole grove. It went underground a little below the waterfall and flowed under the cornfield, too, to emerge again as a spring in a wild chasm on the river bank.

He had stopped again. "I'm damned if I'm not going to carve my name," he said. "Yours, too."

He took a penknife out of his pocket and wandered off among the trees. Lucy sat down on a rock. A clump of sweet fern came up beside the rock. She plucked a frond and crushed it in her fist and thought of the stream flowing secretly under the rock, under the dead leaves, making even the pebbles in the path glisten with a light film of water. She kept perfectly still and thought she could hear the plash of the waterfall. It was only a little way off in the woods.

She did not know whether she wanted to go there today. Some days she did not feel like going there. When you felt that way you might as well not go. But some days you went and afterwards you couldn't imagine what it would have been like if you hadn't gone. It made a difference, though, who went with you. She and her mother came here often. The stream flowed in a narrow channel up on the bluff, then suddenly dived between two tall leaning rocks and fell fifteen feet to a flat ledge below. That was what made the waterfall. Her mother would stand, clasping the trunk of a tree and stare and stare until you were afraid she would forget who you were and you went to her and took her arm and said *"Mama!"* . . . Her father had gone there with them once. In the spring, soon after they bought the place. He said that he would go back again some time.

Uncle Tubby had found a young beech tree whose bark shone like grey satin. He was carving "L.L." and "E.M." each in the center of its own heart, but with the hearts intertwined. . . . The next time Lois came to visit her she would bring her to see the initials carved on that tree. If Lois asked her she would say, "L.L—that's Lucy Lewis," but she wouldn't say how old he was or anything about him, just "a man from New York."

He had begun another carving, a very small heart, pierced by an arrow, and now he was carving tiny initials in its center.

"Who's that?" she asked.

He looked at her, smiling, like a person who knows a secret he isn't going to tell. "Imogene," he said, "Imogene . . . Marie . . . Louise . . . Lointaine . . . Don't you think that's a pretty name?"

"I think it's a funny name," Lucy said.

"*Lointaine*? . . . That's her mother's family name."

"Whose name?" she said and kicked her heels against the rock, "Whose family name?"

"My little girl's."

"You haven't got any little girl," she said. "You aren't even mar. . . ." She stopped, remembering something her father had said about him: ". . . just ripe for another disastrous marriage." "You haven't got any little girl," she repeated, to cover her confusion.

"You'd think I had if you could see her bills. The things that girl buys!"

He had finished the last flourish on the L and was putting a period beside it. "What does she buy?" Lucy asked.

"Oh . . . mink . . . and vair . . . and samovair . . . and Lucite. Let her stroll through Saks Fifth Avenue and she will order a thousand Lucite bubbles, each one in its own filigree box. . . ." He fell silent, absorbed in his carving.

"What does she do with them?" Lucy asked.

"Breaks them on people's heads. Or sometimes she lets them float out of the window and they fall down on the heads of the people passing by and break. The police are at the door, night and day. But we pay no attention to them."

"Does she go to school?"

"She did, for a while, but she came home one day and said that Miss Plobscote was an old pelican. Naturally I couldn't deny that." He shut his penknife up and put it back into his pocket. "How does it happen that the MacDonoughs go to school in August?" he asked.

"It's country school," Lucy said. "They start soon as the crops are laid by. And then they get out early in the spring."

"So they can put the crops in again? . . . And where do you go to school?"

"In town. . . . Daddy says I'm not learning a thing."

"And are you?"

Lucy shook her head. "Not much," she said. "Miss Simpson is the dumbest old thing you ever saw in your life. But Mama says it's vulgar to complain about the teacher."

"Your mother is a wonderful woman. . . . Fearfully—and wonderfully made. But I shouldn't think she'd be much help in so to speak living your own life."

"She's got more fool ideas than any white woman I ever saw," Lucy said.

"Yes? What are some of her ideas?"

"She just hates Yankees," Lucy said. "She doesn't think anything Yankees do is right."

"I've noticed that," he said before she had time to be embarrassed.

"And she won't use cube sugar," Lucy said, "and she thinks it's vulgar to have your garage fastened on to your house. And *Christmas wreaths*! We can get 'em out of the woods but we can't buy 'em. . . . She don't even like electric lights on Christmas trees. . . ."

"A very *parfait* gentlewoman of the Old South," he said. "I wonder how she got that way?"

"Well, she stayed out in the country with Mammy a lot when she was little," Lucy said. "Daddy thinks that's what makes her so peculiar."

"Who's Mammy?"

"She's my great-grandmother. She lives 'way out in the country where all the Fayerlees used to live. But she's so peculiar can't anybody live on the place with her except a few colored people."

"Does she raise a special brand of colored people?"

"Oh, they're all almost as old as she is. They've been in the family a long time and know how to manage her. . . . Daddy says she's hell on wheels. . . ."

"And what about you?" he asked. "Are you peculiar like the Fayerlees or peculiar like the Lewises?"

"I don't know," she said with a sigh. "They don't know how I'm going to turn out yet. One thing, I'm not going to be a writer."

"And why is that?"

"It takes up all your time," she said. "You don't have time to go around and have any fun or do anything because all the time you got to be writing. And then days when Daddy isn't writing we all of us have to worry because he can't get any writing done. . . . We just hardly ever get to do anything," she concluded with another sigh.

"And some people think you lead such a charmed life!" he exclaimed and then stopped, pointing to a big-bellied oak that thrust its trunk out into the path, like a pompous person demanding attention. "What's over that way?" he asked.

"The waterfall," Lucy said.

"The *waterfall*!" he said. "We'll have to see about that."

They passed the pompous oak and suddenly were on the bluff overlooking the stream. The trees that grew there were tall and slim, second growth, her father said, but down in the gorge were more big beeches and, glimmering as white as the water that dashed beside it, a giant sycamore that was so old its trunk had split in two.

He stared. "Good Lord!" he said. "Why didn't you tell me you had this up your sleeve?"

Lucy laughed in delight. "It's not up my sleeve. It's in the woods."

But he had grasped her hand and was dragging her with him down the path, slipping, sliding, sometimes falling to their knees, rising to keep on at the same pace until, finally, on the brink of the falls, he caught hold of a low hanging branch and, steadying himself, released her hand.

"There!" he said. "Look what I did for you!"

"Look what I did for *you*!" Lucy retorted.

They watched the water rushing down between the two leaning rocks to fall on the ledge below. It struck so hard that every drop of water that fell leaped off the rock again, some straight into the air, to redescend more gently, others bouncing off into spray. Lucy moved over and stood between him and the falls and felt the cold needles of spray beat against her skin. The rock showed darkest where the water was churned into the wildest froth. She put her hand up to feel how chill her cheek had grown and smiled at him. "It looks like Undine's uncle, doesn't it?" she said.

He stared at her. "Be damn! I haven't thought of *her* in twenty years!"

"She was the foster-daughter of the fisherman and lived on the point with them, but she had an uncle in the forest. . . ."

"A terrible old party," he said. "Name of Kühleborn. The fisherman was always meeting him when he went through the forest to sell his fish. . . ."

"He was really a waterfall," she said.

"So he was! . . . *White and nodding!* . . . Have you got to the place where she gets a soul?"

She shook her head. "She just runs out of the house when they say anything to her and then they hear water dashing against the window pane."

"She outgrows those tricks and gets a soul. Makes a lot of trouble for everybody. But you read on. . . ." He raised his head, his nostrils widening. "What's that I smell?"

She looked at her hand, from which, somewhere on the way, the crushed frond had fallen. "Sweet fern," she said and held her hand out so that he could see the green stain on her palm. He smiled and shook his head, too. "I told you!" he said.

"Told me what?"

"That you were a *belle dame sans merci.* Carrying sweet fern! Aren't you ashamed of yourself?"

"No," Lucy said and heard her own laughter tinkle, high and frail as the spray. "No," she repeated, "I'm not a bit ashamed of myself," and she ran over to the sycamore tree and stood by it, not looking back over her shoulder, for she knew that he would follow.

The tree was so old that its trunk was hollow. It had, perhaps, been struck by lightning years ago. That was what her father said, though her great-uncle maintained that lightning never struck a sycamore. At any rate, it had sustained some injury which had resulted in a cleavage of its bark and outer fibers. But time had smoothed the edges of the wound and curled them back scroll-wise, to show the dark, decaying heart.

It was damply pitted by millions of little holes, the homes and highroads of insects. He stooped and gazed into the glistening cave, then straightened up, sighing.

"*You* could slip in there," he said. "Have you never been in there?"

She nodded. She and Ruby—the most daring of the MacDonoughs, though she had become more sedate since she had turned thirteen—had squeezed in and had stood with their bare feet sunk in the moist, rotting stuff that was heaped high inside. But not for more than a few seconds before Ruby turned to her, whispering, "Snakes!" and they wriggled out into the daylight, beside Magdalene, with only the feel of the wet, rotting stuff on their ankles to remind them that they had been inside. . . . But it would be different to stand in there with a grown man beside you. . . .

She stretched out her hand. He caught it and held it with a warm, even pressure. "This strange light," he said, "and all these great trees. It's magical, isn't it?" He looked down at her, smiling. "You *are* a *belle dame sans merci!*" he said.

She smiled back at him. A few feet from where they stood, a jewel weed, growing on the brink of the waterfall, trembled and bent toward the water, straightened up and, trembling, bent again. The pressure of his hand on hers grew warmer, closer, then suddenly slackened. They stood as they were for a moment before their hands fell to their sides as if struck apart. Mellow notes from some giant anvil were sounding through the woods. He listened. His eyes were still fixed on her face, but their expression had changed. He said:

"Six o'clock! Good Lord! We'll have to hurry."

"Dinner won't be ready yet," Lucy said.

But he had already turned away. "Shall we go back the same way we came?" he asked.

She looked about her vaguely and did not answer.

He took a few steps. "This same path?" he said.

She roused herself. "No," she said, "there's a short cut."

She called Borcke. They walked beside the stream until they came to a footlog. It was the only footlog she knew of anywhere around here, but he did not seem to find it remarkable that it should be there, spanning the stream, and she did not call his attention to it. He looked back once, just after they crossed the foot log, but he did not say anything else about the falls and she did not tell him that they were passing within a few feet of the place where the stream sank underground.

They came to a blackberry thicket. She stopped to eat a few berries, but he kept on along the path and after a few minutes she followed him to the top of the bluff. Up here there were no big trees, only third-growth post oaks, hackberries, dogwoods, gums and a few hickories. The people who owned the farm before her family bought it had been able to get wagons in here and had lumbered off the whole bluff.

They left the woods and entered the plum thicket. The path was one made by small game. He pushed the bushes aside as he went, but did not turn to hold them back for her. Sometimes the green closed in over the path so thick that she could not see his brown shirt. She looked behind her. The woods still blazed in the western sun. Ahead the eastern sky was faintly rosy from the reflection. There were no lights; the house crouched on the hill like an old grey horse lain down to rest. This was the time of day she loved best, when the sun was down but the light had not yet left the hill, the time of evening when the MacDonoughs sometimes suddenly came up over the side of the hill and without a word spoken they would all start running through the thin, cool air while the bats veered overhead. She broke a branch from a plum tree and peeled it. The dog came panting out of the thicket and lay down in the path before her. She bent and gently brushed the top of his head with her wand and walked on. The edges of all the plum leaves were touched with light, like the dew that sparkled on them sometimes in the mornings. . . . *Full beautiful . . . a fairy's child.* . . . She walked more slowly and as she went touched a leaf here and there with her wand.

She would be tall, as tall as the knight if she stood up, but she would be sitting sidewise on the steed, leaning down. Her hair fell over her shoulder in one long wave. Her eyes were grey and shone always with the same light.

"He-ey!" Uncle Tubby called and, raising his hand high in the air, raced out of the thicket and up the slope. She ran, too, with Borcke padding after her. Under the willow tree her father and mother stood talking to a lady and gentleman who had just got out of a car.

Her mother stared at her. "Where have you been?" she asked. "We've looked everywhere for you."

Uncle Tubby laid his hand on Lucy's shoulder. "She took me to her elfin grot," he said.

The lady looked at Lucy before she looked at him. She was

tall, and thinner, even, than Mama. She shook her head and her hair fell farther back on her shoulders. It was the same color as Lucy's and the same length. Her eyes were the color of the periwinkle blossoms that grew in the old graveyard at Merry Point.

She said, "Tubby, *don't* shut your wild, wild eyes!" But you couldn't hear the rest of what she was saying, for Uncle Tubby had put his arms about her and was kissing her. As Lucy gazed at them she would have wept but that all eyes were upon her.

IV

AT eight o'clock Lucy came out on the porch, smoothing down the skirt of her yellow dress. Uncle Tubby sat up in the hammock. "You look mighty pretty," he said. He put his arm out and would have detained her but she walked past him to stand in front of her father. He made no motion; then, as she continued to stand before him, he set his hands on her hips and would have drawn her on to his knee. She wriggled her shoulder blades until she could feel one of them protruding through the open back of her dress. "Button it," she said.

"Oh . . ." he said. "Well, stand still then," and held her against his knee with one hand pressed against her stomach while the other hand slowly fitted buttons to buttonholes.

"I like your hair that way," Uncle Tubby said.

Lucy smiled politely and, turning around, laid her arm about her father's neck. "Daddy, the stars are out," she said.

"In a minute," he answered and leaned over to knock his pipe out on the railing. " 'The Water-Bearer' is still the best thing she ever wrote," he said. "In fact, I haven't been able to see any of the later stuff. She had something in 'The Water-Bearer' that she hasn't had since."

"What about 'Gemini'?"

Stephen Lewis shook his head. "Dull," he said, "and diffuse. I felt that she was trying to get back to the kind of thing she did in 'The Water-Bearer' and couldn't. Something happened to Isabel after that first book. . . . Or maybe something didn't happen. . . ."

Lucy realized that they were talking about the visitor, Mrs. Reardon. She said in a high, scornful voice, "I suppose you want her to hear you. I suppose you want her to hear everything you're saying about her."

Her father laughed. "All right," he said. "Go get the Star-Finder."

She fetched the pasteboard wheel from his study. He stood up and, holding it over his head, turned it slowly from side to side until he had found the North Star, then handed it to her. "Now where's the Little Dipper?" he asked.

"I know those old Dippers," Lucy said.

He leaned over the railing, pointing. "Well, there's the Dragon. See him wind himself around the Little Dipper? See him flip his tail almost over on to the Bear?"

"Naw," Lucy said, "I don't see it."

Holding his pipe in his hand, he looked down at her and suddenly smiled and she knew that he was noticing her white kid slippers, her yellow dress, even the flat green ribbon that held her hair to one side. "Keep on looking," he said and went back to his chair.

She leaned farther out over the railing as her eyes searched the heavens. The sky was still pale; the stars showed only faintly. If she lowered her eyes, even for a moment, to the trees that fringed the river, she lost the Dippers and had to go back and find the North Star and then trace the Little Dipper curving out from it and the Big Dipper curving out from that. And as for the Dragon, it was as she had told him, she could not see it at all until she had looked at the Dippers so long that it seemed as if they actually were giant dippers flung down in a high meadow. After she had looked at them long enough she could see the Dragon rearing up between their handles to wriggle his way across the heavens.

"He's going to eat the Swan!" she said.

Her father glanced up. "Or Hercules." He looked back at Tubby. "God, aren't the heavens crowded!"

"It's the moon I worry about," Tubby said. "It's going to be tough when she breaks up."

"Just exactly what's going to happen?"

"It's pretty complicated. The very tides she's raising on the earth tend to slacken her orbital speed. Then, as her speed slackens, gravity grows stronger. She's being drawn slowly but inexorably closer to the earth. It'll take billions of years but it's bound to come. She'll keep spiraling closer to the earth till she reaches what they call a danger zone. She'll break up then."

"Into what?"

"Meteorites. There'll be a rain of meteorites; the earth will literally be bombarded; death and destruction everywhere. Then what's left of those meteorites will form a great ring and revolve around the earth. . . ."

Her father said:

> "I saw eternity the other night,
> Like a great ring of pure and endless light. . . ."

Uncle Tubby said: "Maybe. . . . Still, I don't believe that's quite what Vaughn is talking about."

A voice came from below stairs: "*Lucee!* Run out in the garden and get me some zinnias."

Lucy did not move.

"I was born under Scorpio," Tubby said suddenly. "You were too, weren't you, Steve?"

"Yes," her father said.

"The House of Death. A bad sign—unless a man is reborn."

"Yes," her father said.

Lucy had left the rail and was about to sit down in the chair near the hammock. Tubby reached out and, clasping her arm, drew her toward the hammock. "What sign has the *belle dame*?" he asked.

"The same as her mother. Libra."

"Libra!" Uncle Tubby punched Lucy in the small of the back. "A girl of very stout kidney."

Lucy wriggled out of his grasp and went to stand at her father's knee. "What's kidney, Daddy?" she asked.

"Kidney?" he repeated vaguely. "Lucy, you know what kidneys are."

"Rognons!" Uncle Tubby said hastily and since he could not get his hands on Lucy's back again set his hands, one on each side of his own waist. *"Rognons!* The reins. Keeps you balanced. See? That's why you're such a smart girl."

"Luc . . . EEEEE!" the call came again.

Lucy glanced at her father. He made a brief, impatient gesture with his hand. She walked to the railing and leaned over. "I'll get my white shoes wet," she cried.

There was no answer, but she could hear quick, darting steps below. When she had come upstairs a few minutes ago her mother had told her that there was nothing else she could do to help her. But she hadn't finished making the cream sauce and there was salad to make, too. Her mother wasn't calling now because she didn't have time to call. Lucy sighed and went into the house.

The hall seemed dark after the pale light outside. She did not realize at first that someone was mounting the stairs to the third floor. She thought that it must be the strange lady's husband. The shadowy figure had paused on the landing. She had the impression that the strange gentleman, if it was he, was gazing down at her as Uncle Tubby had looked down at her from that same landing earlier in the day. She did not look up but went into her own room. A pair of blunt scissors that she used to cut out paper dolls were lying on the table. She picked them up and was about to tiptoe out, then paused.

The door into the next room was ajar. She waited to make sure that nobody was in there before she tiptoed in. Two big brown traveling bags stood at the foot of the bed. One of them gaped wide. She saw grey-striped pajamas rolled into a ball and, stuck in beside them, a sheaf of papers. An oval-shaped hair brush lay on the floor. She resisted the impulse to pick it up and walked past it to the table that stood beside the bed. Somebody had laid a book down there, the way her father and mother had told her never to lay a book down, half open and face downwards. She tiptoed over to the bed and picked it up, muttering under her breath, as she had heard Jenny mutter under her breath one night when she had wanted to go out with Mr. Stamper and had to wait at table for company dinner: "I ain't made of pig iron. . . . I ain't made. . . ." Steps came to a halt over her head. There was the sound of rushing water. She thought, with satisfaction, that Mr. Reardon, whose room this must be—though how anybody could tell, with people sleeping all over the house, she didn't know—Mr. Reardon would have to walk up a flight of stairs every time he wanted to go to the bathroom.

Something white and black and shining lay under the book.

She took it up in her hand—a cross carved out of ebony, with an ivory figurine fastened upon it: Jesus on the Cross. She turned the crucifix sideways. The tiny face was yellowed to the color of old flesh. Light shot from the diamonds that formed the eyes as Lucy examined the figure more closely. The little body sprang upwards like a bow, so taut that its middle part did not touch the cross. She felt the curve of the back delicately with the tip of her fingers. If he had been a real man he would have had kidneys there. It was there, in the small of the back, that Uncle Tubby had said that the kidneys were placed, the kidneys that he said kept you balanced. With the tip of the same finger she touched the feet, pierced, each, with a golden nail, a ruby beside it. They were carved so minutely that she could discern the nails on the tiny toes. She touched the loin cloth; its folds were edged with gold. She turned the crucifix in her hand. The eyes glowed at her. In the bath room overhead somebody turned off a tap. She raised her head and stared at the wall. Her hand closed tightly over the crucifix. She had turned to leave the room when she looked back. It seemed to her that the book was not lying in the same position it had been in when she found it. Still holding the crucifix tightly clutched in her hand, she tiptoed over to the table, lifted the book, laid it down again exactly in the center of the table and went out, softly closing the door behind her.

There were steps on the stairs and then steps in the hall outside her door. She sat on the side of her bed, the crucifix clasped in her hand. When the steps had passed she opened her hand and held the crucifix out before her on her open palm. The Christ's head drooped sidewise. The fine nose, the high forehead, crowned with clotted curls, looked white now, against the black wood of the cross. The eyes still shone, but the cheeks were slightly sunken, the mouth open—as if he were about to gasp out words. A shiver went through Lucy. With an effort she raised her eyes from the figure and sat rigid, staring at the wall opposite. It was patterned with figures: a man and a boy carrying a donkey slung upside down by his tied hooves from a pole, while a woman watched from a casement window were the patterns repeated oftenest. Somewhere off in the fields a calf was bawling for its mother. Her arm was aching. She waited until the calf had bawled again and went noiselessly to the dresser and taking the top off a lacquered box marked GLOVES shoved the crucifix under a heap of handkerchiefs. As she replaced the lid she became aware that somebody was watching her in the mirror. She stood still to meet the strict gaze. The girl had on a yellow dress. There was a green ribbon in her long, light brown hair, but she had not known that her own eyes could hold such an expression. She stared back. The expression in the grey eyes did not change. It was as if the girl in the mirror did not know that it was she, Lucy Lewis, who was looking back at her. She cast her eyes down and stood motionless before the mirror, her finger tips resting, as if for support, on the polished wood until the twilight call of a bird broke the silence and she was able to turn from the mirror and move over to the bed and pick up the shears she had cast there and go out into the hall.

A man stood in the front doorway. He had just stretched himself, she thought, for his legs were spread wide and his arms that held on to the door frame were raised as high as they could reach. Lucy felt as if someone had taken the shears and thrust them into her bowels. . . . Or was it into her kidneys? The wall opposite her flushed suddenly with light; out on the gallery someone had struck a match. Slowly she turned her head. Uncle Tubby was leaning forward to light his pipe. Even while he crouched, cupping the flame with his hands as if it were something precious, he kept his sparkling eyes trained on her father's face. Her father's chair was tilted back against the post. He had his pocket knife out and was whittling. In the pale light his downbent head looked as if it had been carved out of some dark and unusually resilient wood. He had just spoken but it was Uncle Tubby's voice that she heard now.

She turned her head toward the front door. In the west the sky still showed a faint pink where it was not blotted out by the dark, spreading limbs of the man who stood in the doorway. She had a sudden, urgent desire to leave the dark hall, to stand outside on the cool grass or walk about among the crape myrtle bushes under this sky still streaked with rose. She told herself that in any event she could not stay here any longer and started walking quietly to the head of the basement stairs, intending to descend that way, but he had heard her steps and was turning around. "Hello," he said, "do you want to get through?"

She could feel his eyes on her cheeks; they seemed to burn. She stammered her thanks and pushing past him went headlong down the front steps and took the path that wound between the scraggly cedars to the flower bed that her mother had made halfway down the slope.

As she stumbled over one of the rocks that still lay here and there in the flower bed, she fell to the ground. She remained, half-kneeling, and then, with a sob, forgetful of her company dress, prostrated herself on the ground, her arms encircling the rock over which she had stumbled. It was damp and cold to the touch. She closed her eyes and laid her cheek upon it. After a little she opened her eyes. The night air had dried her tears. Her face felt stiff. Still clasping the cold stone in her arms, she looked up at the sky. The moon was riding high over the willow tree: a cold, silver crescent whose horns pointed upwards into the heavens rather than down toward the earth. Two nights ago her father had asked Mr. MacDonough when it was going to rain and Mr. MacDonough, shaking his head, had told him to look at the moon. "Holding all the water in her lap," he said. "She ain't going to let none of it spill down for a while yet."

Mr. MacDonough believed that God put the moon up there in the sky and that she would stay there, cold and silver, till he took her down. But Uncle Tubby thought that she had already left her place and was moving toward the earth and some day would strike against it and shatter into a million pieces. Where would they all be then and what would happen when the moon and the earth broke against each other?

She got up moved about among the flowers. The light was now so dim that she could hardly tell one flower from another but she found the bed where the zinnias grew and cut handfuls of them at random. Her upturned skirt—she had forgotten to bring a basket—was full, but she did not feel like going back to the others. She looked back at the house. Lights were burning on all three floors. A figure showed itself briefly at the front door, then disappeared: Daddy on his way downstairs to get more ice. She pressed her arm against her turned-up skirt and struck her cupped left palm with her clenched right fist and whispered, "Stamp 'em!" That was the game she had played all summer with the MacDonoughs. They had called it "You Stamp 'Em!" You started from the MacDonough house, all running, and found the best hiding place you could on the slope. Lying hid in the bushes, you watched the big house till somebody showed himself at one of the windows or on the gallery and then you "stamped" them, like white horses. That big Englishman and his wife and secretary and the young poet from Boston were all here then. The MacDonoughs thought that the big Englishman was stealing the eggs. He used to get tired of writing on his history of the world and would come out and go into the hen house a dozen times a day, to see if the hens had laid any eggs. The poet lived in a tent in the yard and read poetry over and over to himself; it sounded like a bumblebee buzzing. And then in the evenings they used to go up on the gallery and have their drinks. Sometimes they would read poetry to each other or sometimes they would just talk about their friends, but if you lay down in the hollyhocks and looked up at them you could see each one's face plain through the railings. It looked like they were animals that had been put in a pen. If you were playing "Stamp 'Em" then you just stamped the one that got up and went inside to get ice or whiskey or something. The MacDonoughs thought it was funny just to look at them. Ruby MacDonough used to laugh so hard that sometimes she would forget to stamp them and would get beat, though she was so much older and had practically invented the game. They didn't play it any more. Mr. MacDonough had come by one day and found them all squatting in the bushes and had told Ruby that if he ever caught her mocking the company again he would whip her hard, even if she was thirteen years old.

She lowered her gaze from the house to the circular drive in front of it. It was bisected by a brick walk. The ragged crape myrtles that grew on each side of the walk were almost as tall as trees. She had always had the feeling that they were the guardians of this slope.

In the fading light one of them took the shape of a mediaeval warrior, equipped with sword, shield and streaming plume. A few feet away from him a shorter, stouter warrior half crouched for an upward thrust. The stout warrior was about to throw down his shield! No. Someone passing by had set the crape myrtle boughs shaking.

She stood still, feeling the heavy blossoms chill through the thin fabric of her upturned skirt. She had thought that she had plucked zinnias, but she must have plucked a few marigolds unaware; their odor was rank on the air.

"Are you there?" a voice asked.

"Yes," she answered.

The strange gentleman stood a few feet away from her on the drive.

"I couldn't see where you'd gone to," he said.

"I came down to get some flowers," she told him.

He had turned and was looking off down the slope. "What's going on down there?" he asked and moved toward the fence.

"It's the Brush Arbor meeting," she said and took a few steps toward him.

The MacDonough house stood silent and dark. In the field below three or four dozen people were gathered. Some of them had already taken their places on the wooden benches under the canopy of boughs that Mr. MacDonough and Mike and Mr. Lancaster had spent the afternoon fixing to the poles. Every now and then a bough sprang out gold as men and boys moved about, hanging lanterns on the forked ends of the poles.

The visitor turned to her suddenly as if he wanted her to share his wonder. "It's like something out of the Middle Ages," he said.

"It's just the Brush Arbor meeting," she said again, thinking that he was in no way different from other people who came to that house. Her father's and mother's friends hardly ever said what a thing was, they said what it was like. Mr. MacDonough didn't talk that way. She had sat in the MacDonough house a long time yesterday afternoon, listening to them talking about the meeting. Claude Lancaster was there, drinking beer. "But what if He don't come, Terence?" he kept saying. "What if we git all this brush up and all them benches made and He don't come?"

Mr. MacDonough had laughed softly. He said: "Why, Claude, He made His choice before the foundation of the world. . . ."

"How you know that?"

"He says so. 'I was set up from everlasting,' He says. 'When the Lord made the world, I was there, playing before Him,' He says. 'And my delights are with the children of men. . . .' He comes back here to play with us, Claude, like children sporting in the pasture. . . ."

"I ain't never noticed Him anywhere around where I'm at," Claude said.

Michael grinned at that but Mr. MacDonough said only: "He's thar. Even if you don't feel Him. He's closer than hands or feet."

Ruby's lean face suddenly sparkled. She darted a quick, sidewise glance at Lucy. "Lucy ain't never seen anybody get the Holy Ghost," she said.

Mr. MacDonough looked at Lucy. His brown eyes shone, the way they always shone when holy things were mentioned. "She will," he said, "I've got no fear for Lucy."

That was the way they talked down at the MacDonough house. They hardly ever mentioned the radio or politics or even the Depression. They mostly just talked about God. When Mr. MacDonough or Mrs. MacDonough said "Jesus" you felt as if He were in the next room. And when she was down there, listening to them, she felt the same way. Once she herself had almost seen Jesus, coming around the corner of the house. At any rate, the lilac bush had shaken and there had been a radiance in the air. . . . Up at the house you didn't feel that you were likely to see Jesus, though her father and mother talked about him a good deal, too. *The man who fell among thieves.* It didn't seem like a real man, though, or real thieves. . . . *The grain of mustard seed.* . . . Her father said he wasn't sure that it was the same kind of mustard that Mr. MacDonough planted there on the side of the hill for greens, or not. And those people who went through the field plucking corn weren't plucking corn at all, her father said, just ears of wheat. "In King James' time they had never heard of corn. Corn is one of the plants we got from the New World. . . ." She had never been sure what King James had to do with it. There was a King James who was the son of poor Mary Queen of Scots and after Elizabeth cut Mary's head off James had to go and be King of England. But he couldn't have been living at the time when Christ was. Her father said that Jesus spoke Aramaic. . . . Her father quoted the Bible almost as much as Mr. MacDonough did, but it sounded different on his lips: The Christ of the New Testament, the Jesus of the Second Gospel, the Coptic something. . . . Her mother talked to her about God sometimes, usually when she was worked up about something. Like that time her mother thought that she had told a lie about going in swimming and had come and sat on the side of her bed that night and told her that she needn't mind owning up that she had told a lie, that God already knew it; he knew everything. . . . It didn't sound like the same God, though. Or maybe it was just that the MacDonoughs were closer to Him. She wondered whether their being so poor had anything to do with it—or so dirty. Her father had read aloud from the New Testament once, about some man's rebuking Jesus for not washing his hands before he ate dinner, and Jesus said, "You fool, do you not know that uncleanness comes from the heart?"

She sighed. The man beside her started, as if he had forgotten her existence until she sighed.

"How long does the meeting go on?" he asked.

"I don't know," she said, "it depends on the Spirit." And then, because she was afraid he might ask her to explain the workings of the Spirit, she said hastily: "I better go in the house now."

He fell into step beside her. "I was going to ask you to show me the rest of the garden, but I suppose it's too dark now."

"Yes," she said and added, in unconscious imitation of her mother: "Not much to show. Don't anything much grow on this old dry hill."

"Don't you have plenty of water?"

"Just a well. It goes dry when we have too much company."

He laughed. "It's the same way at Toulon," he said. "They turn on the taps and leave them running. . . . But you have the river here below you."

"Daddy says it would cost too much to get it up here."

"Are there no springs?"

"One down at the river bank and a big one in the woods."

"Those woods down there?" he said and gestured with his hand. "Will you show them to me tomorrow?"

"If some of the rest of 'em don't," she said aloud, telling herself that she would never visit the spring or the waterfall again. No, not even if everybody else went. Not even if they should have a picnic down there, as they sometimes did when they had company.

I will never go there any more. I will never show anybody the names carved on the beech tree. Not even Lois. Least of all, Lois. No matter how long I live. The years will go by and all the time, in the woods, the bark will be growing around our two names, but nobody passing by will know, except me. And I will never tell anybody, as long as I live. . . .

They were approaching the house. She stole a glance at her companion. Light streaming down from the third storey window of her own room fell on fair, sparse hair, ruffled just now as if he had been running his hand through it. He was not as tall as her father. She could not see his eyes, for his head was turned away from her and slightly raised. He was looking at the window above their heads. She hoped that he would not turn to her again before they reached the window. *He's only seen me in the dark,* she thought. *He doesn't know a thing about me. He doesn't know a thing!*

She realized suddenly that she had walked a long way that afternoon in the woods. Her legs ached. She stared up at the lighted windows of the room occupied now by the strange lady. It was not often that she wished herself in bed but she wished now that she had had her dinner and was in her own bed, ready to go to sleep.

They had passed the willow tree when her companion stopped abruptly and looked up at the window. "Isabel!" he said.

The strange lady was leaning out of the window, laughing. "Where have you been?" she asked.

He said, "Isabel!" again and caught his breath sharply. You would have thought that she was not a grown woman who could take care of herself but a child who might leap out of the window and tumble to the ground.

She laughed again. She had on a white robe and she must have been brushing her hair for she held a shining brush in her hand. There was a light clatter as she threw it on the floor and leaned farther out of the window, turning her head from side to side the way Borcke did when he sniffed the wind. "It's so cool now," she said.

"Yes," he said, "yes, it has got much cooler."

She was still turning her head slowly from side to side but when he spoke she stopped. She put both hands on the sill and leaned still farther forward. The folds of silk that fell from her hip fluttered; she was making as if to bring one leg up and thrust it over the sill.

He really thought that she would do it. He jumped. *"I'm*

coming right up," he said sharply. "I'm bringing you some flowers."

Still leaning out the lady looked down at him. Lucy could not see her face clearly in the dim light but she seemed to know the expression that was on it: the same expression she had seen so often on Lois' face when Lois would have some treat, a chocolate bar or something, and instead of dividing it would hold it behind her back and make you choose which hand you'd take, smiling at the thought that you might choose the empty hand.

"Let me see your flowers," the lady said.

"Show them to her," he said in a low voice. Lucy, wondering, advanced until she stood under the window and letting down her skirt, displayed to the downbent gaze the yellow and pink and cream-colored zinnias, with the few bright marigolds scattered on top.

"I like those little yellow ones," the lady said.

Her husband was picking them hastily off the top of the heap as if he would have tossed them to her that moment. "I'm bringing them up to you," he said again.

"Lucy can bring them to me," she said and Lucy knew that even if she couldn't see the smile the lady was smiling sweetly. "Will you bring me some of your flowers, Lucy?"

"Yes," Lucy said, "only I got to fix some for the table first."

She left him standing under the window and went around to the rear of the house. In the kitchen her mother was standing beside the stove, stirring the cream sauce. Her white linen dress was cut almost to her waist line in the back. As she moved her arm vigorously Lucy could see the beads of sweat glisten on her shoulder blades. She turned around as Lucy entered.

"Oh. . . ." she said. "Darling, you ought not to put them

in your skirt that way. . . ." She left the stove and, approaching, pointed to a greenish spot on the yellow linen.

She was holding the spoon with her other hand. A white, glutinous drop fell from the tip of the spoon to the floor. Lucy stared at it a second before she raised her eyes to her mother's face. "Yes, and you ought not to drop cream sauce all over the floor," she said.

Sarah had turned back to the stove and did not answer. Lucy went into the dining room and drawing a chair up to the old built-in cupboard took down from it a glass bowl and a metal "frog" and carrying them into the kitchen filled the bowl with water.

"Can you fix them yourself?" her mother asked without turning around.

Lucy did not answer until she had finished arranging a handful of the flowers so that they were supported by the metal wires. "Does that look all right?" she asked then.

Sarah turned around. Her face was scarlet from the heat. The wispy end of one of her braids showed. "It looks lovely," she said. "Will you be careful not to spill it when you set it down, darling?"

"You better fix your hair before supper," Lucy said and walked slowly into the dining room and set the bowl down in its place on the table. When she stood back to look at it, it did not seem to be in the exact center of the table. She reached and pulled it a little to one side. Water washed up the side of the bowl; a few drops spilled over on the white cloth. Lucy bit her lip as she contemplated them. Pushing closer to the table, she drew the bowl over so that it covered the spots, then went back to the kitchen.

"You want me to do anything else?" she asked.

Sarah was lifting the pot of cream sauce off the stove. She set it down on the kitchen table before she turned her scarlet face to her daughter. "No . . ." she said, "thank you, darling." She suddenly came and knelt down beside Lucy and caught her to her in a quick embrace. "Honey," she murmured, "these people'll all be gone in a couple of days. We'll see about the pony then. Honest, we will."

Lucy stood quiet. She could not speak while her mother's hot arm was tight about her waist, but if she spoke it might slacken its grip. She said in a low voice: "I don't mind 'em being here."

Sarah hugged her again. "You know you could have Lois out if you wanted to. We could bring that cot down from the attic. . . ."

"No use going to all that trouble," Lucy said. She took a minute step backward. Her mother's arm fell from about her waist. Sarah was on her feet, looking down at Lucy, laughing. "Don't tell me you've lost your taste for Lois!"

Her daughter turned on her a look of anger. "I never had any taste for her," she muttered and went over to the sink and, picking up the flowers she had left there, formed them into a clumsy bouquet.

"Why didn't you put them all in?" Sarah asked.

"Because that lady said she wanted some upstairs." She left the kitchen and mounted the stairs to the second floor.

In the upstairs hall the light was not on. The door that opened on to the gallery was a dark blue rectangle, pricked here and there with the gold lights from the houses across the river. She could not see her father and Uncle Tubby but the deep antiphon of their voices smote on her ear. She wondered how they could sit there, hour after hour, talking. Talk was all they seemed to care about. They would talk while Rome burned. She repeated the phrase to herself, but there was something about its rhythm that did not satisfy her . . . Fiddle . . . That was what you did while Rome burned.

Fiddle . . . Fiddle . . . Faddle . . . Faddle . . . That was all their talk was.

From the floor below came the sound of rapid steps: her mother, crossing the little hall on her way to the dining room, bearing, no doubt, the platter that held the creamed chicken. The saucepan had been three quarters full and there were three opened cans of mushrooms on the table. The chicken had had to be pieced out to make it go round. Well, she for one, would not eat any of it. She might not eat anything at all tonight, or tomorrow, either. She might not eat anything for several days. But whenever she didn't eat anything Mama noticed it and started up. *Eat your dinner. Eat your dinner. What's the matter with you? You didn't eat your dinner. No, you can't do this. You can't do that. You know you didn't eat your dinner. . . .*

She was halfway up the stairs to the third floor. Suddenly the wall beside her and the railing under her hand were flooded with light. A door above her had opened. She felt the bright glow strike full on her forehead and recoiled, blinking.

The strange lady stood at the head of the stairs, resting her hand on the newel post. "Where have you been?" she asked.

"I had to fix the flowers for the table," Lucy said as she mounted the last step.

The lady laid her hand on Lucy's shoulder, a touch as light as the touch of a bird's wing and yet comforting. She drew Lucy inside the bright room and shut the door behind her.

"We'll have to hurry," she said.

"You mean to get ready for dinner?" Lucy asked.

The lady stood in the middle of the floor and looked at Lucy. "I thought your dress was *white*," she said.

"It's yellow," Lucy said, "canary yellow."

The lady laughed. "That's all right," she said, "I've got a yellow one, too."

She had taken the flowers from Lucy and laid them down in a great heap on the dressing table while she turned to the closet and with a rapid motion of her hand set the hangers sliding on their rod.

Where she had been standing the air smelled sweet. Lucy waited, motionless, until she could no longer smell the perfume before she went over and sat down on the edge of the bed. Through the open window she could see the lights of the town sparkling. In their yellow shine the river and the intervening fields looked dark blue. Sometimes she herself slept in this room. When she did she went every night to the window just before she got into bed and looked down at the lights. The lights looked as they always did, but it seemed to her that she had never been in this room before. Even the air was different. There were fragrances over here on this side of the bed that she had not smelled when she first came into the room. Perhaps it was all the fragrances in the air that made even the familiar objects look different. She glanced about with brightening eyes. A round, gold-encased traveling clock stood on the night table. Beside it lay a gold pen and a leather portfolio that had IR stamped on it in gold letters. On a chair next to the bed a bag made of pale green satin and shaped like an envelope lay half open. The nightgown that was spilling out of it had tiny white flowers worked in a narrow band about its neck and short, puffed sleeves.

Mrs. Reardon had taken off her white robe and was slipping a yellow organdy dress over her head. It was tight in the waist and had a full skirt. She tied a green sash about her waist. The air turned flowery again as she approached the bed.

"Don't we look like twins now?" she asked.

Saliva gushed up suddenly in Lucy's mouth. A little dribbled on to the counterpane. She bent her head, closing her lips firmly. Mrs. Reardon did not seem to realize that she had not been answered. She sat down at the dressing table and began brushing her fine, blonde hair. When Lucy raised her head their eyes met in the mirror. Mrs. Reardon's eyes were the color of the periwinkle blossoms that grew in the old graveyard at Merry Point. She smiled at Lucy. "This is such a beautiful house," she said.

Lucy had been surreptitiously rubbing the damp spot on the counterpane with the tip of her finger. She put her hands behind her and spoke rapidly:

"Yes, but it's awful funny. Mama says people don't know how to act when they come here. They get out of the car and see a great, big house and they think there ought to be somebody to take their bags and there never is anybody but Daddy, and he's so lazy. Sometimes we don't even have a cook. . . ." She broke off, her laugh sounding false in her own ears.

"What do you do then?"

"Why, Mama has to do it, but it makes her awful mad. One time there was an Englishman visiting here and Jenny was off, seeing her grandmother that was sick, and he left a three-dollar tip on the dresser. Mama told Jenny she was a good mind to take it herself!"

"She ought to have given it to you," Mrs. Reardon said. "Didn't you do a lot of things for him?"

"Well, I'm always bringing 'em ice and cigarettes and things, but I don't reckon they'd ever think of tipping me for that."

"They should," Mrs. Reardon said. "They should tip you good and proper. Why, when I visit my sister-in-law in England I always tip all three of her children a pound apiece."

"That's England," Lucy said with a sigh. "They do different in different countries. I don't expect Mama would let me have the money, anyhow."

Mrs. Reardon smiled at her again. "I hope Jenny's in good health tonight," she said.

"She's down in the cabin, drunk as a hoot owl," Lucy said.

Mrs. Reardon's whole body shook with her delicate laughter. "We'd better hurry and get downstairs then," she said and beckoned Lucy to come over and stand beside her. "Which ones do you like best?" she asked.

Lucy looked down at the flowers, spread on the dark mahogany slab of the little dressing table that had been her grandmother's. They were of almost every color. On top of the heap lay several clusters of yellow marigolds.

Mrs. Reardon's arm, clasping her waist, as her mother's arm had clasped her waist a few minutes ago, tightened its gentle pressure. She smelled the flowery fragrance again as Mrs. Reardon bent her head. "I like those yellow ones," Lucy said.

"Oh, yes," Mrs. Reardon said.

She formed two or three sprays of the blossoms into a wreath and set the wreath on Lucy's head. "Look!" she said.

Lucy gazed gravely at her own reflection. Her eyes seemed to her a colder grey than usual. Above them the fair brows glistened in the lamp light. Her lips, set now in a straight line, were a pale pink. She thought that perhaps Mrs. Reardon would offer her some lipstick. If she did, she would take it, no matter what Mama said. But Mrs. Reardon said only, "See! We're twins." Lucy's eyes went to the other mirrored face. Mrs. Reardon did not look as old as most grown people, and she had a look in her periwinkle-colored eyes that Lucy had never seen in the eyes of any other grown person. Most grown people when they talked with you were thinking of something else and rarely paid any attention to what you said, but Mrs. Reardon was looking straight at Lucy, as if she wanted more than anything else in the world to know what Lucy thought.

She looked, too, as if she wanted you to like her and was half afraid that you wouldn't. "Oh, but I do. . . . I don't care. . . . I do!" Lucy thought, even while she noticed that Mrs. Reardon wore her hair the same way she wore hers, parted on the side but drawn back with a flat silver brooch instead of a bow, and falling straight to her shoulders. It was almost the same color as Lucy's, but it seemed lighter than it was because her face was so brown. Lucy thought that she must take a sun bath every day of her life.

The dinner bell—the old cowbell that they had found on a window sill when they bought the house—was sounding downstairs. Mrs. Reardon finished pinning on her own wreath and jumping up from the dressing-table, held out her hand to Lucy. They ran out of the room and down the stairs. There was nobody on the middle floor. Lucy indicated the narrow flight of stairs that led to the first floor. "Heavens!" Mrs. Reardon said. "How many stairs are there in this house?"

"Thousands," a voice said. Uncle Tubby was standing in the little hall, waiting for them. His eyes shone when he saw them. He said, "Two Cranachs Descending the Stairs," and took them each by the hand and led them into the dining room. He seated Mrs. Reardon beside Daddy, then seated himself beside her, with Lucy on his other hand.

Out of the corner of her eye Lucy observed that Mr. Reardon was sitting next to Mama. She kept her face turned toward Mrs. Reardon who was laughing and saying to Uncle Tubby: "Not his fat Venus, I hope."

His arm was lying on the back of her chair. It slipped down and lay for a second about her waist as he leaned over to look into her face. "No," he said, "you haven't got the *embonpoint.*"

His arm fell from around her waist as she sat up a little straighter. But he still leaned forward, resting his other arm on the table, so he could look into her eyes. "His Eve?" he said. "No, you're too intellectual for her."

Mrs. Reardon held her head with its crown of flowers slightly tilted and smiled at him steadily. "*Tubby!*" she said. "You know how intellectual I am!"

Mama sat a little forward in her chair and began talking very fast: "I can't remember Eve very well. . . . All I remember is that darling buck. *He* looks intelligent. Do you suppose he knows everything that's going to happen?"

Uncle Tubby's green-brown eyes were as bright as the eyes of a frog Lucy had found one day beside a puddle. He laughed, the silly kind of laugh that Rita Trevaine laughed in school when Miss Simpson caught her passing a note to Margaret Powers. He said: "Sure. He's going to rise up from there in a minute and give her the buck laugh." His arm slipped from the back of Mrs. Reardon's chair and fell to his side.

"*Lucy,*" Mama said, "run in the kitchen and get the hot rolls."

"Where are they?" Lucy asked.

"Under the sink," Mama said. Her voice had an edge, her eyes, as they rested on Lucy's face, were hard. Lucy got up and went into the kitchen and found the hot rolls, covered with a napkin, in the oven. When she came back they were talking about Paradise. At least Mama was talking in that light, fast way she talked when she wanted to keep things going while she thought about something else.

"I'm going to make Steve explain the whole thing to me some day. . . ."

Daddy laughed. "I'm obliged to you," he said.

"Yes, but you know you do remember everything. I don't believe I even know what *happens*. I know Adam fell, but suppose he hadn't fallen? Would he have gone on living on earth or would he eventually have been taken up to Heaven?"

"He was already in Heaven," a voice said.

They all looked at Mr. Reardon. The little, smiling, bright-eyed man was looking at the glass of wine that he held in his hand. He gave it a shake, as if the tiny plash of the red wine on the side of the glass made whatever he was looking at easier to see, before he set it down and glanced about him. He saw Lucy and smiled. "He was already in Heaven," he repeated. "God came and talked with him every day. That is being in Heaven."

"Oh . . . ?" Mama said. "That's being in Heaven, is it? I never knew that before."

He nodded. "I didn't, either," he said, "until recently. We have a friend who lives in the same town that we do who instructs us. He has explained a great many things to me that I never knew before."

"Is that that Father Du Fresnay?" Daddy asked. "He's immensely learned, isn't he?"

"I've never asked him a question that he wasn't able to answer."

"He's a wonderfully lucid expositor," Daddy said.

"I don't know about such things," Mr. Reardon said. He looked at Stephen hard. When he spoke he looked as if he had been going to say something else but had changed his mind. He said again: "I don't know much about these things, Steve. I was already converted when I met him."

"Did it come on you suddenly or had you been considering it for a long time?"

"It came on me suddenly," Mr. Reardon said.

"And you were converted at once?"

"Yes."

"Road to Damascus?"

"It was on the road to Tarascon," Mr. Reardon said.

Uncle Tubby's eyes brightened. He looked at Mama, smiling a little. But Mama did not see him. She leaned forward and said to Mr. Reardon: "Did you leave the St. Martha at St. Tropez or did you take her back to Toulon?"

He stared at her, then he said: "How did you know about the St. Martha?"

"You showed her to me," she said impatiently. "Don't you remember? You didn't know whether you ought to keep her at St. Tropez. You felt that maybe you ought to take her back where you got her."

He slowly shook his head.

"It was at the bottom of a long flight of stairs," she said, "in a little close. . . . A woman bending over, holding a rope or chain in her hand. The rope was around the neck of a beast, but the beast was sort of crumbled away. . . ."

"That was her girdle," Daddy said. "Saint Martha took her girdle off and tied it around the neck of the dragon when she subdued him."

"What was the dragon doing?" Lucy asked.

"He was devastating the whole country. Breathing fire on 'em and that sort of thing."

"Was it in the Holy Land?"

"No," Daddy said, "it was in Southern France—not far from where we lived when you were four years old."

"What was Saint Martha doing over *there*?"

"It's a *legend*, Lucy," Daddy said. "After the Crucifixion Mary and Martha and Lazarus and, I believe, the Bishop Maximin, were put into a leaky, rudderless boat and set adrift. The boat drifted over to Marseilles. The saints debarked and divided up the missionary field. Lazarus stayed at Marseilles where he found plenty to do—that country was given over to the worship of Melkarth, who is the Phoenician equivalent of Hercules. Mary took over the region around Sainte Baume and Saint Martha went up into the *Crau*. . . ."

"What's *Crau*?"

"A most desolate place, all full of rocks—to this day. At that time it was given over to this dragon. He was quite a fellow. You could hear him roaring for a mile off. His dung covered a whole acre."

"I don't believe that," Lucy said, "I don't believe a word of all that."

"A good many people believed it for many years," Stephen said. He was looking at Mr. Reardon. "You say the beast is crumbled away? Has any expert ever examined the statue, Kev?"

Lucy looked at Mr. Reardon, too, and realized, with a start, that during the time they had been talking he had not taken his eyes from Mama's face. He said absently, "It's Roman . . . third century, I think."

"It may not be Saint Martha at all," Stephen said. "It may be Brito-Martis, 'the sweet virgin' of the Phoenicians. They held all that country once. When Marius was fighting the Cimbri and Teutons he had a prophetess of Brito-Martis carried along in a litter and he gave Brito-Martis credit for all his victories. That's how she got into so many of the churches later—as one of the three Marys."

"It was *not* Brito-Martis," Sarah said. "It was Saint Martha. The dragon was coiled up beside her. You could tell that it was a dragon by his snout. His head was right there under her hand, but part of his tail was crumbled away."

Mr. Reardon smiled faintly. "You have a good memory."

She said: "You asked me whether I thought you ought to keep her at St. Tropez or send her back to Toulon where she came from."

"St. Tropez used to be Herculaea," Stephen said. "Tubby,

did you ever study Marius' strategy in that battle he fought against the Cimbri and Teutons? Beats Fredericksburg all hollow. He piled up one hundred thousand bodies and burned 'em. The ground was covered with cinders for hundreds of years afterwards."

Sarah was looking at Mr. Reardon again. "You had so many wonderful lemon trees at St. Tropez. Didn't you hate to leave them?"

Mrs. Reardon laughed. "There are more at Toulon. At the *Villa Marthe* the lemon trees are perfect Yggdrasils. So old and so tall you can't prune 'em. And the blackest cypresses on the Riviera."

Sarah said: "*The Villa Marthe!* Why, we lived just down the road from it. . . . There was a niche in one of the pillars of the gate, with a figurine in it and tall cypresses on each side of the gate. . . ."

"And a *tunnel* of ilex," Mrs. Reardon said. "Barbara Dean says that tunnel ought to be labeled: 'All hope abandon, ye who enter here'. . . ."

"I used to go there every day," Sarah said.

"To see my father?" Mr. Reardon asked quickly.

She shook her head. "To steal flowers. It was in October. You know how wonderful the roses are in that country then? And there were great tangles of them, right beside the wall. I thought the place was deserted—and then one day I met a gardener and that scared me and I didn't go there for a while. I asked our real estate agent whether anybody was in residence and he said only the old gentleman and he wouldn't mind my walking there. He said that he would tell him that I was a friend of his and it would be all right. . . ."

"I hope you didn't give up your flowers on account of meeting the gardener."

"I didn't help myself to them as freely. . . . I was always afraid after that I'd meet somebody."

Mr. Reardon was looking at her very intently. "Did you ever meet anybody?" he asked.

"I met the same gardener again, once or twice. I thought that the agent must have told him who I was for he smiled when he tipped his hat. . . . I never saw anybody else . . . except once. An old man, in a shawl, at the window. . . ."

"Kev, that must have been your father," Mrs. Reardon said.

He did not seem to have heard her. He was still looking at Sarah.

"Did he say anything to you?" he asked.

She shook her head. "He didn't get a chance. . . . I came out of an *allée* on to the house quite unexpectedly and there he was, standing there, looking down on me."

"What happened then?" Mrs. Reardon asked.

"I was about to turn and run when he made me a sign."

Mrs. Reardon laughed unexpectedly, on a high note. "The Sign of the Cross, no doubt."

Sarah kept her eyes on Mr. Reardon's face. He said slowly: "Since I was seven years old I have seen my father only once."

"Oh!" Sarah said. She waited a moment then added, frowning a little: "He had a big bald head and he was standing at an upper window. I think he had on a dressing gown under his shawl. He looked as if he might have been writing or reading and had got up to go to the window to think. I remember that when I burst out of the *allée* he was staring down at a tree on his right, but oh, absentmindedly. Then he saw me—out of the corner of his eye, I imagine—and started a little and had half turned toward me when his left hand came up and he made me, well, as I say, a sort of sign, and turned back to his tree."

"What sort of sign?" Stephen asked.

She said, still looking at Kevin Reardon, "I *think* it was benevolent. I had an idea that he was about to bow and perhaps smile—to tell me that I was welcome in the garden—but the effort seemed too much for him, or perhaps he felt that it was not necessary. Anyhow, he got only halfway through the gesture when his hand dropped to his side and he turned his head away—and I knew that it didn't make any difference to him whether I walked there or not."

They were all silent until Mrs. Reardon suddenly held up her hand. "Listen!" she said.

Music was floating up from the field below the house: the voices of fifty or sixty people, with one voice—Mr. Lancaster's tenor?—soaring above the others:

> Bread of Heaven . . . Bre . . . ad of Heaven,
> Fee . . . ed me *till* I thirst no mo . . . oore. . . .

Mrs. Reardon kept her chin propped in her hand. Her eyes roved the table. She smiled first at one person, then at another. "What is it?" she asked. "What in the world is it?"

"A mixed metaphor," Uncle Tubby said.

Daddy laughed. "They're pretty bold when it comes to that." He looked at Mrs. Reardon. "The Holy Rollers are having a revival. They have one every year in August."

"Do you have a chapel here on this place?" Mr. Reardon asked.

"They make an arbor out of bushes, Kev," Uncle Tubby said, "get under it and grapple with the Spirit. Roll on the ground. . . . Like the early saints."

Mr. Reardon looked at Uncle Tubby, hard, for a second, and said: "St. Benedict used to cast himself into a thorn bush when the desires of the flesh got too strong for him."

"I know just how he felt," Uncle Tubby said. "Steve, could I have some more of that chicken?"

"They are too poor to have a chapel," Daddy said as he helped Uncle Tubby to chicken. "But in a sense, they have had a chapel on this place for many years, one not built with hands. . . . There is a sacred grove, or what's left of it, down there in the bottom."

"No . . . o?" Mrs. Reardon said and smiled at him brightly. "Indian?"

He shook his head. "Holy Roller. There are two or three big hickory trees down in the east field. It was under one of those trees that Arnold Watkins received his revelation. About thirty years ago."

"It gives me a turn every time I look at it," Mama said, "to think of people getting revelations right on your own place!"

"What was the revelation?" Mr. Reardon asked.

Stephen Lewis laughed. "It was a case of a little learning being dangerous. A school teacher over in the hollow persuaded Arnold to go to school, though he was then thirty years old. He got through the third grade and then he took to reading the Bible. Mark 16, 18: 'They shall take up serpents; and if they drink any deadly thing, it shall not hurt them.' Arnold thought that meant that he *must* take up serpents."

"And did he take up serpents?" Mr. Reardon asked.

"Sure. Every year, as soon as he had laid his crop by, he'd go over in the hills and catch rattlesnakes for the meeting."

"How long did he keep up this sport?" Uncle Tubby asked.

"Till he was thirty-six. A young rattler that he had just brought in got him. They buried him over here in the woods; he is regarded as a martyr by the faithful. Mr. MacDonough's father knew him. He says Arnold used always to coil a rattler about his neck before he got up to testify. There was one old rattler, who, Arnold thought, was edified by his discourse; it used sometimes to rear its head up and peer into his eyes as he was talking. He got fond of the snakes. He told old MacDonough that one of the hardest things he ever had to do was kicking the box."

"Prepare to meet thy God!" Uncle Tubby said. *"Kicking the box?"*

"The box that holds the rattlers is set at the foot of the pulpit. When the service begins the saints file past and each man gives the box a good ritual kick—to get the rattlesnakes in the mood to strike."

"Say! We really must go down there tonight!"

"Oh, there won't be any snakes tonight," Daddy said. "Old Judge Kimbrough broke that up. Got a bill through the legislature making it unlawful to have venomous reptiles in your possession."

"A *parfait* Christian gentleman," Uncle Tubby said.

"Well, an eighteenth century rationalist. He called himself an Agnostic, I believe, the way they all did in those days. He took a lot of interest in the Holy Rollers. If the old boy hadn't been raised an Episcopalian I believe he'd have got the Spirit. When one of his own tenants was arrested for violating the law the judge defended him. Got him off, too."

"He couldn't have taken any more interest in them than you do," Sarah said. "You'll squat out there for hours, talking Holy Roller theology with Mr. MacDonough."

Stephen Lewis smiled at his daughter. "Lucy here knows more about their religion than I do. Tell them about it, honey."

Lucy was aware of Mr. Reardon's eyes on her face. Slowly she raised her own eyes. She had not looked full at Mr. Reardon before and now she found herself looking straight into his eyes. They were the darkest eyes she had ever seen, yet full of light—the deepest well will brim with light when one leans to look into it. With an effort she lowered her own eyes. "It's being Saved and Sanctified," he said, "and you got to speak three words in the Unknown Tongue."

"It's Pentecost every day with them," her father said. "There are three degrees of grace: Salvation, Sanctification and the Gift of the Spirit. . . . Speech in the Unknown Tongue is the proof that you have received the Gift of the Spirit."

Uncle Tubby had put his arm about Lucy's shoulders and was drawing her closer to him, shaking her a little. "Come on, *belle dame,* speak a few words!"

"I don't know anything about it," Lucy muttered, "but Mrs. MacDonough spoke once."

"What did she say?" He held her closer, trying to make her turn and look at him.

Making all her muscles rigid, she disengaged herself from his embrace. "She spoke four words," she said. "Mr. MacDonough and Ruby heard her." She had not been looking at any of them but now she stole a glance at Mr. Reardon.

His eyes were already on her face. He was smiling. The hair that grew a little back from his high forehead was still ruffled. He held his head on one side, as if, she thought breathlessly, he were considering how best to do her a kindness. It came to her that he was not a large man, not nearly as tall as Uncle Tubby, not even as tall as her father. And in the bright, almost bird-like gaze now fixed on her face there was nothing but kindly interest. *But of course!* she thought. *He doesn't know yet. He hasn't been back to his room. He couldn't know yet!*

Her mother was leaning toward her, whispering: Lucy might remove the plates. She herself would bring the fruit *compôte.*

"Let me help you, *belle dame,*" Uncle Tubby said, but

Lucy shook her head and rising began to remove the plates with alacrity. She was so happy that she felt like singing. She told herself that as soon as she had taken all the plates into the kitchen she would run upstairs. It would not take a minute to get the crucifix out of its hiding place. She would slip into his room and put it on the floor beside his bed. The counterpane would come down far enough to cover it. When he found it he would think that it had fallen off his table. It would not take a minute!

She had piled the plates on the kitchen table and was in the hall, her foot on the bottom step of the stairs, when her mother came out of the dining room, bearing the salt and pepper cellars on a little tray. "Would you brush the crumbs off, Lucy?" she asked.

Lucy hesitated. Sarah's dark brows drew together. "Would you brush the crumbs off?" she asked again.

"I've got to go upstairs and get me a handkerchief," Lucy said.

Sarah repressed a sigh. Her lips set in a straight line. She passed Lucy and went into the kitchen. But Stephen Lewis appeared just then, carrying a stray saltcellar. He glanced at his daughter and he, too, frowned. "Why don't you try to help your mother sometimes?" he asked irritably.

Lucy went silently into the dining room and brushed the crumbs from the cloth. Her mother brought the dessert in. Lucy hurriedly began to eat her *compôte*. If she did not finish when the others did her mother might make her stay behind after they had gone. If they walked out on the lower gallery, to see the view, as they sometimes did after dinner, she would still have time to run upstairs before anybody else went up.

The telephone rang. Sarah answered it. "Jim Eglinton wants to know if you still want that setter pup," she said to her husband when she came back into the room.

"Sure," he said. "Did you tell him?"

"They're coming out here in a little while," she said.

They rose from the table. Uncle Tubby and Daddy walked out on the gallery. "Isabel," Uncle Tubby called, "come and look at the lights."

"In a minute," she said and looked at Lucy and smiled. "Want to come upstairs with me?" she asked.

They went up the two flights of stairs to the third floor. There was no light in Mr. Reardon's room. When they came to the landing on the last flight Lucy lagged behind her companion. She was about to say that she needed a handkerchief and go down to her own room but Mrs. Reardon turned around, smiling, and laid her cool fingers on Lucy's wrist. "I just thought of it during dinner," she said.

"Thought of what?" Lucy said after a moment's hesitation.

"Something I've got for you," Mrs. Reardon said.

She had to look in two of her bags before she found it: a square gold box, whose flowery top, which seemed to be made of china, was ornamented with a scroll of vines and tiny pink flowers. *"Cloisonné,"* Mrs. Reardon called it. "Do you like it?" she asked.

Lucy had to swallow hard before she could answer. "I think it's the most beautiful thing I ever saw," she said. *It's just the right size to hold the little man,* she thought. Do you suppose *she's giving it to me because she knows I've got the little man?*

"What are you going to keep in it?" Mrs. Reardon asked.

"I don't know," Lucy said. "I haven't got much—except handkerchiefs and bobby pins. . . . I *have* got two good hair ribbons."

Mrs. Reardon laughed. "I just thought of it during dinner," she said again and got up and went over to the dressing table and began brushing her already shining hair. When she had finished she brought the same brush over to the bed and brushed Lucy's hair before she disappeared into the bathroom.

Lucy sat on the edge of the bed, the box clasped in her hot hand. Mrs. Reardon kept the water running a long time. There was still time to go downstairs and slip into her room and get the crucifix out of the glove box and then slip into his room and bend down and slip it under the folds of the coverlet. The water was still running—but it might stop any time and Mrs. Reardon would come in and wonder where she had gone. She turned the box back and forth so that it caught the light. It was like the crucifix, seeming to catch the light wherever it was. Laid out on her palm the crucifix had extended to the first joint of her middle finger. The box was a little longer. If she gave the crucifix back what would she have to keep in the box? Bobby pins and hair ribbons? One of her ribbons already had creases in it that wouldn't iron out. . . .

Mrs. Reardon was standing in the doorway. "Do you want to go in there?" she asked.

Lucy shook her head. They descended the stairs. The others were sitting in the parlor, talking about whether they would go to the Holy Roller meeting or not. Sarah looked up as Lucy came in. Lucy thought that she was going to say that it was time for her to go to bed.

She clutched the box tighter in her perspiring hand. "I'm not, either!" she cried shrilly, "I'm not going to stay up here all by myself while you all go to the meeting!"

Sarah sighed. "We aren't any of us going to the meeting, darling," she said. "The Eglintons are coming out here in a few minutes."

"That lovely lady in the big hat!" Tubby said.

"Oh, God!" Stephen Lewis said.

"Well, you liked him when you met him at the Andersons'," Sarah said defiantly. "And he's the only person in town cares anything about the War. And you can't have *him* without *her*. You can't live *altogether* outside the pale of decent society."

"I should say not!" Tubby said. "And the society here so rich and strange! Why is Steve so set on Dr. Eglinton?"

"He's a wonderful shot. He's going to give Steve a setter puppy."

"Exactly what this place needs. It's too big for a dachshund. Is the dog trained?"

"Oh, no," Sarah said. "Steve is going to train him."

"Have you ever trained a bird dog, Steve?" Tubby asked.

"Oh, *no*!" Sarah said again before her husband had a chance to answer. "But he'll have no difficulty. No difficulty at all. All he needs to do is to give up his work and everything else for a couple of years. . . ."

"When I get stuck I always take a walk," Tubby said. "Steve could take the dog out while he meditated."

"You can't meditate when you're out with a bird dog," Sarah said. "You've got to be thinking of him every minute, else you've got no business having him."

Tubby looked at her and shook his head. "Sally, you're a perfectionist," he said.

"I'm *not*," she said, "but I know one thing."

He waited a second before he said, "Let's have it."

"You can't serve God and Mammon," she said.

"I never thought of a bird dog as Mammon, exactly."

"Well, when a person's two years over his deadline. . . ."

Stephen Lewis got up. "Let's not talk about deadlines," he said. "Tubby, you want to help me rustle the drinks before they come?"

They left the room. Mrs. Reardon had moved from the sofa over to a chair near the window where she could look out on the river and the lights of the town. Mr. Reardon went over and stood beside her. Sarah looked at Lucy who had been sitting beside Mrs. Reardon, the hand that held the box concealed by the folds of her skirt. "It's time you went to bed, darling," she said.

Lucy stood up. Sarah bent to kiss her, then straightened up, smiling. "What's that you've got in your hand?" she asked.

"A box," Lucy said in a low voice. "*She* gave it to me." And she nodded her head toward Mrs. Reardon.

Sarah took it from her and held it on the palm of her own hand. She eyed the distant figure thoughtfully before she said: "It's lovely," and then, "Now will you run on to bed, darling?"

"I've just had my supper," Lucy said. "I can't go to sleep right after my supper."

"*Lucy!*" Sarah said. "Please don't whine!"

Lucy walked slowly toward the door. At that moment her father and Uncle Tubby came up the stairs. Her father bore a tray laden with glasses and a bowl of ice. Uncle Tubby carried a bottle of whiskey in one hand and a bottle of gin in the other. He held them out like Indian clubs. "We're going to play charades," he said.

Lucy stopped short and looked at her mother. Sarah groaned. "Oh, God, Tubby, what did you have to do that for?"

"What's the matter with charades?" he asked. "Honest to God charades? You understand I don't advocate 'The Game' or any of those paltry substitutes. . . ."

"This child ought to have been in bed hours ago," Sarah said.

Uncle Tubby set his bottles down and swung Lucy up on to his shoulder. "Not tonight," he said. "Why, this is going to be one of her big nights. She's going to be on my side . . . Steve, you can have Mrs. Eglinton. . . ."

Clutching the box tighter in her perspiring hand, Lucy looked down at her mother. Sarah said, "Oh, Lord!" but she smiled a little when she raised her eyebrows and compressed her lips; she knew that there was no use in arguing. It was understood that Lucy should be allowed to stay up whenever they played charades. The huge room suddenly seemed larger, brighter; Daddy had switched on another light. Mrs. Reardon was coming toward them, smiling. Mr. Reardon still stood with his back turned, looking out of the window.

Lucy glanced at the dark figure beside the window, and felt a surge of triumph. It would be hours before she had to go to bed. The whole house would be in a turmoil. There would even be time—and opportunity—for her to slip into his room and drop the crucifix on the floor beside his bed if she wanted to. She could do it on her way to the attic. They would all be going up there to dress up in all those funny old clothes that were in the big trunk. After they got into their costumes they would begin acting. They would feel sorry for her because she had almost had to go to bed while they were playing and they would probably ask her to be in every act. She signaled for Uncle Tubby to set her down. As her feet struck the floor the blissful feeling swept over her again. For the next two or three hours she would know nothing but pleasure.

V

I THOUGHT at first that it was a dog," Dr. Eglinton said. "The bones were all laid out so neat. Like he'd crawled in there and laid down and died. And then I saw the skull and I thought 'Hell, that's no dog! Might be a wolf. Might even be a bear.' So I just gathered the bones up and put them in my sack. I always carry a sack on these trips. No telling what you may find."

He was a big man, brown all over. Ever since he had come in he had sat in the big chair by the fireplace, his legs spread wide apart, his big, white, clean-looking hands swinging between them, looking from one to the other of them and laughing as he told about how he and some other men had found the bones of a strange animal embedded in a piece of rock in a cave near Palmyra.

"But you never thought you'd find a saber-toothed tiger!" Mama said.

Dr. Eglinton laughed, too. "Evelyn calls it the saber-toothed tiger," he said. "It's going to take us some time to find out what it is. We know it's not a dog or a wolf, because it's got a hole in the thigh bone that is not present in dogs and wolves . . . and is present in all cats, except the saber-tooth. . . ."

"Oh, dear, then it's *not* a saber-tooth?" Mama said.

"Well, the saber-tooth *usually* lacks it," Dr. Eglinton said. "You know, it might be a Jaguar Augusta. Joe Duval just thinks it's a saber-tooth because of that half of a tooth that we found."

"Well, is *it* saber?"

"It's got quite a curve on it. The dentine in it is as good as yours or mine. . . ."

"*No . . . oo!*" Mama said. "Well, Steve's teeth aren't very good; ate too much candy when he was little. . . . But mine. . . . I simply can't get over it! To go out for a walk here in Montgomery county and come on a saber-toothed tiger! I can't get over it!"

Dr. Eglinton laughed. "It wasn't exactly a walk. We left Bob and Joe Duval on top. We've had this cave on our list for quite a while but we couldn't figure a way to get down into it. Had to enlarge the opening, as a matter of fact, before I could get in and then they had to lower us twenty feet before we struck anything we could stand up on."

"Good God!" Mama said. "Jim, I think you were terribly brave."

Dr. Eglinton laughed again. "My feet struck a little ledge first. I hollered to Joe to give me a little more rope and then I climbed down off the ledge and there was the creek. I waited till Tom got down and then we swam up it, oh, not more'n a hundred yards."

"Can you *imagine* swimming in a dark, dank underground river like that?" Mama said.

"No!" someone said. They all looked at Mrs. Reardon who was sitting sunk in a big chair between Stephen and Dr. Eglinton. When they had first started talking she had turned from one to the other, smiling, but now she was shivering, as if she had a chill. Lucy had never before seen anybody shiver like that. The shivering did not seem to start in her body; it was as if something had come up on her from behind and had slipped inside her and would not let her go.

Her husband got up from where he had been sitting beside Mama and sat on the arm of her chair. He put his hand out and clasped her wrist. The shivering went on for a moment longer and then her arm lay quiet in his clasp. He said in a low voice: "It's just talk." She turned her head and looked at him. Her eyes were bright. "I know it," she said, "but I can't *bear* it!"

He held her wrist tighter and put his other arm about her shoulders. He was looking at Daddy. "She doesn't like to think of people going down into the earth," he said.

"Me, either," Mama said. "It gives me the creeps."

"You're antrophobes," Dr. Eglinton said. "Joe Duval is like that. Always stays on top. But he wouldn't miss a trip for anything."

"They're spelaeologists," Mrs. Eglinton said. "Jim contributes to *The Spelaeologist*, and so does Joe. But Jim is going to write the tiger up for the *Medical Journal.*"

"I should think so," Daddy said.

"It'll take me quite awhile," Dr. Eglinton said. "There's a lot of work to do on it yet."

Mama got up and went over and touched Mrs. Reardon on the shoulder. "Come on, Isabel," she said. "Let's play charades."

Mrs. Reardon got up, smiling. "Oh yes," she said. "Let's play charades."

"Tubby, you and Steve take sides," Mama said. "Hurry." She looked at Daddy as she spoke the last words. He started and said, "All right. I'll take Evelyn."

Mrs. Eglinton smiled at him. "I'm sorry, but I've already promised Mr. MacCollum to be on his side."

Uncle Tubby looked surprised, but he said, "That's right," and went over and stood beside her.

"I'll take Isabel," Daddy said.

"I'll take Lucy," Uncle Tubby said.

"I'll take Kev," Daddy said.

"Hey!" Uncle Tubby said. "Can't have husbands and wives on the same side. You keep Kev. I'll take Isabel."

"You're getting all the women," Daddy said.

"I got a harem scene in mind," Uncle Tubby said.

"Well, that leaves Sally on my side unless you take her," Daddy said.

"I welcome her with open arms," Uncle Tubby said.

"No," Mama said briskly. "I'll stay with Steve. There has to be somebody on each side knows where the costumes are. Lucy can be you all's wardrobe mistress. . . . Tubby, you and your gang go on upstairs. Jim, you stay here with us."

They started up the stairs. Mrs. Eglinton kept talking all the way. "I know a wonderful word. Ingratiate. See? Somebody comes in a grey dress and sits down at the table and eats something. In—grey—she—ate. See?" She looked at Mrs. Reardon, smiling. "Have you got a grey dress?"

Mrs. Reardon did not answer. They had entered the attic and were standing beside the great cedar chest in which the charade costumes were kept. Lucy lifted the lid. Mrs. Eglinton bent and picked up Grandpa Mallory's stovepipe hat and set it sideways on her brown hair. Then she saw his yellowed brocaded waistcoat and put that on over her shell-pink linen dress.

Lucy, standing between them, glanced from one lady to the other, asking herself which one she would rather resemble. Mrs. Eglinton looked, if possible, prettier than she had looked this afternoon. Excitement, or the pink of the dress, had brought a wild rose color to her cheeks. Everything about her seemed to sparkle.

Mrs. Reardon had found a green-striped basque in the chest and had put it on. But it would not meet about her waist. She made a little face when she saw that it was too tight and took it off.

"It was lacing made their waists like that," Mrs. Eglinton said, "but their hips were terrible. . . . My mother was still tying her corset strings to the bedpost when she was forty years old. It's a wonder her organs didn't get out of whack. Some of 'em did. But that might have been six children."

"Be quiet!" Uncle Tubby said.

He had gone a little way off and sat on top of a trunk, with his glass still in his hand. Their side was to go on second but Uncle Tubby said now that they couldn't go on at all if they didn't get the word. He was trying hard to get the right word.

Mrs. Eglinton dived into the trunk again and came up holding something white in her hands. *"What in the world?"*

"It's Aunt Portia's drawers," Lucy said. "She weighed two hundred pounds."

Holding the drawers out before her, Mrs. Eglinton took a few prancing steps. "We could have a clown act," she said.

She looked at Lucy archly as she spoke. Lucy looked away. She had spoken in a whisper and hoped that Mrs. Eglinton would take the hint. Laughing was fun—if she and Mrs. Eglinton got started they could laugh themselves weak over those drawers, the way she and Lois did sometimes over nothing at all. But acting was more fun than laughing. She was anxious to get on to it. She knew from experience, however, that certain preliminaries had to be got through first. They always spent a lot of time selecting the word. She had never quite understood the principle of selection, but she could tell by the way they looked when they had hit on a word that suited them. An expression of incredulous delight came over a face. The person who had thought of the word would repeat it over and over, shaking with laughter. Sometimes they would laugh so hard that they would have to put their arms about each other's shoulders in order to stand up. For days afterwards they might go off into gales of laughter at the mere mention of that word. Visitors did not understand how important the selection of the word was and were always suggesting words of their own. But her father and mother hardly ever listened to them. Uncle Tubby, she reflected, was not likely to waste his time acting out one of Mrs. Eglinton's words, even if he did smile at her so often.

"Be quiet!" he said again mechanically and set his empty glass down on the trunk and stared at Mrs. Reardon as if she might know the word. She did not say anything, only smiled back at him.

"We've got to get something that will lay Steve out," he said after a minute.

"Dante," Mrs. Eglinton said. "You could be a Spanish don —and we could have a tea party."

"The Mad Hatter's?" he said.

"I bid to be the dormouse!" Lucy cried. She looked at Mrs. Eglinton. "And you could be the Mad Hatter."

Uncle Tubby shook his head. "Not a contemptible idea. But not good enough. . . . The ideal thing would be a Civil War scene disguised as a literary scene. An incident in the life of Dr. Johnson and all the time it would be the boyhood of Robert E. Lee. . . . Shiloh. . . . Antietam. . . . Malvern Hill. . . . Bull Run. . . ."

"Antietam!" Mrs. Eglinton said. "It's too bad it doesn't end with an R."

"Oh *yes*!" Lucy said. "They have long sticky tongues."

Uncle Tubby was looking at Mrs. Eglinton almost respectfully. "A bold stroke," he said, "but I don't think we could get away with it. There are some tough babies out there."

Mrs. Reardon was not listening. She was moving about the room. She stopped with an exclamation before a picture that leaned against a chair: a twelve-year-old boy who sat with his hands clasped in his lap, his head a little tilted to one side and from under heavy lids stared straight before him.

"Such a strange little boy!" she said.

"He's dead," Lucy said.

Mrs. Reardon turned her head and glanced at Lucy, smiling. Lucy took a step forward and stopped; she did not like to go into that part of the attic if she could help it. "It's Uncle Joey," she said. "They didn't have a picture of him, so they propped him up and took one after he was dead."

Uncle Tubby emptied his glass and set it down on the trunk. "That was quite a custom in the old days," he said. "But sometimes the ones taken in life are just as terrific. There was an old admiral in our dining room had his hand thrust into the bosom of his coat. When I was a kid I thought it was his stomach busting through."

Mrs. Reardon transferred her smiling glance from Lucy to him. "You must have been a strange little boy."

"You ought to make a study of me some time," he said.

His voice had cracked on the last words. The smile was still on his face but it was like something painted and already fading. She had begun to move on before he had finished speaking. He straddled a trunk with his long legs, moving after her, like a big greyhound, Lucy thought, and it seemed to her that when he reached the woman's side he might bend his head for her to set a careless hand upon it.

But he was standing upright before her, in the open space between some trunks, where she had stopped. A deer's head mounted on a block of wood sat on a table. Moths had eaten away a wide patch on the forehead: one of the ears was torn. Grandpa Lewis' Knights of Pythias sword lay in front of it. A stuffed monkey that Daddy had played with when he was little squatted in front of it. Mrs. Reardon put her hand out and touched the deer's forehead lightly with her finger. "Couldn't we use this?" she asked.

The cleared space that they were standing in made a little room. He put his hand out and flicked the deer's good ear. He had made the gesture in order that his hand might, for a moment, cleave the same air that her hand had cleaved. He said: "You could impersonate a fallow doe. Down by yonder auld faill dyke, I wot there lies a new-slain knight. . . ."

She looked at him and shook her head gently, as if he had told her something that didn't much interest her. ". . . Leman . . ." she said. "You could have your incident from the life of Robert E. Lee."

Staring back at her, he spoke absentmindedly: " 'Man' would be dull to act and the 'Lee' would be pretty obvious."

Mrs. Eglinton had set her hat farther back on her head and with her shoulders thrown back, came towards them, swinging an imaginary cane.

"Killarny!" she said.

Uncle Tubby swung slowly around. After a moment he said: "An animal act, perhaps? With you gorging yourself on this stuffed object here?"

"I bid to be a tiger!" Lucy cried. "Couldn't there be two tigers?"

" 'Larn'?" Uncle Tubby said.

Mrs. Eglinton flashed him her wide smile. "You could be a schoolteacher. . . ."

He shook his head. "No," he said, "not even for you. 'Parnell,' " he said sharply, then: " '*Parnell!*' That's the word."

"It's not Civil War. You said it had to be Civil War."

"It'll have to do," he said. "It's better'n anything they can think up."

"Just an old Irishman. How can we act that?"

"It means a priest's mistress."

"Parnell means a priest's mistress?"

"P-a-r-n-e-l". Uncle Tubby said, "Comes from St. Petronella. One of those saints started out as a prostitute. Met up with a St. Peter. . . . Naturally there was talk. But it's a perfectly good word—since the time of Langland."

"What was Langland's first name?" Mrs. Eglinton asked.

"Piers," he said, "Piers P. Langland."

"Sure enough?"

"Quite," he said.

"A priest's mistress! That might not be so bad." She glanced over her shoulder at the chest. "I suppose there are plenty of robes in there?"

"Stoles, reredoses, chasubles." He went up to her. He laid his hand on her arm. "Evelyn"—he called her Evelyn, though he had never seen her before today. "Evelyn, run downstairs and see whether they are ready for us."

Mrs. Eglinton's white teeth shone. So did her dark eyes. When he put his hand on her arm she laughed and laid her hand on his other arm. "Listen," she said, "why can't you talk to our study club while you're here?"

"I will," he said.

"What on?"

"The platform of States' Rights," he said.

She stopped laughing to let him have the full glow of her dark eyes. "Will you really speak to them?"

"In the Unknown Tongue," he said. His hand clasped her arm tighter, then relaxed, then tightened its grip again. "Hurry up. Ask them if they want us to come down now."

After she had gone Lucy sat down on a little cane-bottomed chair that rested against a crazily leaning screen. The screen was of wood, homemade, covered with chintz: a pattern of ferns on a yellow ground. The chintz was rotten; the wine-red of an earlier covering showed through rents here and there, like blood at the roots of the ferns. All these old things that people had used for a while and had thrown away must stay up here, alone. But worn out, abandoned, as they were, they still kept some of the ways of life. That place they were still standing in was like a little room and here before her was another little room. The screen made one wall, an old bookcase whose shelves were crammed with discarded books, made another. Her chair was drawn up beside the bookcase, as if somebody were in the habit of sitting here to read those old books. . . . Downstairs the life of the house that everybody knew went on, but she was up here, above it, in a room of her own, in another house than her own, and a little way off, in another room were people who had forgotten that she was in this strange house, too. She could look at them freely. She asked herself again whether she would rather be Mrs. Eglinton or Mrs. Reardon. Mrs. Eglinton sparkled more. Her white teeth, her dark eyes, her gold-brown hair all shone. She was like the girls in the smooth-fitting bathing suits who smile at you from under enormous hats in the beer or Coca-Cola ads. Mrs. Reardon did not look like anybody you had ever known.

He said: "Well, here I am."

They had not moved from that place that was like a little room. He stood with his hands shoved into the pockets of his coat, looking down at Mrs. Reardon. She would not look at him but kept fingering the worn hair on the dead deer's hide.

"What was it that you had to say to me?" he asked, not taking his hands out of his pockets but moving a little closer to her.

She did not answer.

"You telegraphed and asked me to meet you here."

She raised her head at that. "The Lewises must think it's strange!"

"They have so many nutty friends it doesn't make any difference, but it is getting to be a habit with you, you know."

"Twice!" she said, "twice I've made you leave your work."

"You had a right to command me. I told you you could."

She gave him a long look. "You make me sound whimsical."

"When I got to Paris it did seem that all you wanted me to do was to take you to tea at Rumpelmayer's. I can't say that our sessions at the Sherry-Netherland were any more rewarding."

"You talk as if I were to blame," she said.

His hands came up out of his pockets and went down at his sides, balled into fists. He said in a voice so low that it barely reached Lucy's ears: "Forgive me, darling!"

She stepped back so that the deer's head was between them. She was wiping her eyes with her handkerchief. "It's all right," she said.

"Did Kev see those people?" he asked quickly.

She nodded.

"Do you think he'll go through with it?"

She nodded again.

He drew a long breath. "You'll be in this country some time then. An operation like that isn't concluded overnight."

She began to laugh. "We're going back!" she cried.

"Going back?"

"He's told them that his business won't allow him to stay here more than a few weeks. They've agreed to send representatives to him."

"Business. . . . In the name of God, what business has he got?"

"Nothing." She laughed again, wildly. "Nothing—except tormenting me. . . ."

"Tormenting?" he said. "You wouldn't write! My God, how could I know what was going on? Has it been worse lately?"

She shook her head. Her eyes were so full of tears that one splashed down on the front of her dress. "He's not any worse than he was when you were there," she said. "But I'm so tired of it. I get up in the morning and I think: 'How will I get through this day?' "

He laid his big hand on her shoulder. "You're not going back there," he said. "I'm not going to let you."

She put her hand up and pushing him a little away from her was whispering something that Lucy couldn't catch when Mrs. Eglinton put her head in at the door. "They want to borrow me," she said, "and the hat and waistcoat, too. They think I look good in 'em."

"You do," Uncle Tubby told her. "Tell 'em to go right ahead." He spoke without looking around, but Mrs. Reardon went toward Mrs. Eglinton, laying her hand on his arm as she moved past him. "Do they want us to come down now?" she asked.

"I bet you don't guess it," Mrs. Eglinton said. "It doesn't seem really fair, the way they're working it."

Uncle Tubby turned around then. His eyes were bright, but he looked dazed, too, like a person who has just come to the surface after swimming under water. He said "Tricky, eh? You have to watch that Lewis!"

He put one hand under Mrs. Eglinton's arm and one under Mrs. Reardon's and they left the room. It was not until they were out in the hall that one of them remembered Lucy and called to her. "I'm coming," she said, and got up off her chair and followed them downstairs.

VI

THEY were met at the door by Sarah who asked them to sit in chairs that had been arranged at one end of the parlor. She told them that the word was in four syllables and would be acted all at once. The other end of the parlor had been fixed up for a stage. There was the little round table, covered with a red-checked cloth in the center of the stage; Mr. Reardon was sitting beside it. Stephen was evidently acting the part of a waiter; he had a big white napkin tied about his waist and another napkin over his arm. He kept bending over Mr. Reardon, smiling and whispering, but Mr. Reardon would only shake his head and push farther away from him the pile of saucers. Mrs. Eglinton appeared from the left and came up to Mr. Reardon's table. He asked her to sit down at the table and told the waiter to bring her a drink. Then he got up and went over to the other side of the stage where the palm that Sarah hadn't been able to resist raising from an avocado seed stood, with beside it, a bridge table that was supported on two chairs. Mr. Reardon got behind the bridge table and stood, looking very thoughtful and not seeming to see any of the people who passed by. They were Sarah and Dr. Eglinton. Dr. Eglinton was wearing the hat and the waistcoat and carried Grandpa Mallory's gold-headed cane, but otherwise he looked as he always did, brown and quiet. Mama had a shawl over her head and was pretending that she was an old beggar woman, for she picked up several cigarette butts that were lying on the floor and held her hand out to Mr. Reardon and whined. But he just kept on looking over her head.

Mrs. Eglinton pretended that she had finished her drink. She looked about her and asked the waiter something. He pointed toward the bridge table. It did not make a very good hiding place for Mr. Reardon; you could see the upper part of his body and his legs and feet, too. Still, it took Mrs. Eglinton several seconds to recognize him. When she did he bowed and lifted his hat high off his head and she squeaked and said "Oooh!" and fell back in her chair.

"That's all," Daddy said then and he and Dr. Eglinton went downstairs to mix some drinks while Mama and Mrs. Eglinton and Mr. Reardon came and sat with the audience.

"Are you playing it straight, Sally?" Uncle Tubby asked.

She considered. "Well, there are wheels within wheels."

Uncle Tubby stared at Dr. Eglinton, who, the stovepipe hat pushed far back on his head, was dropping ice cubes into glasses. "Wheels within wheels . . ." he said. "He's a fellow got an old-time look to him, anyhow. Who thought up his part?"

"Steve," Mama said.

"Does Eglinton have anything to do with the rest of the show?"

"Oh, *no*!" Mrs. Eglinton said. "He's never been there and

if he did go he wouldn't act like that. Why, one time when he was sixteen he was sitting in the little house at his grandmother's, reading, and a colored girl came to call him to the 'phone and he wouldn't go back out there again till his grandmother fired her."

"Tippecanoe," Mrs. Reardon said suddenly.

Uncle Tubby slapped his leg. "Of course! That bridge table was a *pissoir*. . . . But that doesn't account for Eglinton."

Daddy came over to him carrying a tray of highballs. "Sarah told you there were wheels within wheels," he said.

Uncle Tubby looked at him hard, then said, "And Tyler, too! . . . Lewis, you dog, I'll get you for that!"

They went up to the attic. "Find me a black robe," Uncle Tubby said. Mrs. Eglinton began lifting things out of the cedar chest and laying them on a trunk that sat beside it. Mrs. Reardon sat down on another trunk, with her hands clasped in her lap. She caressed the thumb of one hand with the fingers of the other. Sometimes she stopped and held both hands out before her and looked at them before she laid them back in her lap. Lucy wondered why Daddy had said that he did not like her hands. She thought they were pretty: the kind of hands that a partridge might have if a partridge were a lady—small, with little, tapering fingers. Lucy decided that Daddy didn't like her hands because they were so delicate. They did not look as if they had ever done much work, or ever could. Daddy never seemed to be doing much work himself, but he had strict ideas about other people. Mama's hands looked perfectly dreadful. She, Lucy, was ashamed of them sometimes when she saw her out with other ladies, but then Mama did not go around with other ladies much.

Mrs. Eglinton was holding up a black silk dressing gown. "That's it," Uncle Tubby said. He put it on and tied a string of black beads about his waist. "My loins are now girded. Bring me my helmet of salvation."

They rummaged in the trunk till they found a little square, crocheted cap. He put it on his head. "While I'm about it I'll have a maniple, too," he said and picked up from the top of the heap a square of embroidered silk, which he draped over his left arm.

"What's that for?" Lucy asked.

"To wipe away the tears that you must shed in this life," he told her. "How about getting yourself fixed up?"

"I don't know what I've got to wear," she said.

"A nice embroidered petticoat. You're going to be an altar boy."

They found a petticoat which would fit Lucy and then Mrs. Eglinton searched in the heap of garments until she came upon Grandma Mallory's nightgown, which they said would do for the other altar boy.

Mrs. Eglinton glanced at Mrs. Reardon. "Make her be it," she whispered.

Uncle Tubby went over to Mrs. Reardon. "Come on, Isabel," he said, "you're going to be my Parnell."

She started and looked around the room before she looked at him. Suddenly she began to laugh. "You do look like a priest," she said.

"I am," he said impatiently. "I'm going to be the priest and you're going to be my mistress."

Her eyes gleamed. She put her finger to her mouth as if trying to push the laughter back. "Father Du Fresnay would love that."

"Your chaplain is naturally the soul of honor," he said. "*I* am a very corrupt priest." He was smiling, but his voice went a little hard, like Mama's when she was determined to make you do something but wanted everybody present to think that you did it of your own accord. He took her hand and pulled her to her feet. "Give me something for her to wear," he said over his shoulder to Mrs. Eglinton.

Mrs. Eglinton brought a faded scarlet shawl that had white flowers embroidered on it in silk. Mrs. Reardon stood quietly while they draped it about her. When they had finished Uncle Tubby passed his big hand over her hair, disordering it a little. She looked up at him and smiled. "What do I do?" she asked.

"Just show yourself at the door when I give the signal."

Mrs. Eglinton was getting into Grandma Mallory's nightgown. "Tell her what the signal is," she said.

He thought a moment, frowning. "When I say '*Introibo ad altare. . . .*' That's the signal. . . . And you . . ." he turned first to Mrs. Eglinton and then to Lucy, "you two are acolytes. Lucy, you can take the amice when I doff it. Evelyn, you catch hold of the tail of my robe when I kneel."

They went downstairs. He made Sarah give him two candles. Then he made them turn off the lights and put the bridge table between the two west windows and set the lighted candles on it and got some chairs from across the hall and put two on one side of the room and two on the other. He said that they would follow the example set by the other side and present the word in one act, and strode down the aisle that he had made between the four chairs, with Lucy and Mrs. Eglinton following him. He was at the altar. He reached up and lifted the helmet off his head. Lucy took it from him. He turned about and faced the audience. He said, "*Dominus vobiscum,*" and clasped his hands in front of him and turned again and knelt before the bridge table. Mrs. Eglinton knelt behind him, holding the tail of his robe.

Lucy faced the audience, pressing the crocheted cap against her breast. She thought that she should have knelt when Mrs.

Eglinton knelt but it seemed too late to do that now. She looked at her father. He was staring at the floor, not even watching what was going on. She met her mother's eyes. Sarah blinked and frowned a little as if she had just come out into a strong light. She made a gesture with her hand, but Lucy did not know whether she meant for her to leave the stage or to stand where she was. Lucy frowned and was muttering, "I don't know what you're talking about," when someone suddenly came forward and took her hand in a hard grip and she felt herself being led off the stage and out of the room.

In the hall she stopped short and tried to wrench her hand away. But the man who held her hand in his went on through the door and out on to the gallery, pulling her after him. He released her there and stood with his back to the screen door that he had just closed, his arms folded across his chest, his head bent slightly downwards.

She could see the brass knob glittering in the light from the hall. She had heard the latch click as the door went shut. But even if the catch were not fastened she could not get back into the hall. She reflected that when she had first caught sight of him he had been standing in a doorway that she wanted to pass through. He had stood aside to let her pass, but she knew that he would not stand aside now.

His head sank lower on his breast. He seemed to stoop a little. He was not a tall man. His eyes must be nearly on a level with her own eyes now. He spoke: "He said *Dominus vobiscum!* That was sacrilege."

She did not answer.

"Do you know what a priest is?" he asked.

She could feel his eyes burning on her face. She moved out of the shaft of light. *He's crazy,* she thought. *That's what they've been talking about all along. He's crazy.*

With an effort she wrenched her gaze from the dark figure.

In the field below the house people were walking about, swinging lanterns and singing. The Holy Roller meeting had broken up. The hymn that they were singing came to her only in snatches, one voice taking up where another voice left off. The lanterns that the church-goers held in their hands gave off flickering lights, like the will-o'-the-wisps that shine before travelers who have lost their way in dark forests. Down in the woods there was a rock almost as big as this house. The man who had been bitten by the rattlesnake was buried there.

Her knees were shaking, her head felt lighter than air. She sat down in the hammock. "I could smash the window with my fist," she thought. "They'd have to come then." She leaned back in the hammock so that she could look through the window in the parlor. They were all still in there. She could hear the drone of Uncle Tubby's Latin above the Holy Rollers' chanting, but it sounded faint and far away. And the people in the room were all so quiet, like people in a picture. Uncle Tubby had risen and stood with his arms upraised, pouring forth more Latin. Mrs. Eglinton still crouched behind him, holding the skirt of his robe in her rosy-tipped fingers. Mrs. Reardon was coming through the doorway.

She must have gone somewhere to look at herself in a mirror. When Uncle Tubby first laid the silk shawl on her shoulders she had let the folds fall as they would. But now only one end of the shawl fell over her shoulder. The rest was wrapped tightly about her body. She had a scarlet ribbon in her hair and she had changed her white high-heeled pumps for flat gold sandals. She came straight forward, looking at Uncle Tubby and smiling. He went to her and put his arms around her.

The man in the doorway spoke: "A priest is higher than the angels."

She kept her eyes fixed on the lighted window. Mrs. Reardon had fallen sidewise in Uncle Tubby's arms. Her head drooped. She was making a thin, strange sound.

"She's crying!" Lucy said in a low voice.

He came swiftly and stood behind her for a second, then he was gone into the house. She followed him.

Uncle Tubby was carrying Mrs. Reardon over to the sofa. He set her down there as if she had been a doll and knelt on the floor at her feet. He said: "Isabel, what in God's name is the matter?"

She stared over his head and kept rubbing her hands together.

Daddy stayed where he was but Mama came over and stood beside them. "I'm *so* sorry," she said. "She must be frightfully tired. I'm *so* sorry. . . . I didn't realize. . . ."

Mr. Reardon pushed past her. "Isabel!" he said.

Uncle Tubby did not move to make room for him. He put his hand out and laid it on her knee. She did not seem to know that it was there. Her head jerked back and forth. She began to laugh.

"Isabel!" Mr. Reardon said again.

She shivered all over. Uncle Tubby's hand fell away from her knee as she jumped to her feet. She looked at her husband. "You didn't fool me for a minute," she said.

Her voice was high, like somebody trying to talk in a loud wind. He kept his voice low. "What makes you think I'm trying to fool you?"

"Not for a minute," she said. "All these other people . . . but not me. . . . Why can't you ever learn that you can't fool me?"

"What is it?" he asked. "What is it now?"

As he spoke he moved, not toward her, but a little to one side. Her head turned slowly in the same direction. When he moved she, too, moved a little. They were like young roosters who are stalking the yard and suddenly one of them will ruffle his wing and scrape the ground with it and begin to walk about the other rooster, who, in turn, begins to ruffle and strut. So they revolved, one around the other. But no matter how far they moved each kept his face full upon the other. It was as if a line stretched taut between them and each movement they made only stretched it tighter.

"You were out of the room when they started acting, but *that* didn't fool me," she said and for the first time took her eyes from his face and stared at the floor, shaking her head from side to side. "Oh, no," she said and laughed.

"What in the devil . . ." Uncle Tubby said, but nobody paid any attention to him, for in the second that she had taken her eyes off his face Mr. Reardon had darted forward and was now standing directly behind her, holding each of her arms in a firm grip. Her eyes started in her head, she shrieked and arched her body out from his and struggled to free her arms, but he was stronger than she was; she could not break his grip.

Uncle Tubby said: "Kev, you can't get away with that," but Daddy put his hand out and held him back. "You keep out of this," he said.

Mr. Reardon looked up at Daddy, as if surprised, as if he had not known till that moment that there was anybody else in the room. "It's all right," he said and indeed his wife had suddenly stopped struggling and lay against him, her head turned a little to one side, her eyes closed. He released one of her wrists and slipping his arm about her shoulder drew her forward. "Come on," he said, "let's go up to bed," and they went slowly out of the room, crossed the hall and started up the stairs.

Mama walked over to the table where Daddy was standing and made a gesture indicating that he should pour her a drink. When he had poured it she did not drink it but took it over to Uncle Tubby. "Here, mate," she said.

He took the glass and drank almost half of it before he spoke. "It's too deep for me," he said. "I've known 'em a long time, but I never saw anything like that before."

"I never saw anything like that before *anywhere*," Mama said, "and I thought I'd been around. . . . Jim, do you think it's because she's tight?"

He shrugged and got to his feet. "Come on, Evelyn," he said.

Mrs. Eglinton's bright eyes were going from face to face. "Yes," she said, "we ought to be going." But she made no move to go until Dr. Eglinton said again, "Well, come on, then."

They said their goodbyes. Mama went with them as far as the front door but Daddy sat where he was, only waving his hand at them as they went past. "Better luck next time," he said.

"Don't give it a thought," Dr. Eglinton said. "I'll call you about that dog."

When they were gone Daddy looked at Uncle Tubby. "Kev went in there mighty fast," he said.

Uncle Tubby was sitting on the end of the table, his legs spread, his hands swinging between his knees. He raised his head and stared at Daddy. "You think he's in the *habit* of manhandling Isabel?"

"Don't get excited," Daddy said. "All I meant was that it struck me that this might not be the first time he'd had to calm her down."

Uncle Tubby was staring over Daddy's head at the wall. "I bet that's what she meant," he said suddenly.

"Meant what?"

"When she telegraphed and asked me to meet her here.

Said there was something she had to see me about, but she couldn't put it in a telegram."

"She didn't *plan* to come here?"

"No."

"What in the hell where they going to Bardstown for?"

"There's a fellow there Kev wanted to see. A priest."

"Well," Daddy said. "I'm still wondering why they turned up *here*. If Isabel wanted to see you there are plenty of other places—Paris, New York, the Riviera. . . ."

Uncle Tubby said: "I think that somewhere on the trip she lost her nerve. . . . After all, it's enough to shake one's nerve."

"What?" Daddy asked. "What's shaken her nerve?"

"How'd you like to be shut up for weeks on end and not allowed to communicate with your friends?"

"Did he do that?" Daddy said.

"Ask Barbara Dean. She had a letter from Isabel asking her to stop by next time she went to Sanary. So she stopped."

"Well?"

"She saw Kev. Said he was as sweet as pie. But she didn't see Isabel."

"Did she ask to see her?"

"Sure. Kev told her Isabel just couldn't see her."

"Didn't he give any other excuse?"

"No. Just said she couldn't see her."

Mama came in from the hall. She looked at them. "Do you think I ought to go upstairs and offer to do anything?" she asked.

Neither of them answered. She went to the table and picked up two ashtrays and emptied them into the fireplace. It was then that she saw Lucy sitting in the corner on the little sofa. *"Lucy!"* she said. "Oh, darling!"

Lucy got up slowly. One of her legs was so fast asleep that

it buckled under her when she tried to stand on it. She cried out.

Uncle Tubby ran over and caught her in his arms. "What a life!" he said. "Even the kids are mowed down!"

"Please," Mama said. "Just take her on across the hall, Tubby."

Lucy burst into tears. She knew that it was already hours past her bedtime and that her mother would not allow her to stay up even a minute longer, but if she left the parlor now she might never find out what was wrong with Mr. Reardon, for it would be no good asking them later. They could talk you blue in the face, but they would never answer a question—even if you were fool enough to ask them something you really wanted to find out. They would make her go to bed now but they would sit up for hours yet, talking about what was wrong with Mr. Reardon. At the thought, she sobbed.

Mama, walking beside Uncle Tubby, put a hand up and caressed her bare leg. "Poor little thing. I had no business letting you stay up so long."

Lucy glared at her. "I'm not sleepy," she muttered, "and you know it."

"I am," Uncle Tubby said. He cast her down on her bed, bent and kissed her cheek, and he left the room. Her mother was at the dresser, getting out a clean nightgown. Lucy sat up on the edge of the bed, her eyes half closed, and let her mother slip her clothes off and draw the gown over her head. As her hands moved over the child's body the mother kept murmuring: "So tired . . . all of us so tired. . . . Going to sleep now. . . . Too tired to say your prayers, darling?"

"Yes," Lucy whispered and closed her eyes tight, but after her mother had left and the room was dark she found herself wishing that she had said her prayers and she opened her eyes and stared into the corner of the room that held the bookcase. It was so dark that you could not tell one book from another, but she knew that *Morte d'Arthur* still stood in its place on the third shelf and that the crucifix still lay behind it, on its side, maybe, with the little face turned toward her bed and the little, fierce eyes glowing upon her. It had lain there all the time she was out of the room, when she stood in the yard with Mr. Reardon to look down on the Brush Arbor meeting, when she sat at the table with the others, when she sat in the attic listening to Uncle Tubby and Mrs. Reardon talking together, when she stood in the parlor before all of them, clasping the Helmet of Salvation to her breast. . . . And on the dresser where she had laid it when she darted into the room just before they started playing charades was the gold box that Mrs. Reardon had given her. . . .

She turned over and lay face downwards, the covers pulled up over her head, her cheek pressed flat against the cool sheet, breathing hard. The frail barrier of sheet and coverlet gave her some comfort. Her breathing grew slower and softer. She slept at last and dreamed that all the people in the house were setting out on a journey. They had said that she could go with them if she got her clothes packed in time. But she could not find her yellow linen dress and it seemed impossible to go without it. She rummaged in her dresser drawers, as Uncle Tubby had rummaged in the cedar chest, and yet at the same time she seemed to be accompanying them on their journey. It was through a forest, such as the Knight Huldbrand had wandered in, but the road was not plain and every now and then they stopped, not knowing which way to turn. Her father went first—and this was a curious thing—he did not walk as he did every day, with his head bent, his eyes on the ground, but held his head high, not looking where he set his feet, and would not listen to her mother when she pointed, saying that the trail went this way or that. Mama left him standing at the foot of a great tree and went on alone, saying that she knew that this was the way. When she came back her hands were full of white flowers. He would not look at her or her flowers, but standing, his head still high, pointed to another way down which Mrs. Reardon and Mr. Reardon and Uncle Tubby were coming. Mrs. Reardon was all in white, and she walked slowly, as she had walked into the parlor for the charade, holding out before her the great silver tray from the sideboard in the dining room. Uncle Tubby and Mr. Reardon kept pointing to what lay on the tray: Captain Green's head. There was no blood on it anywhere; it was as white as bone. The lips kept moving. When Uncle Tubby and Mr. Reardon heard the sounds that came from the lips they cried out and ran away, but Mrs. Reardon kept walking slowly forward and the trees got thinner and you saw that this country they were walking through was no real country at all, only the brink of a great chasm into which they would all fall if they did not turn around and go back the way they had come.

VII

"YOU can fix that one," Jenny said, and with a silver knife she trimmed off the superfluous pastry that hung shawl-wise over the pie pan, and set the pan down on the kitchen table. Lucy took a fork and laboriously fluted the edges of the pie, then with the fork stabbed the middle of the pastry until the berries' red juice welled up through the pricked dough. She would have pricked the dough again, but Jenny took the fork away from her. "No use filling it full of holes," she said, "no use to anybody then. You remind me of some of these people always going around with ice picks. Lord, I got so I hate to see the summer come in."

Sarah Lewis' garden chair was placed so that she could look into the kitchen. She turned her head and fixed her eyes on Jenny's face. "Was somebody hurt last night?" she asked.

"My first cousin," Jenny said. "My mother's sister's baby boy. Just back from Detroit where he had been working in the Ford factory and a nigger named Buzz Collins slipped up behind him and stabbed him in the back. Shattered a kidney. They got him in the hospital now, but they don't have no idea whether he going to live or die."

Sarah groaned. "I bet they were drinking," she said.

"Luther, my cousin, do drink a lot, but seems it just makes him happy-like. That Collins nigger is mean."

Jenny took a clean cotton bag from a drawer of the cabinet and disappeared into the hall. When she came back the bag was full of cracked ice. She folded a towel over it and stepped out on to the gallery where Sarah lay, pale and inert in her long, green-striped chair. Jenny laid the ice bag on her forehead and made her sit up while she adjusted her pillows so that she could rest more comfortably, then tucked the wispy end of one braid out of sight. "Your hair do look awful. Seems like you *could* run into town long enough to get it washed."

Sarah moved her head feebly from side to side. "Yours looks wonderful. When did you get it done, Jenny?"

Jenny turned around so that both Lucy and her mother could see the little curls that clustered over her whole head. "I called Madame Eline up early this morning. Told her you had company and she just got to get me fixed up."

"You must have called her at the crack of dawn," Sarah said. "I heard you in the kitchen around eight o'clock."

"I was in there by six o'clock and out of there by half past seven. Madame Eline say she just like me. Say she don't ever let the morning sun shine on her face while she in the bed. Say it make her sick at her stomach if it do."

"Don't talk about stomach," Sarah said and groaned again. "Oh, Jenny, why did I do it?"

Jenny's smile always made her eyes look larger and darker and more mysterious. "You be feeling better in a little while," she said. "Come on, Lucy. . . ." She held out her hand. Lucy slid down off her stool and took Jenny's hand and followed her upstairs. It was past noon, but Jenny hadn't made any of the beds yet, and it seemed that there might not be any lunch. Lucy didn't care. She and Jenny had breakfasted early on the lower gallery, on bananas and cornflakes and the remnants of a watermelon that they had found in the refrigerator. "Ain't no use cooking nothing now," Jenny had said. "Ain't nobody around here going to feel like eating no breakfast today. But you better look out around supper time. . . ."

"How do you feel, Jenny?" Lucy asked now as they went up the stairs. "They said you were drunk, too. Haven't you got a hangover?"

Jenny laughed and laid her hand on the bosom of her freshly starched blue uniform. "I had a bad old toothache," she said, "but I took some medicine for it and slept it off."

They were at the door of the room in which Lucy had slept. "You made your bed?" Jenny enquired.

Lucy shook her head.

"How you like to go in and make it now whilst I make the strange gentleman's?"

Lucy went into the bedroom. The blue gingham dress and the underwear she had worn the day before were lying on the foot of her tumbled bed. She gathered them up and put them into her laundry bag, then made the bed up as neatly as she could. The door that connected the two rooms was shut. On the other side of it she could hear Jenny singing, "Let a song go out of My Heart. . . ."

Lucy stood quietly in the middle of the room, her eyes fixed on the door. She had waked at sunrise that morning; the whole house was quiet. She had got out of bed and tiptoeing to the dresser had taken the crucifix out of its hiding place and put it into the gold box that Mrs. Reardon had given her. A breeze was blowing in off the gallery. She slipped back between the sheets and lying propped on one elbow held the crucifix in her other hand and slowly turned it back and forth so that the jeweled eyes caught the light. The sun grew stronger. The whole bed swam in a glimmering patchwork of light and shade. But the light that seemed to radiate from the little eyes was stronger than the beams that shimmered on her blue coverlet. She held the crucifix up so shielded by the palm of her hand that the sun's rays did not fall on it. Even then the eyes glowed at her. She laid it down on the sheet, moved her pillow so that it cast a shadow over the crucifix and lay for a while on her back, staring at the wall opposite. The house seemed even more silent now than when she had awaked. It occurred to her that to all intents and purposes she was alone in it. Jenny had not yet come up from the cabin. Her mother and father and all the guests were still asleep. . . . Where did people go when they slept? To some other country? She had had a strange dream last night. She could not remember it very well, but it had seemed that something terrible was going to happen to all of them if they did not do something. But she did not know what it was they were supposed to do. . . . She got up and put the crucifix back into the gold box and slipped the box under the tissue paper that lined the drawer of the dresser in which she kept her underwear.

It seemed to her now, that that was not a good hiding place for it. Her mother and Jenny, too, were always rummaging among her things. She deliberated a moment, then took the box out and swiftly deposited it on one of the shelves of the bookcase, behind a row of books. That, she decided, was as safe a place as she could find. Jenny was not likely to be dusting the fronts of books, much less the backs, with the house full of company.

She had hidden the box none too soon. Jenny was coming

through the door. She stopped beside Lucy's dresser, flicked its top with her feather duster and put out her other hand to push the lacquered glove box into neater alignment with the mirror. "You can give me that box when you get through with it," she said.

"No, I can't," Lucy said. "It belonged to my grandmother."

Jenny yawned. "Well, there's a shell box at Woolworth's I just as soon have. . . . Where you reckon that strange gentleman went? He the only one of 'em up and doing this morning."

Lucy shook her head. "Is his car gone?"

They went to the window and looked out. They could see the nose of the family car protruding from the open garage. Uncle Tubby's car still stood beside the crape myrtle bush, but the long grey roadster was gone.

"He *ran* off," Lucy thought. "He knew that the sheriff would come and get him and lock him up, so he ran off."

Jenny shook her duster to and fro over the hollyhock plants. "I expect he went to town to get some Eno's," she said. "They all going to be needing it. . . . You like to help me shake the rug?"

"If you'll let me beat it," Lucy said. "Let's take it out in the yard and beat it."

But at that moment a call came from below: "Luceee!"

Lucy stood silent. Jenny gave her a little push. "Go on. Go and help your sick mother. You ain't going to have her with you long."

Downstairs Sarah was sitting up in her long chair, holding out the sodden ice bag. "Darling, couldn't you just put some more ice in this for me?"

"I don't know how to crack it," Lucy said.

"You don't need to crack it," her mother said irritably. "Just bring me two or three ice cubes." She leaned farther forward and wrung the ice bag and the towel out on to the brick floor. "Do help me, Lucy. I've just *got* to get myself into shape before dinner time. . . ."

"You ought not to gone and got drunk," Lucy said.

"Lucy," her mother said, "are you going to get that ice, or aren't you?"

Lucy went hurriedly into the house. She filled the bag with ice cubes, then dashed it against the wall until crushed ice spilled through the rents in the fabric and finally folded the bag inside a towel, as Jenny had done, and laid it turban-wise on her mother's forehead. Uncle Tubby came around the corner of the house. He stopped and stared and put his hand out as if to push both her and her mother away. "No more mummery!" he said and sank down in the chair opposite Sarah so heavily that its screws squeaked.

They regarded each other languidly. "Does that stuff help?" he asked after a little.

"Enormously," Sarah said. "Freezes the pain right out of your brain. Lucy. . . ."

Uncle Tubby shook his head. "I'd be afraid to try it. Any beer in the icebox?"

"Oh, God, yes," Sarah said. "Lucy, you go show him."

They went together through the dining room and into the kitchen. A bowl full of ice cubes still stood on the kitchen table. Uncle Tubby folded several cubes up in a dish napkin and clapped the napkin on his forehead. "Try everything," he muttered.

He took two bottles of beer from the refrigerator. *"Belle dame,"* he said, "do you think you could find me some whiskey?" Lucy fetched a bottle of whiskey from the sideboard in the dining room. He had removed his ice cap and was putting the cubes into two glasses he had taken from the kitchen cabinet. Lucy made a face. "You could get some more ice out of the 'frigerator," she told him. "This is no time for protocol." He filled the glasses three quarters full of beer and put generous dollops of whiskey on top of it.

"There," he said as he handed one of the glasses to Sarah. "A boilermaker is what you need."

She held the glass in her hand so limply that it seemed that it might drop on the brick floor at any moment. "I couldn't," she said, "I couldn't, possibly."

Uncle Tubby drew a stool up beside her and set the glass on it. "You'll come around to it in a minute," he said. He settled back in his chair and raised his own glass to his lips. Lucy watched him drain half the contents. It seemed to her that in the interval between the moment when he set his glass down with an "AAAh!" his eyes grew brighter, his cheeks took on a ruddier tinge. She wondered whether spirits could affect anyone so quickly. She herself had never tasted hard liquor except once when she had complained that her legs ached and Jenny had said that she had growing pains and had given her half a tablespoonful of whiskey from the sideboard cupboard. She had had champagne, however, on birthdays and once or twice at Christmas time. It had not made her feel very different, but then they never gave her a real drink. It seemed to her that they themselves spent half their time drinking something that made them feel so bad that they had to drink something else to make them feel better and that something else made them feel like drinking something else again: what Daddy called a vicious circle. She saw the circle, lowering at her from under beetling brows, its full, voracious mouth twisted a little to one side. . . . Uncle Tubby must be reading her mind. He said irritably: "Don't look at me like that, *belle dame*. I don't feel at all well."

"Just don't talk too much," Sarah said faintly, "and everything will be all right."

"Where's Steve?" Tubby asked.

"Sleeping it off," she said in the same faint tone.

Lucy left them and went into the dining room. Jenny hadn't straightened up in here since yesterday. The pillows on the window seat were still crushed in the shapes she had left them in when she quit the house and walked down to the gate to the Holy Roller Rock. That seemed a long time ago. She slipped her hand under one of the pillows and pulled out the blue and silver bound copy of "Undine." It fell open at the right place. The Knight Huldbrand and Undine were journeying through the forest to his castle of Ringstetten, but the wicked Kühleborn kept always beside them, making ugly faces at Undine, who screamed and turned to her husband for help, but when the knight swung his sword against Kühleborn it struck a rock and a torrent came foaming down and splashed them all over and they heard the sound of laughter. It was then, perhaps, that the knight first began to wish that he had married a mortal woman instead of Undine. . . . The gentlemen all seemed to be afraid of these strange ladies, but they were always going around where they were. . . .

She let the book fall on her knee and gazed out over the lawn. It must be around one o'clock. At that hour the shadow of the willow tree was short and squat, like the dwarfed trees Japanese people grow in pots. As the afternoon wore on it would lengthen until it reached all the way to the garage. It was hot today, but there was a little breeze; the willow leaves were all aflutter. She wondered what it would be like to be a knight in love with a woman who was not really a woman but a stream. The god Apollo had wooed a girl who had run from him and had turned into a laurel bush when he tried to embrace her, but he was a god and used to changing into different shapes. The Knight Huldbrand had remained always himself. How had he felt when the cool arms that encircled his neck changed into foam and spray? And did it happen all at once or little by little?

Daddy had joined them out on the gallery. His deep voice sounded just as it always did. He slept his hangovers off while her mother was always taking things to make her feel beter. Her mother was never content to let things happen. She had to do something about them. She was too quick on the uptake, Lucy's grandfather, old Professor Maury, said. He was off fishing somewhere and had not come to see them for a long time. They bored him, her mother said. In fact, he thought they were fools. But he would have come to stay with them, anyhow, if they had not bored him so much. He could not endure to be bored and said often that he liked each day to be a pleasure to him. When anybody bored him or interfered with his pleasures in any way he went right off and left them. She wondered what he would do if he had to stay there, the way she did, and sit around for hours, listening to them talk. If they ever said anything that anybody would want to hear they made you go out of the room. But usually it was about the Civil War or books. *Books, books, books.* Who wrote them and why they weren't any better. None of them ever seemed to be just right, like "Undine" or "The Secret Garden" or "The King of the Golden River." The writer had always done something wrong. If he had only asked her father—sometimes even her mother—he would have done it differently. But they were glad that they didn't know him, for they didn't think that he would ever write well, anyhow. And they didn't like to be around people who didn't write well. She concluded that they felt about writing the way Old Daddy felt about fishing; it had to be done exactly right or they didn't want to have anything to do with it. She told herself that when she grew up she would be a very different person from her father or her mother. For one thing, she would not write books. She might not even read them. If she realized her ambition to become a horse trainer her time would be fully occupied. But how could she ever get started when she didn't even have a horse?

Sometimes her mother would decide that they couldn't afford to buy the pony and would begin to throw out hints. How about letting them send Old Maggie in from Merry Point? Maggie was only fourteen hands high and she *saddled*. "Ponies are hardly ever gaited. Wouldn't you rather have a small mare that saddled than a pony that trotted you to death?"

The last time her mother said that Lucy had got so mad that she burst out crying. And even now when old Maggie's lean, sorrowful, sorrel face came before her mind's eye she felt like crying again. Mama would never say how old Maggie was, but Maggie already had those deep hollows over the eyes that mean a horse is getting along and she stayed out in the pasture all winter and her coat was as heavy as a teddy bear's and her mane and tail were always burred. You could curry her good and get her coat to shining and braid her mane and tail and *maybe* get them to ripple a little, but you couldn't do anything about those hollows over her eyes or the way she stood, with her head hanging down almost to her knees. "I want a pony that's my own age," she had sobbed, "I don't want to ride a pony that's as old as *Mammy*." And indeed, whenever she thought of the old mare she thought, too, of her great-grandmother. The old lady, sitting on the front porch at Merry Point, her hands folded in her lap, and the old mare, standing in the corner of the stable lot, seemed to fix the wide, empty fields, the woods where nobody now ever walked with the same brooding gaze.

Jenny came in with a plate of sandwiches and a glass of milk. "You just set up to the table and eat your lunch," she said. "Them folks out there ain't going to be eating till later."

Lucy pulled the silver *epergne* that stood in the middle of the table over to her, propped her book against it and read while she ate her sandwich. From the gallery came her mother's voice: "Well, maybe I *could* do with another. . . . Tubby, what made them move to Toulon?"

"Just becausce the old man had that place there."

"But Kev never had anything to do with his father. Weren't his father and mother divorced when he was quite young?"

"I believe he was eight years old when they separated. The old man wouldn't give Mimi a divorce."

"What was the old man like?"

"I knew Mimi, but I never knew him," Tubby said.

"He was the strangest man I've ever seen in my life," Stephen Lewis said suddenly.

"I never *knew* you knew him."

"I was in his house once. For two hours."

"At the *Villa Marthe*? Why, Steve, you never told me!"

"I never told anybody," he said, "and I've never mentioned it to Kev since. And he has never mentioned it to me."

"You went there with Kev? What happened?"

"Nothing. At least, nothing you could put your finger on."

Nobody spoke for several minutes, then Sarah said impatiently: "Go on. You've got to tell us now."

"If I can," he said.

VIII

IT was in the fall, right after the Armistice. Kev asked me to go down to Toulon with him, to see his father. Fellow didn't tell me that it would be the first time he'd seen his father—since he was eight years old, you say? I didn't think anything of it. So many people's fathers and mothers are separated these days.

"We flew down. Kev telephoned from the airport and asked if his father couldn't send a car over for us. Old man wouldn't come to the phone. Butler told us they didn't have a car. Couldn't hire one at the field; we went over on the tram. I was beginning to think that maybe the old man wasn't keen on seeing us, but I didn't say anything. I had Kev's medal in my pocket. . . ."

"Whatever for?" his wife asked.

"I don't know."

"You mean somebody slipped it in your pocket and you just found it there?"

"I put it in my pocket, myself."

"Why did you do that?"

"I tell you I don't know. It was when Kev was staying at the Crillon. You know, he never stayed at those plush places till after he came back from the war. . . . I was waiting for him to dress. He went into the bathroom—and this little box was standing on top of a chest of drawers. I just picked the medal up and put it in my pocket."

"You mean you'd always craved the *Croix de Guerre* and thought that this was a good way to get one?" his wife said.

"No," he said, "I tell you I just put it in my pocket."

"You thought it might come in handy after you got down there? But that isn't like you. It's more like me. Or Tubby. It isn't like him. *Is* it, Tubby?"

"No," Tubby said. "Did Kev know you had it?"

"I forgot I had it, myself. Till we got to *Cap Brun*. Around five o'clock in the afternoon. Went in by a side gate. Down one of those *allées* bordered with yew. There was an old bald-headed man walking ahead of us, reading out of a book to another old man who was raking the gravel. A big man. At least he had been big, but he was very thin and stooped over. All in black. At first I thought he was a priest and then he heard us and turned around and I knew it was the old man himself. I suppose it was his eyes. Grey. Sunk deep in his head, but very bright. He gave me one glance—it was like fire crackling in dry branches—and then he came straight up to Kev and put his hand on his arm and said, 'Is this Kevin?' and when Kev said it was he turned around and called to the other old man: 'Giles, Giles, here is my son come back to me!' "

"In English?" Sarah asked.

Stephen nodded. "The other old bird dropped his rake and came and looked Kev over and said, 'It's him, all right', and began laughing and hollering and a third old man came running and they all started talking French. Seems it was St. Cyprian's Day. Kev's mother had taken him away on St. Cyprian's Day. They thought St. Cyprian had brought him back—St. Cyprian was the old man's patron. They thought it was a miracle. Said we ought to go into the chapel and pray."

"Who *was* St. Cyprian?"

"A pagan magician. He tried to seduce the virgin Justina by his spells but was converted by her prayers—I looked him up as soon as I got hold of a missal."

"Say, that's good!" Tubby said. "On Wall Street they regarded the old man as quite a magician."

"They took us into the house and let us wash up," Stephen said, "and then they said it was time for vespers and we went over to the chapel. It was just a little stone chapel that the old man had had built. Rather Gothic in feeling. But it was so dim in there that I couldn't see much."

"It'd have knocked your eye out if you had," Tubby said. "There's a *Sacred Conversation* by Gian Bellini. The old boy was filthy with money."

"Were you the only ones in the chapel?" Sarah asked.

"Oh, no. His whole staff was there. The old butler and the gardener, two or three maids, some little boys. And some ladies, probably neighbors. They all lifted up their voices and sang vespers."

"How does it go?"

"Starts with the *Ave Maria*, then the versicle: *Deus, in adjutorium meum intende, Domine ad adjuvandum me festina*, then the psalm: *Dixit Dominus Domino meo. . . .*"

"Isn't Steve wonderful?" Sarah said. "He remembers everything!"

"We had some dinner," he said. "I remember there was corn on the cob. It's something of a feat to grow it in that country; the old man called the gardener in to receive our congratulations—the gardener was an Irishman who had been with him for years. The old man was fasting—keeping his vigil for St. Cyprian—but he sat with us and coached us on the Litany of the Saints. His idea was that he and I and Kev were to beat it over to the chapel as soon as we had finished dinner and get the Litany of the Saints in before the rest of the gang assembled for the evening prayer."

"And did you?"

He shook his head. "Kev blew up. Came in my room, as white as sheet and trembling all over. Asked me if I thought the old man was nuts. I told him that people sometimes got peculiar when they lived alone and he said that was so, all right, but the more he saw of his old man the more he thought his mother had been right to leave him and that I could stay if I wanted to, but he was getting the hell out of there. I told him that anything that suited him suited me, so we put our stuff back in our bags. . . ."

"You mean you left without even telling him good-bye?"

"He was standing at the foot of the stairs when we came down, all set for prayers."

"Were his feelings hurt?"

"Couldn't seem to take it in. Kept talking about what we'd do tomorrow, half in French, half in English. I don't think he knew that we were really going till we got to the front door. But I wasn't paying much attention to him. I was worried about Kev. And all the time that damned medal was burning a hole in my pocket. When we got to the door I held it out on the palm of my hand, said: 'Mr. Reardon, you may be interested to know that your son has won the Croix de Guerre.' He took the medal and held it in his hand a second, then handed it to Kev and smiled, the way you smile at a child after you've looked at the toy he's in such a sweat about and then he began talking about the dangers Kev was exposed to *now*, and wanted him to promise that as soon as he got back to Paris he would go to some church and put himself under the protection of Saint Martha—seems Kev was born on her day. Kev shook his head. Said he had no faith."

"How did the old man take *that*?"

"Just stood there, blinking—like some old bird that had been roused up off its perch in the middle of the night. That was the last we saw of him."

"Poor old soul!" Sarah said. "I suppose he *had* got a bit loony, living there all by himself! . . . What did you do then, Steve?"

"Got in the plane and flew back to Paris. After we started I handed the medal to Kev. Told him I didn't know what made me bring it along."

"What did he say?"

"Just took the medal and dropped it into some river we were flying over."

"That *is* a strange story!" Sarah said. "A very strange story!"

"I know it," Stephen said. "That's one reason I've never mentioned it to anybody."

"You mean you and Kev didn't even talk about it on the way back?"

"No."

"Or ever after that?"

"No."

"What do you suppose he made out of it?"

"I have an idea what he made out of it at the time," he

said. "I think he's made something different out of it since."

"What do you mean?"

"Well, he's joined the Catholic Church, hasn't he?"

"You mean you think that was his father's influence?"

"It certainly wasn't his mother's. . . . It wasn't anybody's influence. It never is."

Lucy looked at her mother. Her mother's eyes were fixed on her father's face. He was staring at the floor. Her mother looked at him a second longer, then looked away. Uncle Tubby was gazing off over the river. Nobody seemed to know what to say next, then her mother said:

"You know, when you stop to think about it it's funny how little any of us knew of Kev's family background. All the time he was at Princeton his mother was living up at Rhinebeck, but he never asked Steve up once."

"I used to go up there a lot," Tubby said, "but Kev never asked me. She did. I ran into them when they were lunching at the Nass one day and she was talking about the trouble she was having getting her horses exercised and I told her I'd be glad to help her out. She gave me such a good time that weekend that I got in the habit of going up."

"She kept up quite an establishment, didn't she? Who did she marry?"

"She beat it, with a fellow named Wilcox. Regular Côte d'Azur playboy; she had to get rid of him. But she never married again. The old man wouldn't give her a divorce. Said marriage was a sacrament and used to write her once or twice a year, asking her to come back to him. . . . She used to cry every time one of the letters came. I was dancing with her once and she took me out in the hall and showed me this letter she had stuck in the front of her dress."

"What did he say in the letter?"

"Well, looking back on it, I can see that the old boy was

probably pretty lonely and trying to get his wife back the best way he knew how. At the time it struck me that he was just writing her letters to torture her. He always said that he was praying for her and that he offered up his Mass for her every morning. That's what got her: the idea of his praying for her all those years. Made her feel like she couldn't get away from him."

"Just an old hellhound of Heaven!" Sarah said. "But you know, in some ways he reminds me of the Marquis de Montespan.

"He used to write his wife once a year, too, and ask her to come home. But she was too much of a career woman for that. Called it following her star to be Louis the Fourteenth's mistress. When Louis wanted to make the marquis a duke the marquis told him that he had been born a marquis and preferred to die a marquis. . . . He had a waterfall on his place that he loved better than anything, and used to visit it once a day. . . ."

"Sally, I often wonder what you'd have been like if you hadn't run into Steve," Tubby said.

"It wasn't Steve. It was a house we rented one year. Had a whole library of backstairs court gossip, from Saint-Simon on down. . . . Was she pretty, Tubby?"

"Wonderful eyes. And a kind of natural style about everything she did. Not unlike Isabel, when you come down to it. And she really liked men, which kept them coming around in droves of course."

"Were you Wilcox's successor?"

He laughed. "When I first knew Mimi she was having an affair with her head groom."

"That sort of thing so often seems to end in gardeners and grooms," Sarah said. "Poor things! Nobody ever seems to think about *them*."

"This one could take care of himself, all right," Tubby said.

"Well, go on. . . ."

"He was a big Dane named Knudsen. Hair the color of butter. A *Kinder, Kirche, Küche* sort of fellow. Must have burned him up to have to take orders from a woman, let alone the woman he was sleeping with."

There was a silence, then Sarah said: "How did you *know* he was sleeping with her?"

"I was in at the finish."

"You mean there was a public scene?"

"He and I and Kev had been up in Maine, hunting, one Thanksgiving. We were gone three days. When we got back Mimi was down at the stables, cleaning out a stall."

"I don't see anything wrong with that," Sarah said.

"You wouldn't," her husband said, "but most people aren't as fond of manure as you are. Go on, Tubby."

"Oh, she sounded off about how the colored boy hadn't even fed the horses, much less cleaned the stalls. I think, myself, that she probably gave the boy whiskey to get rid of him. Doing Butch's work, you see—we called him Butch. It must have made her awfully jealous to have the three of us go off without her. . . . Unfortunately we'd stopped at a bar and had had three or four drinks. . . . Butch took the shovel away from her and told her to get back to the house."

"You mean he ordered her?"

"He made a kind of pass at her with the shovel. As I recall, the gesture was both proprietary and admonitory."

"What did Kev do?" Stephen Lewis asked.

"There wasn't much he *could* do. He said in that quiet way he has, 'That will be all from you, Knudsen' and went over and stood beside his mother."

"What did Knudsen do then?"

"Oh, Butch was over the edge by that time. He said, 'That's all you know about it'."

"What did Kev do *then*?"

"He looked at Butch and then walked over and took the shovel out of Butch's hand and he said—it comes back to me now—in the *friendliest* way he said, 'Butch, do you want to stay here after this?' And Butch said, 'Hell, no. I hate the joint!' "

"What was Mimi doing all this time?"

"Oh, sobbing and going on about how he neglected the *horses*. Kev cut through all that. He said: 'Mother, he doesn't care anything about you. You'd better let him go,' and then he looked at Butch and said, 'Butch, you know you don't care anything about her.' "

"My *God*!" Sarah said.

"And Butch said, 'I like her all right when she behaves herself. But I'm not nuts about her. I told her that all along.' And Kev said, 'I know it, Butch. I started to tell her the other day.' "

"Oh, God," Sarah said again. "He *didn't*, Tubby?"

"You think I could invent that?" Tubby said. "I tell you he's not called 'Goof Reardon' for nothing."

"At St. Matt's?"

"Yeah. Used to go into awful rages. That was how we came to room together. Old Scoker called me in one day and asked if I'd take him on. Said he was just one of the finest little fellows ever lived, but had kicked a door to pieces the day before. And he nearly bit Bunch Crawford's ear off. I was sore at Bunch myself. Awful bully. So I said 'Bring him on.' We got along all right. Got along all right at Princeton, too, and I spent one whole summer with Kev on his boat. . . . But I can't figure him now. Jim Ferrebee says he thinks it was that lick on the head turned him queer. . . ."

"Didn't you say he was being treated by a psychiatrist?"

"He went to one for over a year. But you know how he is, once he's started something. Kev had read as much as the fellow had. Poor fellow'd feed him Freud and Kev'd come back at him with Jung. Then he told Isabel one day that he didn't see any sense in fooling with the Freud fellow any longer, but he was ready to go to Bollingen and try Jung if she wanted him to. But the poor girl was nearly off her head by that time and she didn't want to pull up stakes and move to Switzerland, so she said no, for him just to keep his latent homosexuality and he said, 'All right,' and then broke the news that they were going to sell the St. Tropez place and move to Toulon."

"You mean he didn't consult her about the move?"

"Not until it was all decided on. He didn't even take the servants from St. Tropez. Gave 'em board wages for a year and took over his father's old staff, or what was left of it."

Sarah said musingly, "That's why she went off the deep end last night?"

Stephen Lewis said: "You mean that the sight of Tubby impersonating a priest made her hysterical?"

"You can't blame her," Tubby said. "She's had it pretty tough for the last two years. He's repeating his father's pattern. I tell you that lick on his head turned him queer!"

"Is Isabel frightened of him?" Stephen asked.

"She's frightened of what he may do. Of what he threatens to do."

"Does he threaten to sell all his goods and give them to the poor?" Stephen Lewis asked.

"You guessed it. He wants to devote most of his life to the founding, or at least the abetting of some contemplative order. That's why he's down here talking to the Trappists."

"Well, I'll be damned," Stephen Lewis said.

"Hush!" Sarah said, but even before she spoke a change had come in the air. Lucy knew without seeing that all their eyes were turned the same way, that the same half scared, half reassured expression was on all their faces. "The matchless Orinda!" she heard her mother whisper.

Lucy waited until the air which had been so still was again full of their voices and laughter before she went quietly out on to the gallery and sat down on the feed box.

Mrs. Reardon had come around the corner of the house and stood at the far end of the gallery. She wore a white bathing suit and her hair was twisted up out of sight under a sun hat so broad that it covered her shoulders. Her arms and legs were as brown as a horse chestnut. Her eyes looked very blue in her brown face. She was smiling. "Who wants to go swimming?" she asked.

"Wait'll I get my trunks," Uncle Tubby said.

Mrs. Reardon walked over and stood beside Mama. "Do you feel up to a swim?"

Mama shook her head. "I couldn't make it down the hill," she said, "much less back." She looked beyond the gate to where the path to the swimming hole went down through the goldenrod to the river. "It's awfully steep," she said, "and river water's warm this time of year. Maybe you'd better try one of the creeks. It's only three miles to Spring Creek. That's delicious swimming."

"I want to see what it's like down there," Mrs. Reardon said.

Uncle Tubby had come back and stood, waiting, his trunks rolled up under his arm. "The river," he said. "We can explore even if we don't go in."

"I want to go in," Mrs. Reardon said.

"Where's Kev?" Stephen Lewis asked suddenly.

"He's in town," she said. "He had to go to town. . . ." She looked at Lucy and smiled. "You come with us."

"If you go down by the river you'll have to take the citronella," Sarah said. "The mosquitoes will eat you alive."

Lucy ran upstairs and found the bottle on the shelf of the bathroom cabinet and then went into the room she was occupying and got her bathing suit out of the closet. When she came back Mrs. Reardon and Uncle Tubby had already gone through the gate and started down the path to the river. She was about to follow them when her mother called to her. "Lucy. . . ." she said, but when Lucy came and stood in front of her she glanced uncertainly from the child to her husband. "Maybe you'd better not go with them," she said.

Lucy gave her a hostile stare. "They asked me," she said.

Stephen Lewis came out of the dining room, carrying two tall frosted glasses. "Oh, let her go," he said.

Sarah put her hand out for the glass and sank back in the long chair. Lucy, as she dived through the tall grass on the brow of the hill could hear her murmuring, ". . . such a strange world. Sometimes I think I'm the only person in it has good sense," and her father laughing as he bent to kiss her: "My homespun Cassandra!"

IX

GOLDENROD began where the grass left off: waist-high. Purple asters were already blooming. Rabbit runs crossed the path now and then, but the path itself kept zigzagging down to the river. She could see the water now, glinting yellow through the willows. But between her and the willow two heads moved, one burnished brown, the other hidden under the huge yellow hat. A big rock jutted out into the path. The lady stopped beside it, so suddenly that Uncle Tubby, walking right behind her, would have run over her if he had not steadied himself by putting both arms around her. She laughed and stood still in the circle of his arms a second before she turned around to look up at Lucy.

"Who made this wonderful path?" she asked.

"The cows," Lucy said, "and Daddy cut it out some with the Lively Lad."

"Which one of the MacDonoughs is the liveliest?" Uncle Tubby asked.

"It's not a boy," Lucy said, "it's what you cut the weeds with."

Uncle Tubby laughed. He had set his hand lightly on Mrs. Reardon's shoulder and pushed her back behind him. "I'll go first," he said. *"Belle dame,* do you come here often?"

"I come every day," Lucy said, "when I can get anybody to come with me. But Mama says it's too hot to swim in the river this time of year."

"What about the MacDonoughs?"

"Mr. MacDonough don't allow them to go in swimming."

"Not even that simple pleasure?"

"They're not supposed to expose their bodies," Mrs. Reardon said. "Like Jehovah's Witnesses. We had them in Minnesota."

He turned around and gave her a quick glance. "I always forget that you are middle-western," he said.

"I was born within fifteen miles of St. Paul," she said.

"They should erect a shrine. Carl Sandburg has one in his natal village and he isn't dead yet. . . . *Belle dame,* what *is* that stuff?"

"Cane," Lucy said.

It grew in a thick fringe on the edge of the bluff, but the earth below it was bare, except for the yellow leaves fallen from the big sycamore. Willows grew along the bank, but there were no saplings anywhere, not even any weeds. The earth under their feet was slick, moist, yet tight packed: the first rise. But most years the river rose higher than this and overflowed into the small meadow.

Uncle Tubby had stopped to break off a stalk of the wild cane. "This is what Davy Crockett talks about," he said. " 'Those men of the western waters, those men who have cut the cane.' It used to cover the whole country. Did you know it would pop like a gun if you throw it on a fire?"

"The MacDonoughs do it sometimes," Lucy said.

They went on down the slope. He saw the raft, riding high on its four empty oil drums, moored to a stout willow, and had started toward it when Mrs. Reardon said, "Look!" and walked away from them up the bank to where the spring rose in the big gully.

They followed her. The earth was packed even harder than the earth they had been walking over. Above their heads a bunch of driftwood dangled, caught in the lower branches of the sycamore tree. Uncle Tubby put his hand up and broke off a piece of the dry, rotten stuff. "Sinister spot," he said.

Mrs. Reardon walked ahead of them. She had taken off her hat and was slapping lightly at her legs as she went. Lucy hurried and came abreast of her. "Here," she said and held out the bottle of lotion, but Mrs. Reardon did not seem to hear her. She was looking down into the gully.

It was as big as a house. The water looked blue where it flowed out, over a rock, but turned yellow as it flowed over the slick, marbled sides of the gully. There were fissures in the side of the gully so deep that you could not see all the way back into them: caves, with the people who lived in the caves standing on little flat porches in front of their houses. The water had carved the earth into strange shapes. One peak, that had a base as round as any statue, looked like the bowed figure of a woman, another resembled a huge, hunched bird.

Uncle Tubby had come up behind them. He said: "*In Xanadu did Kubla Khan. . . !*" and laid his hand on Lucy's shoulder. "Is this what becomes of our waterfall?"

"Yes," she said, "Daddy says it flows under the whole bottom."

"Through caverns measureless to man, no doubt." His

hand, resting on her shoulder, shook her lightly to and fro. "Every time I go out with this girl she shows me some natural wonder." He slid a few steps down the slick slope and finding a ledge wide enough for his feet to rest on, turned and held out his hand to Mrs. Reardon. "Come on," he said.

They slid down the slope. At the bottom of the gully Mrs. Reardon stopped before the cave that had the woman's figure standing in front of it. "Look!" she said. "It's a statue."

"But look here!" Lucy said and ran a little way up the gully to the cave that she claimed for her own. There were two heaps of earth inside it, just touching each other. Sometimes she and the MacDonoughs played that they were lions escaped from a zoo, sometimes that they were wolves or wild dogs that lived off here by themselves. Mrs. Reardon came up behind her and stooping, looked into the cave. "I like this one," she said. "This is the one I want!"

Uncle Tubby had not followed them up the gully. "Isabel!" he called now.

She did not answer. Still stooping, she picked up a stick and began making marks on one of the piles of earth. "Let's make him a mane," she said.

"You mean the lion?" Lucy asked.

Mrs. Reardon nodded. "Yes. Doesn't he look like a lion to you?"

"Yes," Lucy said. "Sometimes we play like it's a dog, but I like a lion best."

"Isabel!" Uncle Tubby called. "Do you want to go swimming?"

Mrs. Reardon looked at Lucy. "Do you?"

"I reckon we better," Lucy said and they walked back up the gully to where he stood waiting.

"I didn't come down here to make mud pies," he said. "Come on. Let's go out in the boat first."

Mrs. Reardon smiled at Lucy. "Are you going to put on your suit first?" she asked.

"I guess I will," Lucy said, and walked a little way up the bank, behind a clump of willows and cast her bathing suit down on the smooth mud floor. The strings of her halter were tied in a hard knot. She thought that she might have to ask Mrs. Reardon to untie them for her and then she looked at her cotton drawers, lying on top of her faded blue skirt and her fingers went to work again, so patiently this time that the knot came undone. She threw the halter on top of her other garments and wriggled into her bathing suit. It was the one she had got at the end of the season last year. Blue-green, then, but faded now to a greenish-yellow, with a few whitish spots on it: mildew, her mother said, from lying in a wet ball on the bathroom floor so many nights.

Through the green willow boughs she could see them still standing where she had left them. Mrs. Reardon's clear voice came to her: "Well, aren't you going to change?"

He stood looking down at her as if she had just asked him something very important, something that he was not sure he could answer. "In a second," he said.

She laughed. "Men never really like to get wet," she said.

"With that layer of fat over your entire body you're ready to go in, any time, day or night," he said and went up to her and put his two hands on her slender waist and squeezed it until she looked up at him like a cat that doesn't want you to pick it up and her mouth opened and a little sound came out and he let his hands fall away from her waist.

When Lucy came out from behind the willows he had changed into his trunks and they were in the boat, Mrs. Reardon in the bow, Uncle Tubby in the stern. He held the boat up against the raft with the paddle while Lucy got in and squatted in the middle with her back turned to Mrs. Reardon.

"Down she came and found a boat, amid the willows left afloat," he said and looked over Lucy's head at Mrs. Reardon. "Are you all right?" he asked.

"I'm fine," Mrs. Reardon said.

"Really?"

"Of course."

His eyes had that shining-frog-in-the-puddle look as he continued to gaze at her. "Do you think Lucy is more like the Lily Maid of Astolat or the Lady of Shalott?" he asked.

She laughed. "When you were little were you in love with the Lily Maid of Astolat?"

"Up to the age of six. After that I transferred my affection to the Lady of Shalott; it seemed to me that she had more on the ball."

"An awful introvert," she said, "weaving night and day."

"A conscientious craftswoman," he said. "The trouble with you is you don't recognize the importance of honest work."

"It didn't do her any good. The minute she stopped weaving everything went to pot."

"That was Launcelot's fault. The dope! Goes out on the bridge, takes a look at her, muses a little space and goes back to his gin and tonic."

"You think he ought to have gone down and got her out of the boat?"

"Of course. She'd done her part. Got the boat and floated down to Camelot. If he'd had any sense he'd have rowed her back to Shalott. It was quite a nice little property, by all accounts. They could have had a fine life there."

"But she was dead by that time," Mrs. Reardon said.

"Not at all. Just in a trance. He could have brought her out of that with a few well chosen passes."

"But he was in love with Guinevere."

"That old hag! Well, he ended up wood . . . or was it in a monastery? Same thing."

She said: "God! . . . monasteries!"

"Is it all set?"

"I think so."

"And do the Trappists get the boodle?"

"Probably. He'd like to give it to the Carthusians, but there are none in this country and he thinks he ought to do something for his own country."

"What's the difference between them?"

"The Trappists are Reformed Cistercians. They just keep perpetual silence. *He'd* like to adore perpetually."

"Does he want to be a monk?"

"He *says* he hasn't got a vocation."

He plunged his paddle deep into the water and sent the boat farther out into the stream. "It's a strange thing," he said, "to know a fellow as long as I've known Kev and then to have him turn into an entirely different person. He doesn't seem to me the man I've known all these years. Does he seem entirely different to you?"

"Oh, yes," she said, "*yes!*"

"What does the fellow want to do?"

She laughed. "I *told* you. He wants to promote contemplation. He says that there is not enough contemplation in the world."

"What does he want to contemplate?"

"God," she said and laughed again. "God! That's all he thinks about. *God!*"

He said: *"Isabel!"*

She turned her face away from him. "I don't want to talk about it. You promised me you wouldn't talk about it."

He did not answer for several seconds, then he said: "Quite

right," and pointed with his paddle to the cornfields on the far bank. "Nice country."

"If it weren't so hot."

"You could get used to that. The Lewises have. You never hear *them* complain." He stared at Lucy as if he had not known till that moment that she was sitting there in front of him and then he looked out over the cornfields again. "Must have been quite a sight when Lucy's great-great-great-grandmother first came out here, riding pillion behind her husband. The horses' hooves were stained red from the wild strawberries that grew all over the fields. At night Sarah Crenfew kept up her Greek by the campfire. Kept up her other homework, too, or we wouldn't have Lucy."

"Didn't they ride through woods?"

"No. This land around here was called 'The Barrens.' The Indians kept it burned off, to pasture game. Those Indians around here lived the life!"

"How do you know all this?"

"Steve lent me a bunch of old letters once. Some of them were beauts."

She said: "You love the past, don't you?"

"Not immoderately."

"You couldn't write things you write if you didn't love the past more than the present. You like to get out of this age you're living in."

"I always come up for air, though. I couldn't have stuck with the Civil War ten years, the way Steve has. I'm interested in the past chiefly for the sake of comparing it with the present. Steve sees no use in that. He thinks men have always been pretty much the same. . . . Now, there's a funny fellow. Did you ever hear how we met?"

She shook her head.

"We both used to go out for practice. I was on the second

scrub. Steve couldn't even make that, but he came out every evening just the same. One time in the locker room he dropped a piece of paper out of his pocket. I picked it up. I can see it now. That piece of paper!"

"What was it?"

"A poem. A poem about John Donne. I'd never heard of John Donne but I went straight to the library and looked him up. Meeting Steve was the most important thing that ever happened to me. You see, I'd never known anybody before that who wrote poetry."

"Weren't you writing poetry, yourself, then?"

"If you could call it that. But my Muse was lurking underground. What I admired about Steve was his nonchalance. He didn't seem to see much difference between poetry and football. He'd be telling you one minute that Jim Sloan should have run an off-tackle play in the third quarter and the next minute he'd be comparing 'Ode To The Nightingale' with 'Ode To The West Wind.' I wrote three odes, myself, that fall."

"And now you write better poetry than he does," she said.

"He doesn't write poetry any more. If he did, it would be better than mine. At least, I'm pretty sure that it would."

Neither of them said anything for several minutes, then she said, "He doesn't really like my poetry."

"He doesn't understand it. He doesn't like to have anything around that he can't understand."

"I don't understand it, myself."

"What I can't understand," he said, "is why you stopped writing. How long has it been since you've written a poem?"

"Eight years . . . ten years . . . I don't know. One day I thought of nothing else, and the next thing I couldn't see how I'd ever written even one poem."

"If you lived with me I'd see to it that you worked every day."

"How?"

"That's my secret."

She did not answer for a long while, then she said: "I believe you *have* got a secret."

"I've got one, all right."

"It's going to make you successful—and happy."

"It hasn't made me either, as yet—except once. You remember that last night at St. Tropez?"

She said in a soft voice: "Tubby, don't talk like that."

This time it was he who did not answer.

Lucy had turned so that she was not facing either of them and sat facing the water. They were in the current now but still in the shade of the willows. The yellow water was laced all over with quivering flecks of green; the willow leaves kept turning in the mild breeze that always blew down here on the river. Uncle Tubby gave a deep thrust of his paddle and sent the boat farther in toward the bank, so close that the branches brushed their shoulders. Lucy put her hand over the side of the boat to feel the cool water ripple between her fingers. In here the water was almost olive green, except where it was fretted into points of light by the shifting leaves. The false Bertalda had held her golden necklace above the water, to make just such a shimmer, on that voyage that she and Undine and the Knight Huldbrand made down the Danube. A hand had come up out of the water and snatched the necklace from her and a scornful laugh had echoed from the depths of the river. The Knight Huldbrand had cursed Undine for having such mischievous kindred and when she, trailing her hand in the water, brought up a beautiful coral necklace to give Bertalda in the place of the one she had lost, he tore it from her and flung it into the river shouting: "Stay with them and their gifts, in the name of all witchcraft, and let us mortals be at peace, sorceress that you are!" It was then that poor Undine cried: "Woe! Woe! What have you done?" and vanished over the side of the boat. . . .

"Lu-ceeee!"

Lucy looked at Mrs. Reardon. Mrs. Reardon frowned and said, "But we haven't gone in the water yet."

Uncle Tubby laid the paddle across his knees. They sat silent.

The call came again, louder and more prolonged.

"That's Daddy," Lucy said. "I better go."

"You don't think you could dip in just once?" Uncle Tubby asked.

She shook her head. "Sounds like he's mad."

He nodded. "That's the way it is in this life," he said and sent the boat back toward the raft with long, swift strokes. It bumped against the raft. He held it steady with one hand while Lucy stepped out and would have sent it out into the current again but Mrs. Reardon told him that she wanted to get out, too. "Tell them we'll be up in a few minutes," she said.

"All right," Lucy said and started up the bank. They were standing on the raft, side by side, hands lightly interlaced, when she left them. As she passed the last willow and started through the cane she heard a splash and knew without looking around that they were diving from the raft into the green water.

X

"HERE'S Lee's headquarters," Daddy said. He had been leaning against the mantel, his long ruler in his hand, but now he went over to the big map that he and Uncle Tubby had fixed on the north wall of the parlor. "In the rear of A. P. Hill's corps," he said. "Here goes Pickett's Charge!" and he gave the ruler a long, downward sweep. "But there were only fourteen thousand of them. Lee had counted on thirty thousand."

"How do you suppose Longstreet figured he could get away with disobeying orders?" Uncle Tubby asked.

"I don't believe he thought it out. He just couldn't bring himself to sacrifice his men. Thought all along that it was hopeless. The irony is that if he had sent in the thirty thousand that Lee ordered the charge might have succeeded. . . . As it was, Pickett's Division was annihilated."

Mr. Reardon got up from the sofa where he had been sitting beside Mama and came and stood in front of the map, too. "How many got back?" he asked.

"A bare thousand. There's an old Mr. Williams here in town was in the charge. He says they knew when they went in that it was hopeless."

"A thousand out of fourteen thousand. It's as bad as Thermopylae!" Uncle Tubby said.

Mama looked up quickly from the dress she was mending. "You might write a new poem: 'Go tell The Virginians'," she said. Nobody said anything for a second, then Uncle Tubby laughed. Mama's face turned red. She took up her sewing again. She was wearing her new white linen shorts, with a halter that she had made out of a bandanna handkerchief. Her hair was twisted up on top of her head as high as it would go, but even then she was hot; her upper lip and her forehead were as thickly beaded with sweat as the lemonade pitcher that she had set down on the table. Her face had a breathless look.

They had been talking about the Civil War for a long time now, ever since right after lunch, when they had come in here to have Daddy demonstrate the Battle of Gettysburg on the map that he and Uncle Tubby had spent all morning fixing up. Mrs. Reardon said that she had a headache and went upstairs after lunch to take a nap, but all the rest of them were here in the parlor.

Lois and Lucy had come in with them and were sitting on sofa pillows on the floor under the east windows. It was the hottest day they had had. Mr. Reardon was dressed the way he always was, but Daddy and Uncle Tubby didn't have on anything but shorts. Lois was wearing her new pink muslin. It had a white, scalloped band for yoke and smaller, white scalloped bands on the sleeves. Lucy had on a green percale from last summer. She had wanted to put on her new blue dimity but Mama said there was no use putting it on just to romp around in.

Mama was over at the table, making herself a Planters' Punch: she liked more Grenadine than Daddy would ever put in and almost always made her own. Lois and Lucy got up off the floor and took their glasses over to her. She looked at Lois—the way she always looked at Lois—as she filled their glasses with lemonade. "What makes you children sit around in here all the time?" she asked crossly. "Why don't you go outdoors and play?"

Lois sighed. "That's what I told her. But she says it's too hot to play outdoors."

Mama frowned at Lucy. "What's the matter with you, Lucy? Why, when I was a child I never even thought about its being hot. If I got hot I just climbed up in the trees."

"Yeah, and broke your ankle," Lucy said.

"I didn't break my ankle because I was awkward," Mama said. "My cousin pushed me out."

"Was it a girl cousin or a boy cousin?" Lois asked.

"A boy cousin, naturally," Mama said and walked over and sat down in the little rosewood chair that had the stuffing dropping out of its bottom. She took her mending up, then let the dress fall back into her lap as she looked up at the others. "You know, I think it was partly the time of day," she said. "Three o'clock *is* a devilish time of day!"

Mr. Reardon started and looked at his watch. "I'm going in to town," he said. "Can I do any errands for anybody?"

"No, thank you," Mama said, but Lois caught hold of Lucy's arm. "Ask her if we can't go with him," she said. "I've got forty-five cents. We could get two banana splits."

But Mr. Reardon was already going out the door.

"You never asked her," Lois said. "I bet if you'd asked her she'd have let us go."

Lucy was silent. She was trying to imagine what it would be like to ride in to town with Mr. Reardon. She could not imagine herself even getting into his car, much less riding with him. Most of the people who came here to visit talked to her, or asked her fool questions about whether she liked living 'way out here on this river or whether she was going to write poetry when she grew up and all that, but he had never said anything to her since that first evening when they had walked about there in the dusk, under the trees. She, too, gave a start, seeing suddenly the rows of books on the white shelf and one whose faded lettering still shone gold in any bright light. She had not thought of *Morte d'Arthur* and what lay behind it for two whole days. *She had forgotten it.* Was that why he hardly looked at her any more, or was it simply that he was a strange man, the strangest man who had ever visited here? What was it about him that made her feel that she would not dare to ride in to town with him alone? Was it his dark eyes that nearly always had such an odd brightness, or was it because he was so silent? Her father was silent, too, a great deal of the time, but with him that was absentmindedness; he was thinking his own thoughts and didn't care about anybody else's, her mother said. Sometimes she or her mother had to shake his arm to get his attention. But whatever Mr. Reardon was thinking about it was not himself; he listened every time anybody else said anything. He listened to what they said, but all the time he was thinking about something else, too. What was it, she asked herself, what was it that he was always thinking about while he sat there, listening to them talk? What was it that he never could stop thinking about, no matter how hard he listened?

They could hear his car starting. Mama said: "Where is it he goes every day about this time?"

"You yourself just pointed out that it is a witching hour of day," Uncle Tubby said, "the hour of *None*, when *Accedia* is at high tide."

"*Accedia*?" Mama said.

"Cassian defines it as 'perturbation of the heart,' the enemy of solitaries and such as dwell in the desert. He makes the Stations of the Cross every day at three o'clock."

"No?" Mama said. "Why, I'd love to do that. Only I don't know how . . . Tubby, does he really have all the offices said in his chapel?"

"Not Matins or Lauds but Prime and Sexte, None, Vespers and Compline," he said, "and the *curé* to dinner every other evening."

"I can't get over it!" Mama said, "I suppose it's just a phase he's going through. . . . But how odd!"

Daddy had not paid any attention to what they were saying. He was standing in front of his map, gazing at it as if the battle were still going on in his head. He turned around now and said to Uncle Tubby:

"When Lee got into Emmitsburg. . . ."

But Uncle Tubby was not listening. He was looking out into the hall, where she was coming down the stairs, in dark slacks, with a green halter, her hair done up high on her head, her big hat trailing behind her on the steps.

He went to the door as if he would have met her out in the hall, then had to stand aside so she could speak to the others. She stood just inside the door, the yellow hat held up against her breast. Her periwinkle gaze went from one face to the other and did not stay on any face long. She said: "We're going to walk in the woods where those wonderful beech trees are."

"It's horribly hot this time of day," Sarah said. "The flies'll eat you up."

A faint, persistent smile was trembling on his face. He looked at Sarah and then looked away quickly. "I never saw anybody so bent on running things down," he said. "You told us yesterday that the mosquitoes would eat us up."

"And didn't they?"

"Not a bite. Lucy here is my witness."

But he did not look at Lucy where she sat, cross-legged on the floor beside Lois. He was reaching to take the hat from the woman's hand and to lay his own hand on her arm and to turn her around so that she faced the hall. "Come on," he said. "Long as we're here we've got to see the sights."

"I had no idea you were such a passionate sight-seer!" Sarah said.

Isabel Reardon turned her head over her shoulder and smiled at all of them and none of them. Her companion did not answer. You could hear their feet moving in the hall and then the screen door banged; they were going down the front steps.

Nobody said anything until the sound of their feet had died away. "I call that a bit cool," Sarah said.

Her husband shook his head slowly. "Kev had better change the hour of his devotions," he said. "Lauds, perhaps, or Matins . . . though," he added, "I don't know that that would do any good. The case seems pretty far advanced."

"And yet you laughed at me when they first came," she said.

"I'm not laughing now," he said.

Lois leaned over to whisper to Lucy. Mama looked up. "Lucy," she said sharply, "I want you and Lois to go down stairs in the dining room and play. Or if you don't want to play there, go to your own room or out on the gallery. You *cannot* sit around with grown people all day long."

They went downstairs and sat down on the window seat in the dining room. Lois put her hand up and fingered the stiff green taffeta bow that held her side parting back. "You said you wanted me to come out here the first chance I got and I told you I thought I could get Ellen to bring me Thursday afternoon when she got the car to take her music lesson. I *could* have spent the week end with Mary Lee Shattuck. They were going to Dunbar's Cave. They have glass boats on the lake. It costs fifteen cents to ride. But I told you I'd come out here first chance I got and Ellen had the car to take her music lesson. I wouldn't have made her bring me out but she had the car to take her music lesson and you said you wanted me to come out first chance I got and she had the car to take her music lesson. . . ."

She had been talking like that ever since she arrived, yesterday afternoon at half past four, and had found Lucy down at the river instead of waiting for her up at the house. She maintained that Lucy's mother had been calling her for half an hour before Lucy came up from the river. She did not think that Lucy would have come then if her father hadn't gone out on the gallery and yelled at the top of his lungs. She, Lois, had been on the point of going to the telephone and asking her sister to come and get her when Lucy finally came up the path. It did not make any difference, she kept saying, but she could have gone to Mary Lee Shattuck's. . . .

Lucy did not say anything. Lois had turned around and was kneeling in the window seat. "I don't think she's very pretty," she said, "and his nose is too big for him to be really cute. . . . I bet he'd put his arm around her if he didn't know that we were looking at 'em."

Lucy felt faint. She turned around, too. They had come to the end of the gravel path and were starting down the slope to the gate. Mrs. Reardon had taken her hat back and was carrying it herself. Uncle Tubby had one of Daddy's sticks from the hall stand and kept lunging at the lemon lilies as he went. *They asked me yesterday. . . . No, it was she who asked me. He didn't want me to go along then, either. But she asked me—so he wouldn't look at her that way. She likes for him to look at her that way, but she doesn't think we like it, so she tried to keep him from doing it yesterday. But today she doesn't try to keep him from looking at her that way. . . . Something happened when we were out in the boat. It was when I had my face turned so that I wouldn't have to look at them. Something happened then. . . . What was it? What was it?*

"Where are they going?" Lois asked.

To the waterfall! . . . "I reckon they're going to walk in the beech woods," Lucy said aloud.

"Is she going to divorce that little man and marry Mister Tubby?"

"I don't know," Lucy said.

"Well, she can't, because he's a Catholic and I guess she's one, too. Catholics can't marry but once. They can get married just one time and they have to stay married to that person whether they like him or not. . . . I wouldn't like that, would you?"

"I'm not going to get married at all," Lucy said.

"That's silly. You want to be an old maid?"

"I want to be a horse trainer," Lucy said with a sigh.

"I wouldn't want to get all sweaty and dirty, jumping around on horses. I'd rather be a crooner with a name band. I could be married, too, and have a lot of children."

"Let's go down to the cabin and see what Jenny's doing," Lucy said.

They left the cool dining room and walked down the slope to Jenny's house. The shadows of the trumpet vines were all over the porch. As they went up the steps a humming bird darted out of one of the cup-shaped blossoms and whirred away over their heads. The door was open. Jenny lay in bed, on her back, her arms flung up over her head. On the wall above her was a calendar: a picture of a girl in a red bathing suit, crouching on her knees while she tied the strings of a floppy yellow hat under her chin. A frog had come up out of some green water to look at her. DOWN BY THE OLD MILL STREAM the letters said. Jenny's good dressing gown, green, with big purple flowers all over it, was thrown over the back of a chair. Jenny didn't have on anything but her slip. The room was full of the smell of carnations and that smell that Jenny always had. They could hear her snoring before they stepped up on the porch.

Lois stood in the doorway, looking at Jenny's dresser. There was a box covered with pink and yellow velvet that always sat on it, and a silver bulldog with ruby eyes—his back was hollow and Jenny kept bobby pins in him—and a picture of Mr. Stamper in a silver frame and pictures of Jenny's father and mother in gold frames. Jenny did not love Mr. Stamper as much as she loved her mother and father. If she ever made up her mind that she loved him that much she was going to put his picture in a gold frame, too.

Lucy had seen all the things on Jenny's dresser so often that she did not need to look at them. She went over and sat down on the side of Jenny's bed. The smell of carnations was stronger now, mingled with the smell that came from under Jenny's armpits. The bedstead shook a little every time Jenny snored. Lucy sat thinking how pretty Jenny always looked, even when she was asleep. The bedstead was shaking harder. Lucy giggled and bending over laid her hand on Jenny's moist forehead. "Wake up!" she whispered.

Jenny's eyelashes lifted slowly. Her big, black eyes fixed the ceiling for a second, then her lids sank. She groaned and rolled over in bed with her back to Lucy.

Lucy put her hand on Jenny's shoulder. "Jenny, *please* wake up," she said.

Jenny groaned again. "What y'all want?" she asked drowsily.

Lois had come over and was standing by the bed. "We want you to play something with us," she said.

"I don't know no games," Jenny said in the same drowsy tone.

"Well, sit up, anyhow," Lucy said.

Jenny sat up, surveying them through drooping lids. "What y'all doing walking around this time of day?" she asked. "Don't you know you likely to get sunstroke?"

"I'd just as soon get a sunstroke as sit around here, doing nothing," Lois said.

"That's what *you* think," Jenny said. She wiped the sweat from her forehead and from her upper lip, crossed her arms on her bare breast, and motioned to Lucy to hand her her dressing gown from the back of the chair. "Well, go on and sit on the porch," she said. "I got to take me a little bath before I can play anything."

They sat down in the swing that hung at the south end of the porch. The trumpet vines grew thick there. But the other end of the porch and the whole south wall of the cabin were exposed to the full glare of the sun. As they sat there, Daddy drove past the cabin and through the gate and turned and headed for town.

"He didn't even ask us to go with him," Lois said. "I think that's mean!"

"He's probably just going in to the grocery for something Mama forgot to order," Lucy said.

They began playing a game that Lois had made up called "Car-Go." Each one of them picked out a car as soon as it came in sight on the other side of the river and before it rolled up on the bridge guessed whether after it had crossed the bridge it would continue along the river road or turn off on the road to Palmyra. Inside the house they could hear Jenny splashing the water in the basin. The scent of her carnation perfume drifted out on the warm air. Presently she came out, in a freshly ironed white dress and sat down in the swing between them. She was wearing her string of pearls looped three times around her throat.

"You going to wear those beads when you wait on table tonight?" Lois asked.

"That's a long way off," Jenny said, yawning. "You chillun got no business waking me up here in the middle of the evening."

"Let's walk down to the filling station," Lois said, "I bet they've got icecream cones, and if they haven't we could get some pop or some coke."

Jenny shook her head. "Miss Sally don't like for Lucy to be walking on the big road this time of day," she said. "Too much passing. There's some peach icecream in the refrigerator. You can have it if you'll walk up the hill for it."

"I don't care anything about peach icecream," Lois said.

"I don't either," Lucy said.

"Well, set still, then," Jenny said.

A car came in sight on the other side of the river. "I bet he goes the river road," Lois said.

"I bet he don't," Lucy said, for she had recognized Mr. Reardon's grey convertible.

Nobody said anything for several minutes. It was so still that you could hear the little plunk the bridge made every time a car passed over it.

"What makes it do that?" Lois asked.

"It's fixed so it gives," Jenny said. "At Memphis they got a bridge with a loose floor swings out and lets big steamboats go through it. . . . Ain't that the strange gentleman's car over there in front of Patterson's?"

The grey convertible was slowing up as it approached Daddy's car. The two cars came to a halt, then each spun on its way. "Don't they look like bugs?" Jenny said. "Lord, sometimes it seems to me the world's just got full of bugs, beetles kind of like, all of 'em rushing every which a way. Don't hardly know where they're going and don't much care."

The grey convertible crossed the bridge, turned in at the gate and rolled past the cabin. Mr. Reardon did not look to either side as he drove and did not seem to know that there was anybody on the porch of the cabin.

"What he go in to town for every day around this time?" Jenny asked.

"He goes in to church," Lucy said.

"Church at three o'clock in the evening! What won't they think of next?" Jenny said. "Mr. Stamper been after me to go to the Shady Grove Revival with him, but I don't care nothing about going, long as we have to take his baby brother along. . . ."

"What's the matter with *him*?" Lois asked.

"Starts climbing. Soon as he gets in a car starts climbing. And who wants to drive up to a revival with something like that in the back of they car? . . . But Mr. Stamper promised he mother on her deathbed he take him with him everywhere he go on Sundays. . . ."

"You mean every time you and Mr. Stamper go out you got to take him with you?" Lois asked. "I wouldn't like that."

"Me and Mr. Stamper don't like it, either. But that was the way the promise run. Everywhere he go he have to take him with him. On Sundays."

"You don't have to take him other days?" Lois asked.

"Naw," Jenny said, with a sigh, "but he done about ruined Sundays for me."

"Does he climb all over you, Jenny?" Lucy asked.

"Climb all over everything. We was taking an old lady home from church the other night and nothing would do him but he had to set in her lap. For three solid miles he set on that poor old soul's lap and cry like a baby."

"Would she let him?"

"She couldn't help herself. Can't nobody help theyself when he start to climbing."

"What makes him climb, Jenny?" Lucy said.

"Canned heat. He taken to drinking it after he mother died. Mr. Stamper done all he could to stop him. But Mirabow, he was his Mama's pet. Can't nobody do nothing with him. . . ." She put her finger out and lightly flicked Lucy's cheek. "That's one reason I'm always after you to do like your Mama says and not be so pettish."

"I don't think I'm so pettish," Lucy said sullenly.

"You're a heap more that way than I am," Lois said. "That's because you're an only child."

Lucy eyed Lois coldly for a moment, then turned her head to stare into the woods. Big, twisted roots made a sort of stairway down into the grove. Their bark had been worn off by the passing of feet. When sunlight fell on them they glistened as white as paper. At the foot of the stairway there was a carpet of moss as big as this house. She laid her hand on Jenny's arm. "Let's go for a walk in the woods."

"Hot in the woods this time of day," Jenny said. "Flies'll eat you up."

Lucy pressed closer to Jenny's soft side. She put her arm about Jenny's shoulder and leaned forward so that she could look into Jenny's face. *"Please,* Jenny!" she said. "We could wade in the branch and get cool. Please!"

Jenny laughed. Her dark eyes enveloped Lucy's face in their glow. She reached out and with her hand lovingly traced the curve of the child's cheek. "Listen at you!" she said. "Well, come on. You done ruined my nap. Might as well be moving around as settin' here."

"That's what I say," Lois said. "I like it out here all right as long as there's something to do."

"Well, get your feet wet, then, and see if that won't satisfy you," Jenny said and then, as if afraid her tone had been too harsh, she leaned forward to straighten the bow on Lois' hair. "How come you can't get your bows to stand up nice and stiff like hers?" she asked Lucy.

"Oh, come on," Lucy said and ran down the steps.

Jenny rose with a sigh. They went through the plum thicket and down the ladder of roots into the grove. The moss was cushiony under their feet. Lois sat down and took off her shoes to feel the cool softness between her toes. Lucy, too, sat down on the moss. She did not take her shoes off at once, but bent and, parting the moss with her hands, examined a single tuft. She thought that it looked like a little pine tree, but a pine tree in bloom; the blossoms that depended from the upward-thrust branches were a clear scarlet and shaped like tiny bells. A week ago the moss had all been a deep green, but now everywhere she looked, it was flecked with scarlet.

She sat and gazed about her. When they had come down into the grove a while ago they must have walked over this same carpet of moss. He must have felt its softness under his feet, but he would not have noticed that the moss was in bloom. His face would have been turned to that other face, his eyes would have been fixed on those other eyes. He would not have looked down at the minute, forked branches, at the tiny bells.

Lois was already wading in the branch. There was a place where the current was always full of bubbles; a spring came out from under a shelving rock to join the larger stream. Underneath the rock the sand was deep, furrowed a little where the two little currents met and whirled together before they settled into an easier flow. Lois was standing beside the rock, her feet sunk ankle-deep in the sand. She tucked her skirt higher about her waist and shrieked as the water eddied about her knees. "Come on," she cried, "it's *so cold*! *Come on!*"

Lucy did not answer her but took her seat beside Jenny on the bank. Lois had bent over and with the flat of her hand was splashing water downstream. Her pants were soaking wet and her skirt was wet, too. As she bent over, the top of her green taffeta hair ribbon brushed the surface of the water. She smiled at Lucy through her fallen brown hair and pointed downstream. "Let's make a dam," she said.

"I don't feel like it," Lucy said.

"Go on," Jenny said in a low tone. "She your company. Play with her."

Lucy made no answer except to turn her head and stare up the path. The trunks of the beech trees shone like grey satin, their roots were encircled with ferns. Here in the hollow the ferns grew no higher than your knee, but a little farther up the path the bracken began. And above the bracken tier on tier hung the laurel leaves, slick and green and dark, except where the edge of some leaf caught a splinter of light. Once it started the laurel grew all along that path. Some of the bushes were as tall as saplings. They made the way quite dark until you came out on the bluff and looked down and saw the white sycamores and the whiter stream plashing on the rocks. . . . *Were they already at the waterfall or were they still moving along the path, her face turned up to his, his brown head bent to hers?*

Lois had quit wading and sitting down on the bank dried her feet and began to put on her socks and shoes. Lucy kept her own face expressionless. Lois' face had fallen when Lucy told her that she did not feel like making a dam. Lucy had marked the change in her expression with satisfaction. This was perhaps the first time Lois had ever heard those words from Lucy's lips. Lucy was ready to play anything. It was Lois who was hard to please and would sometimes sit through a whole afternoon, saying only with a sigh, "I don't feel like it," to whatever Lucy suggested. Lucy had often wondered how Lois felt when she said that. She thought that she knew now. She wants to play but she's willing to give up playing herself, just to keep me from playing, she thought.

As if reading her thoughts, Lois gave a long sigh. "If we're not going to play anything I'd just as soon go back to the house," she said.

Lusy stood up. Jenny got up, too. "Let's go the back way," she said, "I want to speak to Mrs. MacDonough a minute."

Lucy looked from one to the other. The *back way*; she thought. But that leads to the waterfall, too.

She could not trust herself to speak and walked off rapidly along the path. There were no beech trees along here, only saplings and a wild growth of laurel until they came out in an open place where all the trees had been cut down and blackberry briars grew in a great thicket. In some places the bushes had been trampled down or slashed with knives, where the MacDonough children had stood to pick berries. Something pink fluttered from a bush, a rag torn from the dress Ruby had had on the other day. Jenny stepped gingerly in among the bushes and picked and ate a few berries. "Humph," she said, "MacDonoughs done about cleaned this patch out."

Lucy looked over the top of the thicket to where the path forked. The left hand turn would take you down over the side of the bluff into the ravine. At the foot of the bluff there was another thicket. Buckberries and sumac grew there and that green vine whose briars tore your legs more viciously than anything else in the woods. Innumerable winding paths ran through that thicket. The other day when she had strayed from the main path, they had found themselves in a big patch of blackberries. Berries that ripened in the shade were always the best. But by that time he had wanted to get back to the house. He would not wait to pick berries. *Are you sure this is the way? It's one of the ways. . . .* "Come on," she said aloud. "I know a place where there are still a lot of berries." And she raced on ahead of them.

"If the MacDonoughs ain't beat you to them," Jenny said, following more slowly.

"They don't even know where they are," Lucy called back.

They had come to the edge of the bluff and now they started down. The way was steep. They had to catch hold of roots and saplings as they went to keep themselves from falling. At the foot of the bluff Lucy went more slowly, eyeing each tree she passed. There were rabbit runs all through here. She was not sure she could find that particular path again. And then she remembered that they had come out of the blackberry thicket on to a lot of down logs. She saw them now: big logs, all that was left of the oaks, hickories and beeches that men had come in here long ago and cut down but had never taken out. They lay rotting all over the ravine. But you could not tell now whether they were oak or hickory or beech, for the honeysuckle vines that grew all over them. The honeysuckle was taking all the live trees, too; the dogwood tree in front of them was bent almost double under a mass of vines. *The vines were moving!* Each pendent spray whipped the air as if it were blown by a wind. *But the leaves everywhere stayed still.* She could feel no breeze on her cheeks. She stepped backwards and felt something warm pressing against her body: Jenny had come up behind her, with Lois. She could feel the rasp of Jenny's indrawn breath. Sharp words smote her ear: *"Something in there! Come on, children!"*

But Jenny had not moved and Lucy, too, stood quiet while the wreathed leaves fell away to reveal the brown, burnished head. Glossy as a new chestnut, the head hung motionless among the softly oscillating green leaves. The eyes stared straight into theirs, the lips, slightly agape, were still molding words not meant for their ears, then it sank and rose again and sank once more before Jenny's fingers closed tightly on Lucy's arm and she whirled her about and dragged her around a fallen log and back to the path.

Lois stumbled over the log. A small cry broke from her. "Shut *up*!" Jenny whispered. "*Child*! Shut up!"

They were back at the foot of the bluff where the rabbit runs began. A clump of chestnut oaks grew out of a big rock; a young oak lay splintered beside them. Lucy slowed her pace, pointing with a shaking finger.

"This is the place I was trying to find."

"*Place?*" Jenny said. "What place?" She shook her head to and fro, keeping her eyes on the ground as if she, too, might stumble if she did not guard every movement of her feet. But she had let go of Lucy's arms. "What place?" she said again, not turning her head to Lucy as she spoke.

"Where the blackberries are," Lucy said.

"Blackberries!" Jenny said. "God in Heaven!"

She stopped and turned to Lucy. "You got us in here," she cried, "now you git us out. You know the way out?"

"It's this way," Lucy said and catching hold of a low-growing bough, climbed up on the rock. As she stepped up, she noticed that her feet felt lighter than usual, and brittle. When she leaped from the rock on to the ground they gave way beneath her and for a second she wondered what it would be like not to get up, but to lie there with her cheek pressed against the brown leaves, the cool earth, but her light feet were already bearing her up and she stepped out on the path, as if floating among the leaves that pressed in on every side.

It was very still. In all the woods you could not hear anything except a child's voice. Lois was walking behind Lucy, but she stopped every now and then and turned back. "Jenny, what were they doing? . . . What do you think they were doing?"

"People so mean these days they'll do anything," Jenny said. She took a deep breath. When she spoke again, cautioning Lois not to tear her dress on some briar, her voice sounded the way it always did and Lucy knew that if she turned her head she would find on Jenny's face the expression that was nearly always on her face when she looked at any of them, kind and wise, but a little sad, too. Jenny knew something that would make you feel better if you knew it, too, but she didn't know how to tell it. That was what made her always a little sad.

She said now: "Lucy, we better hurry. I got to start dinner."

"All right," Lucy said and walked faster. Her hands, swinging at her sides, brushed against the blackberry briars as she went; she half paused once, noting abstractedly how darkly green they grew. Only a few minutes ago they had been speckled with light, but the sun had left the ravine; it was later than she had thought. Her fingers tingled. She raised her hand and saw a drop of blood oozing where a briar had pierced her finger, and let the hand fall again at her side. The finger began to throb. The tiny pain seemed to augment the lightness that she still felt in her hands and feet. Behind her Jenny was remonstrating in fluting tones with Lois, who was sobbing. Lucy raised her hand to her lips and sucked the blood away. She wondered what they would say if she told them that she did not know the way out of the woods. This path they were on did not seem like any path she had ever walked on before. But that was because all the leaves kept swaying so. . . . You had not seen the other head. How did you know that another body lay under his? It was the eyes, she thought. They had stared straight into hers. But his gaze had merely happened to fall upon her face. He had seen her and he had not seen her. And if she and the others had not stood there he would have stared straight before him in the same way, as if he were looking beyond whatever was before him, at something that was not there and never could be there, no matter if you looked all your life.

XI

THEY went past the MacDonoughs' house and through the little side gate into the yard.

"I want to go home," Lois said.

"Why'n't you take a nice bath?" Jenny asked.

They had come to the edge of the brick porch. Lois walked closer to Lucy. "Will you ask him to take me home?" she asked.

"Yes," Lucy said.

"Why'n't you take a nice bath?" Jenny said again. "You feel a lot better if you take a nice bath. Lucy, you fix it for her. I got to get supper."

She stopped in the kitchen. Lois and Lucy went up the stairs to Lucy's room. "You want to go to the bathroom upstairs or the one downstairs?" Lucy asked.

Lois sat down on the side of the bed and kicked off her sodden shoes and wet socks. "I don't want any bath," she said. "I just want to go home. Will you ask him?"

"Yes, but you better put on another dress first," Lucy said.

Lois looked down at the skirt of her yellow linen dress. It was stained with mud and torn in one place. "I reckon I will take a bath first," she said and standing up began to strip off her clothes.

Lucy got her own dressing gown from its hook and handed it to her. Lois wrapped the dressing gown about her naked body and they went through the hall and down the stairs to the bathroom on the first floor. Lucy got out a fresh towel for Lois and turned the water on in the tub. "Don't take too much," she said automatically, remembering how her mother complained about the way people from town let the taps run.

"All right," Lois said and reached up and turned the tap off before the tub was a quarter full.

Lucy turned it on again and stood waiting until it should be half full. But Lois had already slid down into the water. "What're you standing around for?" she asked irritably.

Lucy started and went out, closing the door softly behind her. She had traversed the hall and was about to start upstairs when she suddenly stopped. A long shudder went through her body. She stared dully about her, as if wondering what to do next. From the ell came a murmur of voices. Her father and mother were in their bedroom. She knocked on the door.

There was silence, then a voice said, "Come in."

Lucy opened the door. The blinds were drawn but the western sunlight spilled in through the blinds and lay across the floor in bright bars that wavered upon the old-fashioned double bed that Mammy had sent in from Merry Point. Her father lay in bed in his pajamas. His face was flushed, his hair tousled; he looked as if he had just been roused from sleep. Her mother sat on the side of the bed, still wearing her bandanna halter and linen shorts.

As Lucy came in she was bending down to untie the string of one of her sandals, but she straightened up, leaving it untied, to look at her husband. "I couldn't sleep," she said.

He glanced at her and his face set the way it did sometimes when he looked at her. "Well, take your clothes off and lie down," he said, "we might get a little nap before dinner time."

But she sat upright on the side of the bed, the half-fastened sandal dangling from her foot. "I *couldn't* sleep," she said again.

"Why don't you just lie down then?" he asked wearily.

"I *can't* lie down," she said, "I'd get so nervous! I tell you, you don't know what it was like."

He sighed and raising himself on his elbow took the pillow out from under his head, doubled it up and propped himself against it. "You keep saying that," he said, "but you don't get around to telling what happened."

"There wasn't anything *happened*," she said. "I mean. . . . I was just lying there in the hammock and he came out on the porch. . . ."

Lucy had gone around to her mother's side of the bed. Stephen looked at her. "Lucy," he said, "your mother and I are talking. Why don't you go to your own room? You've got a nice bedroom of your own. You don't need to come into ours if you want to take a nap."

Lucy sat down on the side of the bed without saying anything. Sarah, still keeping her face turned toward her husband, slipped her arm about Lucy's shoulders. Lucy put her arm around her mother's waist and hid her face against her mother's back. Sarah turned around. "What's the matter?" she asked. "You and Lois quarreled?"

Lucy did not answer, but drew her legs up off the floor and

stretched herself face down on the bed. Sarah ran her hands caressingly over the child's hair. "Lucy, what is it?" she asked, but Lucy kept her face hid and did not answer.

"Well, go on," he said impatiently.

"He came out on the porch," she said. "I think he thought that there was nobody there. And then he saw me and he started to go back into the house, and then he came back again. . . ."

"Well?"

"He said that he wanted to tell somebody what had happened to him."

"Well, what did happen to him?"

Lucy realized with astonishment that her mother's body was quivering, as her own body had quivered out in the hall a moment ago. Sarah did not say anything for several minutes. When she did speak her voice was cracked and harsh, as if she were already resenting what her husband would say next:

"He had a vision."

The mattress creaked a little. Lucy knew that he was raising himself higher on his pillows. "The Church recognizes various kinds of visions," he said. "Was it an intellectual vision, such as St. Theresa often had, or was it an apparition?"

"You mean did he *see* something? No. He felt it."

"What was it?"

Sarah Lewis put both hands down on the mattress to still the trembling of her body. "A woman," she said, "very large. Larger than any human being could ever be. She might have had a crown of stars on—if he could have seen her head. There was something larger than she was crouching beside her. . . ."

Lucy did not need to see her father's face to know the expression that would be on it. He would have blinked at what her mother had said, and then his gaze would narrow, as a candle set on the window ledge will flicker before it settles to a steady flame, and his voice, when he spoke, would grow gentler, as it always did when he thought that the person he was talking with didn't know what he was talking about.

He said: "This happened in the *Crau*, I suppose, where they had that accident?"

"He came to himself lying upon a pile of rocks. He didn't know what had happened. The chief thing he was conscious of was his thirst. And then he knew that this woman had been sitting beside him for a long time. But it was a longer time than any time he had ever known, longer, even, than his life. She showed him where the water was."

"How?"

"She never touched him. But when he tried to raise himself to crawl to the brook—you know his ankle and collar bone were broken—he could *feel* how strong *she* was. It was almost as if she carried him in her arms, though she never touched him. He thinks he fainted several times. Anyhow, there were times when he saw her face plainer than at others. It would be misty at first and then it would be so close to him that he could look into her eyes. . . ."

"How did they look?"

"Starry was the word he used. All the stars you ever saw on a bright night, gathered in one place, and shining. Shining, not glittering."

"Is that all?"

"No. She left him. He doesn't know just when it was. But he had got some water in his hat and poured it over Isabel's face and hands. He thinks he must have fainted. When he came to, the woman wasn't there. He says the pain in the broken bones was nothing, compared to the thought that she had left him. He thought that he could not bear it and then he realized that she was still there—but different."

"How do you mean?"

"It's hard to explain. He says that before she was bending over him—or would have been bending over him if she had had a body—but now she stood straight and looked at him."

"What did he do then?"

"Nothing. But he says he can still feel her looking at him. He hasn't been the same since. That's why they moved to Toulon. He says that he felt that he couldn't go on living the way he'd been living. . . ."

"I never thought of Kev as leading a debauched life," he said.

"No. But they were always going from one thing to another. . . . And they'd been staying with the Arch O'Neills. They were on their way back from their place when they had the accident."

"I never could take Arch O'Neill's diabolism seriously," he said. "I found him pathetic."

"I know," she said. "Always going around, muttering about how fairies had their cafés, while Sadists had no place to lay their heads. But he *did* have a cage at the Villa Rose. I know, because he locked Helen Barker up in it. . . . You remember that night she came to our place, sort of gibbering? Well, she'd really been frightened by Arch's goings on."

"Helen Barker is a goose," he said.

"I know it. So is Isabel, when you come down to it. But they did see a lot of the O'Neills. And I can't imagine Arch's passing up an opportunity to get Isabel into his cage. Kev must have been pretty sick of the whole business. . . . And then this happened. He says that several times since then he has made an effort and put the woman out of his mind. When he does that he feels a kind of severing pain and goes through a period of desolation and then, one day or one moment, he feels her with him again. Sometimes she is beside him and sometimes she just stands and looks at him."

He said slowly: "He is evidently a born mystic. All mystics have such experiences. I believe the intellectual or inner vision is regarded as higher than the apparition, which is thought to come to those whose spirits burn with a grosser flame. But there are many records of instantaneous conversion. St. Margaret of Cortona was converted instantaneously. Her lover went off to the hunt and never came back. Three months later she was walking in the forest with his greyhound and the dog sprang into a brake, whimpering, and there was the decomposing body of her lover and Christ rising out of it."

She had left the bed and was walking over to the window. There was a rasping sound. She had pulled the blind up.

"What's the matter?" he asked in a low voice.

"Nothing."

"Yes, there is."

She was looking out the window. She said: "You know everything, don't you?"

"You have had plenty of opportunity to find out how limited my knowledge is. You're merely trying to be rude."

"I'm not. But you know what everything is like. Just mention anything and you can tell us about something else somewhere else just exactly like it. . . ."

"That's all anybody knows," he said. "Except, of course, great brains like Kev Reardon's."

"That's unworthy of you," she said. "He's just a poor little man. . . ."

". . . worth about twenty million dollars."

"He's going to give it all away."

"I respect his courage," he said, "but I don't understand what has happened to him."

"You won't *let* anything happen—even to me!"

"That's unworthy of *you*. You know well that I have never interfered with your spiritual life."

"I haven't got any. . . . Neither have you."

"Kev's revelations have evidently aroused the spirit of competition in your breast. Perhaps if you tried you could produce a few visions, too. . . . I don't think, however, that the Lord has given you the gift of discerning spirits. In fact, I think that you are singularly obtuse in that respect."

She left the window and came towards him. "Can't you *see*?" she whispered.

"See what?"

"How you keep things from happening."

He did not say anything.

"You could if you wanted to," she said, "but you don't want to."

There was a silence, then he said, "I think you are the most arrogant woman I have ever known in my life."

"And you are the most selfish man. If you could ever think about anybody else just once in your life . . . just once. . . ."

". . . I might attain to the high spiritual eminence on which you stand?"

She sat down on the side of the bed and put her hands up before her face. She was sobbing. "I just try to do the best I can," she whispered.

"And sit in judgment on everybody else continually. But the world is not necessarily the way you picture it. What do you know of anybody else's spiritual struggles?"

She raised her head. "I've always looked up to you so!" she cried.

"Well, you can look up to Kev Reardon now."

Lucy fixed her father's face with bright, despairing eyes. He had been staring at his wife as he spoke and when he finished speaking he continued to stare at her. His eyes were hard. Lucy had seen him look at other people like that, but she had never before seen his eyes hard when he looked at her mother. And there was a note in his voice that she had never heard before. Sometimes they *sounded* as if they were quarreling, but they usually ended by calling each other "Darling," or one of them would suddenly run over and fling his arms about the other's neck. But her father was looking at her mother now as if she were somebody he didn't like.

The child buried her face in the covers. It seemed to her that her life up till now had been only a dream, a happy dream. They don't love each other, she thought. They never did. . . . What is going to become of me?

The sheet was wet where her open lips had pressed it. She turned over and lay on her side. She could not see either of their faces. There was only the white-washed brick wall that looked grey in this dim light. Set high in it was the little window whose blind her mother had just pulled up. She had not pulled it all the way up but you could see a strip of green: the leaves of the willow tree moving a little in a breeze that had sprung up. The other blind was still down. Everywhere else in this room was grey. Her mother had chosen this room for her own, but she always said that it reminded her of a prison cell. Somebody had told them that in the old days Negroes who wouldn't behave themselves were locked up in here. She wondered how long they left them in here at a time. Suppose it was like that now, only she and her father and mother didn't know it. Suppose somebody had locked them up in here and then had gone away with the key? Suppose they were locked up in here forever? Suppose nobody ever came to let them out?

Her mother's voice broke the silence. "There was something else," she said drearily. "But you probably won't believe that, either. . . ."

"You know beforehand, of course, whether I'll believe you or not," her husband said in his new, dry voice. "You know everything!"

"Well, I'm not going to tell you," she said.

Lucy raised her head. She wanted to see how her mother's face looked when she said that. The bedsprings creaked as her father sat up against his pillows. His face was even more flushed than when Lucy had come into the room. His blue eyes bored into Lucy's. He leaned over and catching her by the shoulders, shook her to and fro. "What are we going to do with you, Lucy?" he asked. "You are always hanging around, listening to grown people talk. What are we going to *do* with you?"

"I don't know," Lucy said and sliding from the bed ran out of the room and left them there together.

XII

LOIS had to spend the night. Daddy said that he would be damned if he would make another trip to town that day. When Mr. Reardon went in to Mass the next morning he took Lois, in time for Sunday School. Daddy stayed in his study all morning. Uncle Tubby and Mrs. Reardon went swimming in the river. But Mrs. Reardon had not got up till late. They did not start down to swim until nearly twelve o'clock, and they did not come back for nearly two hours. At one o'clock Mama told Jenny that she could go, that she and Lucy would put the lunch on the table themselves. There were broiled chickens and hot rolls and new potatoes and butter beans; the dessert was lemon sherbet.

While they were eating lunch Mr. Reardon was called to the long distance telephone. When he came back he said that he and Mrs. Reardon would have to leave the next day—as soon as they finished breakfast, he added.

"Why, you've hardly come!" Mama said.

"We thought you'd stay longer than this," Daddy said. "Why, we haven't had a chance to show you the country yet."

Uncle Tubby looked at Mrs. Reardon without speaking.

Mr. Reardon was looking at Mama. "What about seeing something of the country this afternoon? You know that drive we were talking about?"

Mama looked at Daddy. "He means that equine drive," he said.

"Oh. . . ." Daddy said. "Well, I don't see why we shouldn't go this afternoon. About four o'clock?"

They left the table and went upstairs, all except Mama and Lucy. Lucy helped Mama clear the table and brush the crumbs off and set the chairs back against the wall. Mama stacked the dishes in the sink. She said that she would wash them when she got back from the drive. "I can't stand it if I don't get a nap now," she said and had started out of the door when suddenly she came back and caught Lucy's hands and began dancing her around the room.

"What's the matter, Mama?" Lucy asked, "what's the matter?"

"Didn't you hear what they said?" Mama whispered and picked up an apple from a bowl on the sideboard and threw it up to the ceiling and caught it, and ran out of the room.

Borcke had jumped down off the window seat when they started dancing and now he followed Mama upstairs. You could hear their feet on the steps, Mama's soft in her rubber-soled sneakers and Borcke's lighter than hers but with a little click each time his nails slid on the wood. Those were all the sounds in the house and then you could not hear them any more, and a silence, that had been waiting until even those light sounds died away, floated in from somewhere and filled all the room. It was a silence that Lucy had felt before—at this same time of the afternoon—that day they all came, but it seemed to her now that that silence, that stillness she had felt then was only the beginning of this silence, this stillness, as if she had been walking beside the river and seeing one wave come in had thought that that was all the current. The whole room was full of it. It was rising. She could feel it cold against her lips. . . . But silence, any silence, could be broken. She walked over to the window seat. *Undine* was lying on top of one of the pillows. She sat down and opened the book. It fell open at the place where the knight goes into the Black Valley in search of Bertalda:

> The twigs cruelly whipped his brow and cheeks with the cold dews of evening, a distant thunder rumbled beyond the mountains, everything looked so sinister that he began to feel a species of awe as he approached the white shape which now lay near him on the ground. But he could quite clearly distinguish that it was the figure of a sleeping or swooning woman. . . . He bowed down to her; the darkness of the valley and the approach of night forbade him to distinguish her features. But now, as with a kind of sad uncertainty he pressed close beside her on the ground, a flash of lightning suddenly illuminated the valley. He saw quite close to him a hideous and wasted countenance, and a dull voice cried: "Give me a kiss, you love-sick shepherd!"

She raised her eyes from the page. It was the curtain moving in the breeze that had made that slight sound. She looked away from the curtain to the spot on the wall at which Stonewall Jackson unceasingly stared, then back at his eyes. They were like blue marbles. He had been alive once: a great and good man, her father said. *But he was dead now.*

Her clasp tightened on the blue and silver cover of the book. She opened it again, read a few more lines, then put it down and walked quickly toward the door.

It seemed a long time before her feet rested on the hollowed-out bricks of the gallery. The door had clanged to behind her. Back behind the door it had been cool, but out here the air was warm with the sun. She felt it beat, like something alive, against her cheek. Before her the huge, rectangular shadow of the house thrust forward over the grass. Where it stopped the grass looked brown; if you stooped and gathered a handful it would be brittle to the touch: all the life burned out of it, her mother said every day, sighing: *If only I had water. I cannot raise anything on this dry hill without water. Not even a petunia. Without water. . . . I know it. I know it. But I don't see how we can get it this year. Just to instal the pump would cost a thousand dollars. . . .*

She walked around the side of the house. There was plenty of shade here. The crape myrtle bushes were as tall as trees. Some of them were a hundred years old: her mother would not allow them to be trimmed; they were too old to take on new ways, she said. The willow tree was old, too, one of the oldest trees around here, but it had never grown very tall—because there was no living water on the hill, Jenny said. Plenty in the bottom. Springs everywhere you turned. But water can't run uphill, Jenny said. If you want water you got to get down to its level. They ought to have built the house down in the bottom, Jenny said.

Through the leaves she caught a glimpse of a man's head and shoulders. On the other side of the crape myrtle bushes somebody was walking to and fro. He walked slowly, his eyes bent on the ground. She thought that he had not seen her and was about to tiptoe away when he stopped and turned his head, and stared at her over his shoulder.

She stood still, too. Where was there for her to go? she asked herself. In all this green summer world there was nowhere she could go to escape from him. Always, wherever she went, he was there or coming toward her, as he was now coming toward her. Had he spoken her name? It seemed to hover in the air between them. But she had not seen his lips move. That was because she had not been able to take her eyes off his eyes that were always so bright but so dark. If he would look away, for only a second, the pain would stop.

The darkness of his eyes was shattered, as if a live thing had stirred at the bottom of a well. He came to a halt beside the crape myrtle bush. He said:

"Do you remember the night I came?"

"Yes," she whispered.

He bent toward her. He smiled. "I think it must have been that night," he said. "You remember we walked about out here under the trees?"

"Yes," she said.

He had turned his head away at last and was looking off over the yard. "Do you remember just where we walked?"

She raised her hand quickly. The gesture started the pain again. It was not in her stomach but in her very bowels. . . . *Rognons, the reins, a girl of stout kidney.* . . . Something had got inside her and was moving about on delicate, piercing feet.

He had moved off in the direction in which she had pointed. She walked slowly after him. He stopped beside the big maple tree. "Here?" he asked. "Under this tree?"

She stopped, too, her feet gripping an arched root of the old tree. She felt the breath going out of her with a sigh. He seemed to think that she had spoken. He turned to her again. "You're right," he said. "We stood here and watched the Holy Rollers. . . . You had your skirt full of flowers. . . ." In his eye the spark had grown until the whole pupil brimmed with light. He said: "I lost something that night. . . . It must have been that night. . . . I thought you might have seen it shining."

The thing that was inside her was clawing to get out. But if it got out her whole life might spill out, too, here on the grass.

She said in what seemed to her a high, thin voice: "No, I didn't see anything."

He was still looking at her and as always, whenever he looked at her, he smiled a little. "It is a crucifix," he said and with his hands he measured off a space in the air. "No larger than that. Ivory. On an ebony block. The eyes are made of little diamonds and the nails in the feet and hands are of rubies. I can't find it anywhere in my room. I must have dropped it outside. . . . You haven't seen anything shining when you've been playing in the yard?"

"No," she said and heard with surprise how low and harsh her voice was and heard with even more surprise her next words: "Jenny. . . ."

"Jenny?"

"She makes up the beds."

"Oh . . ." he said, and his lips withdrawing from the name, made in the air a kind of whistling sound. "Is she in there long at a time?"

"I don't know," Lucy said.

They had been standing side by side on the big, gnarled root of maple tree and they stood there a moment longer. The bottom was in corn this year: all green, from the foot of the hill to the big bend in the river. And on the other side of the river there were more cornfields. It was still green there, too, till you got to the red bricks of the town. He studied the view, as if he had been suddenly released from some more pressing obligation and was only now able to give his full attention to it. "Beautiful, isn't it?" he said and sighed. "Well, in that case there's nothing to do." She felt the air about her stir slightly as he shook his head. "No," he said thoughtfully, "there's nothing to do." All at once he laughed. "But I wish I could make some sort of deal with her. . . . If she *has* got it, I mean. It's not worth much—to anybody but me. I value it because it belonged to my father. He hardly ever had it out of his hand during the last days of his life, his old servant told me. . . ."

A call came from the house: "Lucee!"

"I've got to go," Lucy said.

He laughed. "They're always calling you, aren't they? Do you suppose it's because you've got such a fine name?"

"I'm named after my great-grandmother," Lucy said.

"And after another Lucy. Didn't you know that?"

She shook her head.

"She was very strong. Stronger than ten men. . . . Or ten oxen. In pictures she carries her eyes in her hand. Do you know why?"

Poised on tiptoe, her body already inclined away from him, she turned reluctantly to shake her head again.

"Her name means Light. She sees what other people cannot see. . . . Would you like me to send you a statue of St. Lucy when I get back to France?"

"No," she said faintly, "I—don't like statues." And she ran toward the house.

It was cool in the hall. The warm air that soughed about her in her passage dropped from her like a cloak when she opened the front door. She stood quiet, her hand pressed against her mouth, until the coolness had flowed all over her, then she pushed open the door of her bedroom.

Her mother stood, in her green dressing gown, in front of the open closet. "Hurry up," she said and without turning around took a dark blue gingham dress from its hanger. "It's four o'clock now."

The room was full of dust and bars that were striped and shimmered; the blinds were drawn against the sun, but the sun kept sliding in. It had set the bars whirling. In a moment the floor would start going up and down. She sat down on the side of the bed, her hand still pressed to her mouth. A sound broke from her.

Her mother had come over to the bed to put the dress down and looked at her sharply. "What's the matter with you? Are you sick at your stomach?"

Lucy shook her head, still holding her hand pressed to her mouth.

Sarah threw the blue dress on the bed and stood looking down at Lucy, her lips compressed. "I bet you are," she said. "You look funny to me. Lucy, I *wish* you'd stop careering around in the middle of the day. It's positively suicidal—even for a child. But nobody can ever tell *you* anything!"

The spasm had passed. Lucy took her hand away from her mouth and got up off the bed. "Mama, I don't have to go driving if I don't want to, do I?" she asked.

"You certainly do," Sarah said. "Jenny isn't here. . . ."

"I could stay with the MacDonoughs."

"Not while the meeting's going on. There's no telling *who'll* turn up there. Your father wouldn't allow it. Lucy, don't be difficult. Now of all times!"

"That's what you always say."

Sarah grinned. "There *isn't* any time when it's convenient, is there?" She leaned over and put her arm about her daughter's shoulders in a quick caress. "They'll all be gone tomorrow," she said. "Think of that!"

Lucy stood like stone in her mother's embrace. "I don't care when they go," she said, "but I don't want to go driving."

Sarah moved impatiently. She set her teeth on her lower lip and shook her head to and fro. "Lucy, do you think *I* want to go driving? Do you think *Daddy* wants to go driving?"

"What are you going for then?"

Sarah threw her hands up over her head, then clasping them behind her neck, shook her head even more violently to and fro. "My God! I'll be glad when you're grown, even if it does make an old woman out of me. Now you get dressed and stop this foolishness!"

She wrapped the green robe tighter about her and left the room. "Hurry up!" she called sharply from the hall. "I'm all ready now, except for my dress. Hurry *up*!"

Lucy slowly took off her dress. She decided that she would take a bath. That took her ten minutes and it took her another ten minutes after that to dress again. The others were all outside, waiting, when she came down the front steps.

Mr. and Mrs. Reardon were in their own car, but Uncle Tubby was in the car with her mother and father, on the back seat. Mama sat in front, beside Daddy, holding Borcke in her arms. "Do you think we'd better take Borcke?" Daddy was asking as Lucy came down the steps. "My God, yes! He *never* has any fun," Mama said. She moved over beside Daddy and let Lucy sit next to the window on the front seat. As soon as Lucy was settled Borcke crawled over into her lap and standing on his hind legs put his head out of the window so he could sniff the wind. "See!" Mama said, "He loves to ride. Don't you, Angel Dumpling Darling Diddle?"

Borcke turned his head to look at Mama out of his great, dark eyes, then his nose started working, and he dug his toenails deep into Lucy's leg as he clambered toward the window again. Hugging him to her, she raised him up so that he could rest his front paws on the open window. But he was not satisfied and kept digging his nails deeper into her leg as he climbed higher. She hugged his warm body closer and was glad every time his sharp nails sent a flash of pain through her leg. Suddenly she found herself laughing. "He's like Mr. Stamper's baby brother, isn't he?" she asked, looking up at her mother.

Sarah put her hand out to perk up the bow on Lucy's hair. "How is he like him, Lucy?"

"Climbing," Lucy said. "Soon as he gets in a car he starts to climbing. Jenny is ashamed to take him to Shady Grove with them for fear he'll start climbing where all the church people can see him."

"But they climb, too," Uncle Tubby said from the back seat. "Don't they climb all over the furniture and froth at the mouth?"

"It's a different kind of climbing," Sarah said. "His is induced by alcohol, theirs by the Holy Ghost. . . ."

"It's canned heat," Lucy said. "Has that got alcohol in it?"

"It certainly has," Sarah said, "and it will burn his insides clean out if he keeps on drinking it."

The car rolled through the gate. Uncle Tubby raised his right hand in salute when they passed the Holy Roller rock. "Prepare to meet thy God!" he said. "Do you two ever start anywhere and then just turn back?"

"You mean because of that motto?" Mama asked.

"Well, it would give me pause if I had to face it every time I went through the gate."

"It nearly drove me nuts at first," Mama said. "That's why I planted that ivy around it. But now I'm used to it. In fact, I think it's kind of distinctive. I don't know anybody else who has such an impressive entrance to their place."

"Except Cerberus," Uncle Tubby said.

They were on the bridge. Daddy slowed up. "Fort Donelson is about twenty miles upstream," he said. "We might drive up there tomorrow. After the Reardons leave."

"I may have to pull out tomorrow, too," Uncle Tubby said. "There's a man in New York I've got to see. . . ."

"Oh . . ." Daddy said. "Too bad you can't go to Donelson while you're here. It's quite interesting. The breastworks are pretty much the way they were then."

They talked about the Civil War all the way to town and all the way through town and were still talking about it when they left the town and started out on the road that led to Mammy's place. But they did not go to Mammy's place. When they came to the Red River they turned off on a side road and drove for a while along the river.

Borcke had got tired of looking out of the window and curled up in Lucy's lap. Every now and then a shiver ran through him and he would give a long snore, but for the most part, he lay quiet in her arms. Her legs were sweating from the warmth of him but the upper part of her body felt cool. A breeze was blowing from the river. She leaned closer to the window so that she could feel it on her cheeks. The road was narrow, sunk deep between fences that were hung thick with honeysuckle. Locust trees grew on each side of the road. The shadows of their leaves laced all the dust. But the dust on this road was not as dry as the dust on the other road. Even when you could not see the river you could feel the dampness coming up from it. She was glad that they had come this way.

They rounded a bend and the road widened. On one side a barred gate made a break in the honeysuckle. On the other side the fence had stopped. There was a grove of tall trees and under them a cave. A stream ran out of the cave to make a branch across the road.

"Mama," Lucy said, "isn't this the way to Mr. Warfleet's?"

But Uncle Tubby was leaning forward to set his hand on Daddy's shoulder. *"Do you see what I see?"*

Just outside the entrance to the cave a very fat old man sat in a big split-bottomed chair. He had on his hat and a white shirt and white pants but his naked feet were ankle-deep in the water that ran out of the mouth of the cave. A Negro boy was rising from where he had been stooping beside the stream, holding a bucket of water in his hand. As they watched, he up-ended the bucket so that the water poured down over the old man's shoulders and over his fat stomach and knees on to the ground.

"I might as well tell you now that that is my great-uncle, Fillinger Fayerlee," Mama said.

"And your third cousin, Sylvester Beauchamp," Daddy said.

Mama had made Daddy stop the car and was getting out. As she stood, her back turned to the old man, her foot still on the step, she looked at Uncle Tubby. "Steve hadn't been in our family a year before he was telling everybody what kin they were to each other," she said. She turned to Daddy. "He is *not* my third cousin. He's about my fifth or sixth. I asked Mammy and she said that his grandmother was Aunt Daphne, not Aunt Betty, like you think it was. Strange as it may seem, you don't know everything!" and she made a face at Daddy.

Uncle Fill had seen them coming. He made a kind of grunting sound and acted as if he was going to get out of his chair, then fell back, gripping the arms tight with both hands. The water was still running off his forehead and off the ends of his long white moustache. He was panting and looked, Lucy thought, like an old bloodhound, heavy as he was, with his eyes faded to the milky brown to which an old dog's eyes often fade, and with the lower lids red-lined and drooping away from them.

They were up in front of him. He quit struggling to rise and lying back in his chair stared up at them out of his bloodshot eyes. "Steve and Sally!" he panted. "If this ain't a pleasure! And ain't this little Lucy?" He reached out his arm and with surprising agility drew Lucy to him and pressed his wet moustache against her cheek.

Sarah bent over and kissed him on the forehead, then Stephen shook hands with him and introduced Uncle Tubby. "All the way from New York!" Uncle Fill said. "Now ain't that inte*rest*ing!" He snapped his fingers at the Negro boy. "Sylvester! Sylvester! Get 'em some chairs so they can set down."

The boy went behind some big rocks that were piled in the entrance of the cave and brought back four chairs and set them in a row in front of Uncle Fill. Daddy and Mama sat down but Uncle Tubby stood with his hand resting on the back of Lucy's chair, looking at Uncle Fill who was wringing the water out of first one end and then the other of his long white moustache.

"The Lord moves in a mysterious way His wonders to perform," he said. "I was just thinking of going up to the house and taking me a little nap. If I had, I'd have missed you sho."

"That would have been a pity," Uncle Tubby said. "Mr. Fayerlee, do you own this splendid cave?"

"Well, it's on my land," Uncle Fill said. "They call it Crenfew's Cave, after my grandfather, Edward Crenfew, was the first man ever went in it. . . . It's always been a custom with the family to sit here in summer. Delightful, ain't it?"

"But I see you still have to cool off with your bucket of water," Mama said.

"Yes," Uncle Fill said. "It's my blood. Always been too derned rich."

Uncle Tubby touched Lucy on the shoulder. "Let's go look at the cave," he said.

They went along the little path that led into the mouth of

the cave. Sylvester walked beside them. He was staring at Borcke. "Miss Lucy," he said, "do he call hisself a dog?"

"He's a bugle, Sylvester," Mama called, "a German bugle."

"Do he hunt rabbits?"

"He ain't worth a damn, Sylvester," Daddy said. "Nose got blunted, sleeping under the covers."

They were inside the cave. A rocky ledge formed its roof. Little twisted trees and buckberry bushes grew there and long creepers of some vine trailed down at one side almost like a curtain. The floor of the cave was drifted deep in white sand. The branch ran along the right hand side, then disappeared behind a wall of rock. The wall was hairy with green moss. Water dripped off it. Flat rocks covered with the same slimy green moss lay all about. Uncle Tubby took Lucy's hand and jumped her from rock to rock until they came to the place where the stream flowed through the opening which was just big enough for a person to squeeze into. Still holding Lucy's hand, he bent down and peered through the opening. They could see the water glinting where the light fell but everywhere else it was dark.

"How far back have you been in here?" Uncle Tubby asked Sylvester.

"Two, three miles."

"And does the stream go all the way?"

"Yes sir, till it sink in the ground."

"Damn it," Uncle Tubby said, "I'd turn spelaeologist if I stayed around here. I feel it coming over me now . . . *Belle dame,* shall we take a little turn inside?"

Lucy did not answer. Balancing on the slippery rock, she gazed past the trailing vines and bushes to where the others sat ranged in their chairs beside the stream. They seemed a long way off and they sat so still. The gaping rocks, the trailing vines might have framed a photograph except for the sound that still echoed through the warm, outer air: her mother's voice.

"I *am* coming to see you one day next week, but we have to go to Mr. Warfleet's this evening."

"Warfleet's!" Lucy thought. "They never said anything about Warfleet's till now."

"We're thinking of buying a pony."

Uncle Tubby looked down at Lucy, his eyes shining. "Now what do you know about that?" He had let go of her hand, but now he caught it again. They ran toward the others.

Uncle Fill was talking: "What do you want to *buy* a pony for? Ain't they anybody 'll *lend* you a pony?"

Mama laughed. "Well, have *you* got any ponies to spare? If you've got a nice pony we won't buy one from Mr. Warfleet."

"I ain't got any pony on hand right now, but there used to be a lot of them little Morgan horses over at Merry Point. . . . Why'n't you ask Sister ain't she got a horse she can send in for the little girl to ride on?"

Lucy stumbled over a root. Uncle Tubby, coming up behind her, put both hands under her elbows and swung her off her feet, then set her on the ground again. She did not even thank him, but ran on up to Uncle Fill.

"She's got Maggie," she said. "But I don't *want* her."

He leaned forward, fixing his bloodshot eyes on hers. "What's the matter with Maggie?" he asked.

"She's too *old*!" Lucy cried, "too *old*! I don't *want* her!"

Uncle Fill's lower lip was sagging until you could see all the inside of his mouth; it was the same color as his lower lids. "Maggie *is* getting along, now you come to think of it," he said. He shut his mouth up tight and ran his hand over his long, straggling moustache and leaned farther forward and laid his hand on Daddy's knee. "Steve, the author of the Gospel of Matthew is not a clear thinker. No, you couldn't say that he was a very clear thinker. . . ."

Daddy looked straight before him and didn't say a word.

"Why?" Mama yelled. "Why isn't he a clear thinker, Uncle Fill?"

Uncle Fill took his hand off Daddy's knee and leaned back in his chair. His fat old hands came up in front of him. He put the fingers together to make a little tent. He said:

"In the first chapter of Matthew, Verse 18, it says: 'Now the birth of Jesus was in this wise: when as his mother Mary was espoused to Joseph, before they came together, she was found with child by the Holy Ghost. . . .' "

The pebbles creaked under Lucy's feet as she walked over to stand behind her mother's chair. She waited a minute but Sarah did not give any sign to show that she knew she was there. Lucy bent over, whispering: "Mama, are we going to Mr. Warfleet's? Mama. . . ."

Sarah turned her head until her lips were close to Lucy's ear. "In a minute," she whispered. "Just wait a minute. . . ."

Uncle Tubby caught Lucy's eye as she straightened up. He clapped one hand over to the other and, holding them up in the air, shook them to and fro, smiling, as he looked away from Lucy to Uncle Fill.

Uncle Fill spread his legs wider so that his stomach wouldn't be in his way, and pointed his finger at Daddy who had picked up a stick and was making marks on the ground.

"Joseph knows it's not his child, for as the Book says, they have not come together. *But* how does he know that she is with child by the Holy Ghost? How, I ask you?"

Daddy still wouldn't look at him.

Uncle Fill leaned back in his chair and brought his hands up to form the little tent again.

". . . By a *dream*," he said. "The angel of the Lord appears to Joseph in a *dream* and tells him not to fear to take her to himself for that which was in her was conceived by the Holy Ghost. And she shall bring forth a child and call his name Jesus, for He shall save his people from their sins. . . ."

You could hear his breath wheezing under everything he said: an old pump that somebody was letting run down. He sat here, like this, every afternoon during the summer. If nobody came by for him to talk to, he talked to Sylvester. Her eyes went to the Negro boy, who had sat down on a rock in the mouth of the cave. He had a slingshot beside him; his hands had been making slow, languid motions over it, but now they had dropped on each side of his spread knees. His eyes, as large and dark as Jenny's, rested on Lucy's imperturbably before they sought the far horizon. She looked over his head at the rocky ledge that formed the roof of the cave. Tufts of sedge grass grew there between the buckberry bushes. The grasses in one of the tufts wavered; a little lizard moved swiftly out of them and came to rest on the rock. His back shone in the sun as if it were wet. Once he seemed to open his mouth. Something that might have been a tongue flickered in the air before he disappeared under a leaf. "They just sit here in summer," she thought, "but he runs back and forth over that ledge, every day, winter and summer. . . ." Her hands clasped the back of her mother's chair so tightly that it shook a little. Sarah turned her head long enough to say *"Lucy!"* in a low voice, then turned to her great-uncle. "But the Jews had been looking for a Messiah for a long time, Uncle Fill."

"You are mighty right. They had been a sinful race and they knew it was up to them to make peace with the Lord Almighty. But was not this an insult even to *their* intelligence? Here was the most stupendous event in all history, for it *would* be the most stupendous event in all history *if* a virgin were to conceive and bring forth a child. Here was this stupendous event announced to them in a *dream*. Do you suppose that if the Lord God Almighty wanted to tell Joseph anything as important as that he wouldn't have waited till he woke up or had him waked up? Why, I dreamed the other night that I was a rhinoceros! Sylvester here'd been right surprised if he'd come in the next morning and found me walking on all fours. Dream, forsooth!"

Sylvester started and said, "Yes sir?" when his name was called but when Uncle Fill didn't pay any attention to him he shut his eyes and seemed to go to sleep. Uncle Tubby bent over, as if he were going to pick up something off the ground. When he straightened up his face was red, his eyes shone. He looked at Daddy but Daddy kept on making marks with his stick and would not look at him. Mama began talking fast:

"Then you don't really believe in the Virgin Birth, Uncle Fill?"

Uncle Fill looked at her for a second. "I'd like to," he said, "I'd *like* to! The best in the world!"

He had got his handkerchief out and was wiping his forehead. His clothes were dry except for a few places under his armpits and the deep folds where his legs joined on to his stomach. His face was getting redder all the time. Lucy imagined that a little steam rose from the spots on his clothes that were still damp. "I'm glad he's not a tea-kettle," she thought. "I'd hate to drink out of him."

He snapped his handkerchief out tight between his hands, then draped it over one knee. *"Now!"* he said. "Let us suppose this prophecy was true. I don't believe it for a moment, but let us suppose it was true."

Daddy's lips moved. Lucy thought he was saying ". . . for the sake of argument." But Mama began talking again.

"Of course everybody isn't as intelligent as you or me, Uncle Fill, but nevertheless, I think it's a good thing for people to have a religion. I don't think people get along very well without any religion at all. . . ."

Uncle Fill would not even look at her. "God Almighty gave me my intellect," he said, "and He expects me to use it. But what does the author of the Gospel of Matthew use *his* intellect for? For glozening and cozening, forsooth! He says that all this dreaming and going on was in order that it might be fulfilled which was spoken of the Lord by the prophet Isaiah, saying: 'Behold, a virgin shall conceive, and shall bring forth a son, and they shall call his name Immanuel, which, being interpreted, is *God with us*. . . . He shall eat butter and honey.' "

"That butter and honey," Uncle Tubby said, "what do you make of that butter and honey, Mr. Fayerlee?"

But Uncle Fill would not pay attention to him, either. He looked at Daddy who was bent over making a kind of moaning sound as he marked on the ground with his stick. "You notice that this prophecy wasn't spoken *by* the Lord," Uncle Fill said. "It was spoken *of* the Lord, by his prophet Isaiah. The first we know of Isaiah he comes on the scene, ranting and roaring, making his bowels to sound like a harp, saying the Lord is speaking. . . . *Who* was the Lord speaking to through the prophet Isaiah? Ahaz, king of Judah. . . . Pekah, king of Israel and Rezin, king of Syria, had joined themselves to make war on Ahaz and Ahaz and his people were alarmed. The Bible says that their hearts were moved as the trees of the wood are moved with the wind. . . ."

"You know, that's *good*!" Uncle Tubby said.

". . . They wanted to know which side was going to win," Uncle Fill said, without even looking at Uncle Tubby. "So Isaiah took two faithful witnesses, Uriah, the priest, and

Zecheriah, the son of Jerebechiah, and went and lay with the prophetess. As a rule, a man don't want any witness when he's out on business of this kind, but Isaiah took two men along with him when he went to lie with the prophetess. . . ."

Uncle Tubby said a French word that sounded like *"Voyeur!"* Mama showed her teeth at him.

". . . We are not told the name of the prophetess," Uncle Fill said, "but we are told what the name of the child of that union was. The Lord told Isaiah to call him Maher-shallal-hashbaz. That's what He told him to call him, and He said that before that child was old enough to cry 'Mammy' or 'Daddy' Ahaz should be delivered from the danger with which he was threatened.

"Before that child was old enough to cry the name of his father or mother! To come true the prophecy had to be fulfilled within a year, or even less than a year—some children talk at eight months. . . ."

"Girls," Mama said, "girls talk earlier than boys. . . ."

"How then could the prophecy have anything to do with a child born seven hundred years later?" Uncle Fill said. "I ask you that."

Nobody said anything. Daddy suddenly put the stick down and stood up. At that Uncle Fill hitched his chair forward. "What's more," he said, "what's more, the word translated 'virgin' in Isaiah don't mean virgin at all, but merely a young woman. 'Behold a young woman is with child and beareth a son.' That's mighty different from a *virgin* bearing a son. Isaiah's not the first man to get in trouble with a woman and lay it on somebody else. Only most men'll lay it on another *man*. Isaiah's not content with that. The impudent scoundrel has to lay it on the Lord!

"Did human presumption ever reach farther? But that's the way it goes. All through the Old Testament you'll find man cutting the Almighty down to his own stature. One minute the Lord'll be telling 'em to exterminate a whole nation, the next minute he'll be giving minute directions how to butcher and roast a he-goat: the fat and the caul are to be burned on the altar, but the flesh and the hide have got to be burned outside the camp. And they got to put frankincense and oil on it. You reckon Almighty God is going to worry about how you season a kid! Sylvester here's grandfather was the best barbecuer we ever had. Took him two whole days to make his sauce. But God Almighty's time is more valuable than Uncle Aaron's. He established the firmament and divided the waters. He ain't going to bother himself about how you cook a he-goat —or a she-goat, either."

Mama stood up. "Sylvester, how long has Uncle Aaron been dead?"

Sylvester opened his eyes. "Pappy been dead ten years, I reckon."

"Do you have that recipe for his sauce?"

"No'm. But Sister know how he made it."

"Steve, give me a quarter," Mama said. When Daddy had given it to her she walked over and handed it to Sylvester. "That's for the stamps," she said. "Now you get your sister to tell you how he made it and you write it down and send it to me. Will you? You know what my name is now?"

"No'm."

"Mrs. Stephen Lewis, Route Six, Gloversville. . . . Now, Sylvester, you won't forget?"

"No'm."

" 'T won't do any good," Uncle Fill said. "You got to have hickory to barbecue right and anybody got any hickory these days ain't going to cut it down just to make a barbecue fire. . . . I tell you, the man that can swallow the God of the Old Testament has got a strong stomach. And if we can't put any credence in the Old Testament how we going to put any credence in the New?"

Daddy had been standing with his face half turned away from Uncle Fill, staring at the ground. "That's right," he said and leaned over and took Uncle Fill's hand up off his knee and shook it and put it back again. "Well, we got to be going now, Uncle Fill," he said. "You come to see us," and he walked off toward the car.

"Don't go!" Uncle Fill cried. *"Don't go!* Why, you hardly got here! Sylvester, you step up to the house and see if Aunt Maria ain't got any cake. This little Miss here'd like some cake. . . ."

"I don't want any *cake*," Lucy said.

"We've *got* to go," Mama said. "Really, we've *got* to, Uncle Fill." She leaned over and kissed him on the forehead. Uncle Tubby said, "That was mighty inter*est*ing," and shook hands with Uncle Fill, then walked off after Daddy, who was in the car by this time. Lucy ran after them. Daddy had the motor running and drove off very fast as soon as Mama got in. Lucy did not realize until after she was in the car that she hadn't told Uncle Fill goodbye but Mama did not seem to notice it. She had turned around and was looking at Uncle Tubby who was doubled up on the back seat. Uncle Tubby straightened up.

"Cozening and glozening," he said. "Forsooth!"

"It's funny the first time you hear it," Daddy said.

Uncle Tubby was still laughing, but Mama didn't laugh. "You could make something nice out of him for *Now*," she said, ". . . 'In Montgomery county, Tennessese, the citizens all go barefooted. . . .' "

". . . 'And have their body servants trained to pour a bucket of cold water over them every hour' . . . Is that his own idea, or *is* it a custom?"

"He's been doing it ever since I can remember," Mama said, "but then he's the only person I ever knew that did it." She had turned around and was looking straight ahead of her. You could tell just by the set of her shoulders that she was mad. She turned to Daddy. "I don't care," she said, "I think it was mean of you. You never said one single word the whole time. I think it was *mean*!"

"How could I have got a word in?" Daddy asked.

"He'd have stopped talking a minute if you'd ever said anything. But you never said a word. A single word. I think it's damned mean. That's what I think it is. . . . Damned mean!"

"Forsooth!" Uncle Tubby said.

"I can't take it," Daddy said, "I just can't take it."

"It isn't as if you had to take it every day," Mama said. "My God! You don't see him sometimes for months."

"It's something about his voice," Daddy said. "As soon as I hear it I feel as if I'd been hearing it for years. And I feel as if it would go on for years. . . . I tell you, I just can't take it. There are some things I can't take. That's one of them."

"You can't take anything that puts you out the least little bit," Mama said.

"I thought you did awfully well, Sally," Uncle Tubby said quickly. "I had no idea you were such a staunch little churchwoman."

"Somebody had to do something," Mama said. She looked at Daddy again. "The poor, lonesome old thing! He never used to sit down at the big road like that when Aunt Mattie was alive. He just can't stand it up at the house. That's why he sits down there."

"Lurks," Daddy said, "like a fat spider so he can hand out that baloney to anybody that comes along. He'll make a teamster get down off his wagon so he can harangue him about the

Holy Ghost. It's a fact. Joe Crenfew told me he sent one of his hands in to town for some fertilizer and the man didn't get home till nearly dark. Said Mr. Fayerlee made him stop."

"It's been so awful for him ever since Uncle Tom died," Mama said.

"Was Uncle Tom hipped on the Virgin Birth, too?" Uncle Tubby asked.

"That's all either of them cared anything about. Uncle Tom believed in it. At least he said he did. I always wondered."

"If both of them had disbelieved it they couldn't have had any arguments," Daddy said.

"Anyhow, Uncle Tom taught in Sunday School. He was raised an Episcopalian—everybody in this country who took any interest in religion turned Methodist or Baptist or Campbellite or something in the forties. . . ."

"You mean to say that if you didn't turn Methodist or Baptist or Campbellite that showed you had no interest in religion?" Daddy asked.

"That's just what I said. . . . Anyhow, Uncle Tom turned Methodist in his old age. . . ."

"So he could teach in the Sunday School," Daddy said.

"Yes, it was so handy. Right at his front gate. In fact, he gave them the land to build the church on. . . . And every Sunday morning, just before it was time for him to go to church Uncle Fill would send a Negro boy over with a note. . . ."

"Aspersing the Virgin Birth?" Uncle Tubby asked.

"Yes. Then when church was over Uncle Tom would get in his buggy and drive over to Uncle Fill's and they'd eat a good dinner and then sit out in the yard all evening, arguing. . . ."

"Sounds like a pretty good life," Uncle Tubby said.

"Yes," Mama said, sighing, "but it's all over now. Hardly anybody in the neighborhood now cares anything about the Virgin Birth. . . . Uncle Fill was so happy when Steve first came. . . ."

"I can't take it," Daddy said. "I just can't take it!"

"I know you can't," Mama said, "but it would be nice if you *could*." She turned around and looked down the road. "I wonder what's become of the Reardons?"

"I wish they'd been along," Uncle Tubby said. "I'd like for Kev to have heard that. Think of the heights the old boy'd have risen to if he'd had a Papist in the audience!"

Daddy shivered. "The Lord occasionally shows mercy, even in these degenerate days," he said. "We'd better wait for 'em," he added. "They won't know the turn."

They sat in the bend of the road and waited. It was not as cool along here as it had been back beside the spring, but it was cooler than it was in most places at this time of day. That was because the shade was so thick. The branches of the trees almost met over the road. Mama had her head thrown back and was gazing up into them. "It's heavenly along here when the locusts are in bloom," she said. "Steve, let's be sure and drive out here next spring when the locusts are in bloom."

"All right," Daddy said.

"What I like about Uncle Fill is the scale of his operations," Uncle Tubby said. "Now that crack about the impudent scoundrel laying it on the Lord. That's pretty good, you know. . . ."

"The doctor had a keener sense of humor than Uncle Fill," Daddy said. "Honey, tell him about Ananias."

Mama had turned around again and was looking back up the road. "Ananias was a Negro man worked for Uncle Tom, had a lot of children. Uncle Tom told him that if his wife had any more children it would kill her, but Ananias came in one day and told him that she was pregnant again. Uncle Tom gave him the devil, but Ananias said: 'It's the Lord's will, Doctor.' 'Lord's will!' Uncle Tom said. 'Don't you hand me any of that foolishness. The Lord never had but one child, himself.' "

"That's what I mean," Uncle Tubby said. "They don't fool around with trifles. Everything on a big scale. Cosmic humor, what?"

"It's humorous, all right—the first time you hear it," Daddy said.

Lucy watched two birds that had squatted down and were fluttering their wings in the soft dust of the road. They were brownish, with black bars on their backs and scarlet necks. Occasionally, as they fluttered, they turned and spoke to each other, soft chirps, subdued, it seemed, by their knowledge of the presence of human beings. "Wick . . . wick . . . wick . . ." from the woods on the other side of the road came the same sound, louder and punctuated every now and then by a cry that was almost a squeal. Screened from them by the honeysuckle but only a few hundred yards away up the road was the gate that led into Mr. Warfleet's place.

Borcke was sleeping again. She rolled him over on her mother's lap so she could lean out and watch the birds. But they were already flying away. The sound of a car coming along the road had startled them.

They waited until the Reardon car came abreast of theirs. Mrs. Reardon leaned out, smiling. "I'm *so* sorry!" she said.

"Did you go over a bridge?" Mama asked.

"Yes. A long, covered bridge."

"Oh, Lord!" Mama said. "The Red River bridge. Steve, they went over the Red River bridge."

"We ought to have waited for them," Daddy said. "Well,

come on now." And he drove a little way down the road and turned in at Mr. Warfleet's gate.

When they had come here before it had been by another way. For all their talk, Lucy had not been sure until this moment that this was the road to Warfleets'. But there was the same gate, a fancy kind that you could open without getting out of the car. And on the other side of the gate, at the end of the sandy drive, the little white, one-storey house, surrounded by its picket fence. Inside that fence there was another, smaller yard: Mrs. Warfleet's rose garden. She had had that yard made when Mr. Warfleet started raising mules. A mule could wrap his tongue around an oak tree and pull it up if he wanted to, she said. It took two fences to stop any mule, and then you had to watch him.

The larger enclosure, through which they were now driving, was the biggest pasture Mr. Warfleet had and the one he used the most, because it had the best water. They were approaching the pond: on the left hand side of the road, beneath an embankment, long, rather than round; Mr. Warfleet had made it himself, with a steam shovel. On the other side of the pond there was a grove of locust trees. It was full of dark figures, some upright, some recumbent; the horses and mules always gathered there in the shade during the heat of the day.

"There she is!" Daddy said and Lucy, slowly turning her eyes, glimpsed between the black rumps of two mules, the round barrel, the forward-pricked ears, the white-starred, Arabian head.

The pony stood with her head half turned away, her eyes shut; she had fallen asleep, chewing on a long blade of grass. There was a patch of white on her chest and another big splotch on each side of her barrel, but her head and neck were dark brown, almost black. Her nostrils were dun-colored.

They swelled in and out, gently, with each breath. Saliva, mixed with the green juice of the grass blade, dribbled from her soft lower lip.

Mama suddenly laid her hand on Lucy's arm. "Be sure and thank him," she said.

"Who?"

"Mr. Reardon. He's the one that's giving you the pony."

Lucy sat quiet, staring into the grove. The locust trunks that a moment ago had all been standing still were racing beside the car so fast that they all ran together. Daddy had slowed down so that they could look at the pony, but now he was resuming speed. Slowly, cautiously, she lowered her eyes to the water. It was the color of blood, mixed with dirt. A big burdock, growing on the bank, was actually red half way up its stout stem. Ponds were always that color. It was the red clay in them . . . If she were to turn her head now she might still catch through those thin, racing trunks, among all the dark forms, a glimpse of white and brown. But she would not turn her head. There was no use looking back now.

Had he known, when they walked about out there in the yard, and he asked her about the crucifix, had he known then that this would happen? Had he known all along? His eyes had been so dark and yet so bright! He knew something that she didn't know. Was this it?

Her mother was pointing across the fields to Uncle Fill's tall, grey house. There were locust trees about it, too, and an avenue of ragged locusts ran through the brown field to the gate.

"He always had a pony for me to ride when I went out there," Sarah said. "And they made icecream every day. In a two-gallon freezer." She sighed. "Aunt Mattie hated locusts so!"

"Why?" Uncle Tubby asked.

"So brittle. She always had the branches picked up after every storm. I don't suppose he's had 'em cleaned up since she died." Her body suddenly stiffened. Lucy was aware that she was looking down at her hands which lay clasped in her lap. "Lucy," she said quietly, "did you hear what I said?"

"Yes ma'am."

"And you'll thank Mr. Reardon as soon as we get out of the car?"

"Yes'm."

Sarah sighed again and turned her head toward Uncle Tubby who was leaning forward, his arms folded on the back of the front seat.

"When my mother was a little girl her father took her and her sister to a hotel in Nashville," she said. "They had never been in a hotel before and they thought it would be something out of this world. When they had bread pudding for dessert they took it up and threw it at each other. . . ."

"What did your grandfather say?"

"He said, 'Ain't chillun funny?' "

"It's joy," Uncle Tubby said in a low voice. "It stupefies."

Lucy turned her head to look at him. In that instant his eyes met hers. He winked at her. She looked away. Lois was right, she thought. His nose was too big for the rest of his face. It made him look topheavy, even a little foolish, particularly when he was laughing. He was laughing now but then he was always laughing or just about to laugh. She wondered how it was that he always found something to laugh at.

Daddy halted the car under a big sugar tree. They got out and walked across an oval of dusty grass toward the gate. The branches of the sugar tree swept so low that until this moment none of them had seen the half-grown boy who sat on the horse block, whittling. As they approached he laid his knife down and stared at them unwinkingly.

Uncle Tubby did not seem to see the boy even yet. His head tilted back, he was staring at the house. "Isn't it *neat*!" he said.

"Yes," Mama said. "Such a contrast to Uncle Fill's."

"I'd like to see the inside of his."

"I'm sure you would," Mama said. "Would you like to go there tomorrow?"

"Tomorrow?" he said. "I may have to leave tomorrow."

"Oh . . ." she said, "too bad."

Daddy had stopped in front of the boy. "Is Mr. Warfleet at home?"

"Yes, sir."

"Where is he?"

"I think he's in the stable lot. But he might be in the house, taking a nap."

"Will you go and tell him that Mr. and Mrs. Lewis are here to see him about the pony?"

The boy had rust-colored hair that curled over his forehead and forward around his ears; his face was freckled all over. He said "Yes, sir" again, slipped his knife into his pocket and went through the gate around the corner of the house.

"The son and heir?" Uncle Tubby asked.

"Named Earl. Looks like a limb to me," Daddy said.

"Doubtless the present owner of the pony. Do you suppose he's reconciled to parting with it?"

"That boy's too big to ride that pony," Daddy said.

He went over to where the others stood, talking about what time tomorrow the Reardons would leave. Lucy walked over to the horse block. It was just a big rock out of the fields. Somebody had driven an iron rod right through the middle of it. A horse's head was mounted on the rod. The horse was snorting; one of his nostrils still showed a little red. Lucy sat down on a shelving edge of the rock. The dust at her feet was drier than the dust on the river road. And if you looked out over the pasture the grass was all burned brown. The road coiled along through the brown, burned grass like a big snake. Little spurts of dust kept rising on each side of the snake. The Reardons had passed through the gate and were driving toward the house. She became aware that her mother had left the others and was standing beside her.

"Lucy," Sarah said in a low voice, "do you want that pony?"

Lucy looked up. Her mother's eyes, looking down into hers, were the same dark, demanding eyes that they had ever been.

"Yes," Lucy said, "I want it."

"Well, stand up, then, and tell him so," Sarah whispered fiercely.

"All right," Lucy said and got up.

He was helping Mrs. Reardon out of the car. She had started walking toward them, across the dusty grass, but he stood, one hand on the door, his head a little bent, gazing at the ground.

He did not seem to know that Lucy was coming toward him until she stood directly in front of him. He started, then, and pushed the door to and leaned toward her, smiling. She had dreaded his bright gaze. She had thought that when it enveloped her she would be lost. But she found that she could look into his eyes without flinching. Their glance today was clouded and seemed to flow over and around her, without encompassing her. His brows drew together. Even as he smiled, he was frowning a little, as if he were having a hard time remembering who she was. "I'm sorry we held things up," he said.

She could not answer that. She said only: "Thank you for the pony," and held out her hand. He took it in both his own and gave it a quick squeeze before he let it drop. "Where is the pony?" he asked.

"Here comes Mr. Warfleet now," Daddy said.

Mr. Warfleet was coming around the corner of the house, with Earl behind him. He was a tall, thin man with black hair and bright blue eyes. The other time they came here he had been wearing a seersucker suit, like anybody else, but today he had on overalls. His big farm hat was clapped on to the back of his head. He was chewing on a sassafras twig.

"Well, Mr. Warfleet, here we are back again," Daddy said.

"Come on in," Mr. Warfleet said, "come on in the house." And he swung the gate wider open, stepping back a little.

"Oh, Mr. Warfleet, we'd love to," Mama said, "but we have to be getting along. We thought we'd just take another look at the pony."

Mr. Warfleet stepped through the gate, letting it swing to behind him. "Earl," he said and jerked his head back over his shoulders toward the boy who had come up silently behind him. "Earl, go get me the bridle. And three, four ears of corn, Might as well bring the saddle, too."

Daddy introduced Mr. Warfleet to the visitors. They had started walking across the pasture toward the grove when Mr. Warfleet paused, looking down at Mrs. Reardon's white, high-laced sandals. "This old field's hard on ladies' shoes," he said.

She smiled at him. "They're made for walking," she said.

"Well, God knows there's no mud," Daddy said. "Mr. Warfleet, I reckon you been praying for rain?"

"This old pasture here *is* about burned up," Mr. Warfleet said, "but I got me a stand of bluegrass in the north pasture looks like no drought can touch. And one thing, we ain't going to run out of water. You know this land around here is all limestone, Mr. Lewis."

"That means there's water under most of it, don't it?" Daddy said.

"I been watching the water circulating underground around here for forty years," Mr. Warfleet said, "and it stays about the same, take it up one side and down the other. If a pond dries up on my place a new pond'll come on Mister Fill's. One year one of my ponds started drying up. Same time a wet spot, size of a dollar, came in the middle of his sixty-acre field. I used to walk over there every two, three days just to watch it. Started in February. By August he had him a pond half the size of that one over there. Had a bad drought that year. I just turned my stock right in on him. 'I don't owe you any thanks for watering 'em,' I told him, 'It was my water when it started out. . . .' "

"How many mules you got now?" Daddy asked.

"I got thirty head of mules. And two, three mares. And the best jack in this country."

"How you going to pasture 'em if the drought don't break?"

"Oh, I could sit down and worry if I took a notion to," Mr. Warfleet said, "but I'm a man that raises mules for a living . . . Mr. Lewis, a man that raises mules has got the advantage over other men."

Daddy laughed. "You mean he's prepared for anything?"

"He's prepared for the *worst,*" Mr. Warfleet said. "Yes sir, a man that takes to raising mules had better prepare himself, right at the start . . ."

Mama had walked up beside them. "I *love* mules," she said, "I always have . . . Mr. Warfleet, I bet you like 'em better than horses."

"I don't see how anybody could *like* a mule," Mr. Warfleet said, "when you come down to it. But I'm used to 'em. . . . Now, my wife, looks like she just can't get used to 'em. Says she don't know as she'd have married me if she'd known I was going to persist in raising mules. 'You can't say I tricked you,' I told her. Mr. Lewis, I had me eleven head of mules when I was nineteen years of age, two years before I was married."

They walked on toward the grove, their shadows racing ahead of them. Mr. Warfleet, first, and Mama with Daddy on each side of him, then Mrs. Reardon, with Uncle Tubby and Mr. Reardon on each side of her. Lucy had been walking beside Mrs. Reardon when they started out but now she fell a little behind as she walked more slowly.

She was thinking of the water that ran beneath their feet, deep underground, water on whose waves no sun ever glinted, no human eye ever rested, and yet it flowed ceaselessly from one cavern to another, until the very earth over which they moved was borne upward on its dark flood. But the earth itself was dry, the grass so burnt that it made a rustling sound under your feet. And in all the pasture there was no shade, except along the fence rows and under those trees where you did not like to look. Deliberately, she raised her head and stared into the grove.

A few of the mules, startled by their approach, were already moving off, but the pony and the old bay mare stood still and gazed at them. Lucy, as she went forward over the burnt grass, gazed back.

She had thought, a while ago, when her mother told her that it was he who was giving her the pony that that could not be, that something, somehow, would happen to prevent it, that she herself might be able to do something to prevent it, but she had not been able to think of anything to do and nothing had happened and the moment had passed. And now, as she walked over the brown grass, other moments were passing. That was the strange thing: how time went on as if everything had not changed. Nothing would ever be the same. She knew that now. But everything would go on as if nothing had happened, and she would forget what she had done, as they forgot the dark water that they had not ever seen and never would see that at this moment flowed on beneath their feet. She would forget. She could see that now. There would be long stretches of time, whole days, weeks, even, when she would not remember at all, she told herself, moving steadily forward over the famished grass.

A shadow fell athwart hers. Earl was walking beside her. His right hand held the little McClellan saddle and bridle up behind his back. The left hand, dangling, held three ears of corn, looped together by their shucks.

"Will she come to you?" she asked.

"If you give her an ear of corn she'll come," he said.

She felt his eyes glancing sidewise on her face and turned her head to look at him. His eyes were rust-colored, like his hair. In that instant when he had glanced at her something that she had not seen before had flickered in them, but it was gone now, like a mouse which you see out of the tail of your eye only as it is vanishing.

Her mother was looking around to see where she was. She hurried and caught up with the others. Mr. Warfleet was telling how he had got his start in mules. ". . . an old blood mare from Mr. Fill. Name of Daphne. Got some of that stock yet. Every one of 'em's a pacer. . . ." He stopped and snatching one of the ears of corn from Earl brandished it at a big sorrel mule that was coming toward them. "Git!" he yelled. "Git away from here, John!"

"Mr. Warfleet, is it true that you have to talk to mules differently from horses?" Uncle Tubby asked.

"Of course," Mama said. "You say 'Whoa!' to a horse, but nobody but a fool would say 'Whoa' to a mule."

The mule had moved off a little way, but now he stopped again. His ears were laid a little back. His nostrils quivered. His big, black eyes were fixed on the ear of corn.

"You got to say more'n 'Whay' to a mule," Mr. Warfleet said. "Anything you say to a mule you got to back it up. The difference between a horse and a mule is a horse, he ain't thinking all the time, but a mule he's thinking all the time and he ain't ever thinking of but one thing: how he knows better'n you do. . . . Look at that son of a gun!" He ran forward a few steps. "John," he said in a low, savage tone, "if you don't git away from here I'm going to bust your head wide open. YOU HEAR ME?" And he flung his arm out as if the ear of corn were a missile that he was about to hurl at the mule.

The mule let out a squeal and cantered off around the side of the pond. Another mule that had been standing behind the pony and the bay mare took off over the fields, too. The pony and the bay mare moved forward a little.

"Well, there she is!" Mr. Warfleet said. "Cu . . . up! . . . Cu . . . up!" and he held the ear of corn out before him.

The pony turned her head and glanced at the mare, then her thick, dark lashes veiled her eyes, and she stepped demurely forward. The mare followed her. At that two or three mules and an old grey horse moved forward, too.

"Look at that now, would you?" Mr. Warfleet said. "Everywhere she goes on this place everything follows her. . . . That pony's of considerable use around here."

"You don't mean to say you ever work her?" Daddy asked.

"No, but she's a lot of use to toll the other stock. You know how they'll follow anything spotted."

"How old did you say she was?" Daddy asked.

"Around ten, ain't it?" He glanced at his son. "When'd we get her from Sadlers', Earl?"

"She's ten years old," Earl said. "She was four when we got her."

"That's right, Earl rode her to school four years. Now he's started going in to town to high school we been lending her out. Billy Robinson rode her to school all last winter . . ."

The pony was standing directly in front of him now, the mare just behind her. He slowly raised the ear of corn until it was on a level with her nose. Her soft nostrils quivered. Her head sank. Suddenly her lips parted and she snatched the ear of corn from Mr. Warfleet's hand at the same moment that he reached out his long right arm and caught hold of her foretop. "Ho, there, now!" he said and motioned to Earl who came forward and, taking the ear of corn away from the pony, slipped the bit between her teeth and the bridle over her ears.

Mr. Warfleet threw another ear of corn down on the ground before the pony and tossed the other ear at the old mare.

"Saddle her, Earl," he said.

The pony had lowered her head and was grinding the corn between her teeth. As Earl fastened the saddle girth, she put her ears back a little and heaved her sleek sides out.

"Uh-uh!" Mama said. "I hate a horse to swell up when you try to cinch the girth."

"Don't mean anything," Mr. Warfleet said, "she's gentle as can be."

He stepped toward Lucy, lifted her in his long, lean arms and set her on the pony, and gathered up the reins and put them in her hand. "You want to ride her along the road?" he asked.

"All right," Lucy said, and took up the reins. The pony tossed her head and stepped off along the path by the pond. Uncle Tubby ran beside the pony. Lucy looked beyond him at the other faces that hung now on a level with her own, moved slowly forward. Her mother had stopped watching her and was gazing off over the fields. Her father was looking straight at her and smiling. Mr. Reardon was smiling, too.

She let her hand fall slant-wise on the pony's rump and at the same time gripped the round belly with her legs. "Clllkk!" she said, "Clllkk!" and drew her right leg up toward the saddle involuntarily as a tremor ran through her whole body. . . . She had not meant to raise her leg so high; her stirrup had actually grazed the pony's flank. She was straightening up to thrust her feet deeper into the stirrups when she felt herself leaving the saddle and the brown ground came up to meet her with a thud and they were all standing there talking at once.

Daddy's face was closest. He said: *"Baby!"* When he picked her up in his arms the jangling got worse. Fire crackers were still going off in her head.

"The little devil. . . . I thought *when she put her head down . . .* No! *She's just lost her breath. . . . It would take more than that to knock* her *out. . . . But she* is *white. . . . All right,* all right, *why don't you go and get the car, then?"*

She shut her eyes. Daddy's arms tightened about her. "You're all right," he was saying. "You're all right. They'll be here with the car in a minute."

There were fewer fire crackers now and they went off more slowly. She kept her eyes shut as her breath eased in and out. The splintering pains had left her head, but her chest burned, as if all the breath that the earth had knocked out had come back on fire. She waved her legs and struggled feebly in her father's embrace. "I'm all right," she whispered.

He set her on the ground, then put his arm about her shoulders and held her up against him. "See?" he said. "There comes Uncle Tubby now with the car."

Uncle Tubby was halting the car on the road just opposite

the pond. "Can you walk?" her father asked. "Don't you want me to carry you?"

"I can walk," she said and they started over to the car.

Mama went in front, with Mr. Warfleet. He kept shaking his head. "It was touching her in the flank did it. . . . Somebody must have taught that pony to buck like that." He turned around sharply. "Earl, did you ever see that pony buck before?"

"I saw her buck Billy Robinson off once," Earl said, "but I didn't think anything of it."

Mama turned her head, too, to stare at him. "The pony is *ruined*," she said coldly. "Nobody would feel safe to give a pony like that to a child."

"Not to a little girl," Mr. Warfleet said. "Nobody don't care much what happens to boys, but girls are different."

They were at the car. Uncle Tubby got out. Daddy helped Lucy in, and went around to the other side and got into the driver's seat. The Reardons had started walking back to their car. Uncle Tubby followed them. Mama held her hand out to Mr. Warfleet. "Goodbye. We'd better get this child home as soon as we can."

He shook his head again. "I wouldn't a had you waste your time coming out here, Mrs. Lewis, if I'd known she was going to buck like that."

"It wasn't your fault," Mama said. "Goodbye." And they started off.

"I hope he tans that Earl's hide," Daddy said.

"I believe he will," Mama said. "He had a kind of a glint in his eye. And you noticed that Earl took off on the pony without saying anything to any of us."

Lucy lay back, feeling her mother's and father's shoulders on each side of her. There was an ache in her chest, and her legs were still trembly, but otherwise she felt as she always did.

She turned her head to look back over the pasture. Earl was cantering about on the pony, rounding up other stock.

Mama saw her looking after them. "That's not the only pony in the world, Lucy," she said. "You're going to get another pony. You know that, don't you?"

"All right," Lucy said and set her face toward the gate.

"Little scoundrel!" Daddy said. "Probably spent months training her to buck like that."

"Let's don't talk about it any more," Mama said.

They passed through the gate, leaving it open for the Reardons, and drove on down the road. When they got to Uncle Fill's gate the other car drove up beside them. Uncle Tubby leaned out.

"How's Lucy feeling?" he asked.

"She's fine," Mama said.

"You don't want to stop by Uncle Fill's for just a minute, then?" He winked at Lucy. "I thought I might get some ideas on how to train Pompey. The scoundrel has been giving me a lot of trouble lately."

Mama looked at Daddy. "Tubby wants to take a look at Uncle Fill's squalor at closer range," she said. "Do you think you could stand a few minutes of it?"

"I don't want to gloat over the old gentleman," Tubby said, "but I must admit that his way of life fascinates me."

Daddy looked at Mama. "I've had enough of him for one day," he said. "Why don't you stop with Tubby?"

"I have to get Lucy home," Mama said.

"You're not going to carry her home on your back," Daddy said, "and I can take care of her after we get there. . . . You feel all right now, don't you, Lucy?"

"Yes, I do," Lucy said.

Mama bent over her. "Lucy, will you lie down as soon as

you get home? Even if you don't feel like it. Will you do that? Just to please Mama?"

"Yes."

"Promise?"

"Yes."

Mama got out and went over to the other car. The Reardons had not said a word all this time. Mrs. Reardon just sat, looking straight ahead and smiling. But Mr. Reardon's eyes had been going from one face to the other while they were talking. He got out of his car and came over to theirs. He looked at his watch. "It's half past five," he said. "I have to be in town before six o'clock. Steve, could you drop me as you go in?"

"That's right," Daddy said and put his arm around Lucy's shoulders and drew her over closer to him. Mama got out. Mr. Reardon got in. They drove off.

Daddy drove fast. Nobody said anything until they got to town. When they turned in to Jamison street Mr. Reardon looked at his watch and said, "Could you drop me at the church?"

"Sure," Daddy said and turned right on Glover and went past the tobacco warehouses and down toward Vinegar Bottom, where the colored people lived. The Catholic church stood on a little hill, just above the colored section. Lois said it was out there because nobody went to it except shanty Irish and the Verdiers. They were Catholics because their grandfather had come from France and didn't know any better.

The church was wood, instead of brick or stone, like the other churches. There was a cross on top of it and another little house joined on to it and, a little way off, another building that Lucy thought must be the Catholic school.

The car stopped. Mr. Reardon was getting out. "Don't wait," he said. "I'll take a cab."

Daddy laughed. "How long'll it take you?"

Mr. Reardon looked at him and laughed, too. "Five or ten minutes," he said. "But there might be a line ahead of me. Wait a second, will you?" He went up the concrete walk and disappeared into the church, then came out and walked a few steps toward them. "There's only one person ahead of me," he called. "Want to wait?"

"Sure," Daddy said, "go ahead."

Lucy watched Mr. Reardon go back up the walk. A little girl in a blue-checked dress was coming out of the door, holding a smaller child by the hand. He took off his hat and stood aside while they passed through, then he, too, passed through and the door shut behind him.

Lucy stared at the arched door. When it had opened a moment ago it had been on darkness, but something bright had glinted through the gloom. The altar, probably. She, herself, had never been in a Catholic Church—except in France and she had been too young then to remember what she had seen, except sometimes when it all seemed as if it might come back to her at any moment, though it never did—but Lois had gone to the Catholic church once with Anne Verdier and had described some of the things that were on the altar. There were more than in the Presbyterian church, she said; some of them were gold. Was Mr. Reardon praying in there at the foot of the altar or just talking to the priest? And what was he saying?

She laid her hand on her father's arm. "Daddy, what's he doing in there?"

Her father started and fixed her face with unseeing eyes. His own face, in that instant, was so haggard, so drawn that she thought she knew how he would look when he was old. "God knows," he said and groaned, so loud that a Negro man, starting down the path to Vinegar Bottom, paused and stood still in the bright light to stare at them.

XIII

WHEN they got home Lucy went to her own room while her father went downstairs. Lucy lay down on the bed, as she had promised Mama to do. On the way home, sitting between her father and Mr. Reardon, with nobody saying anything and the countryside flying by so fast, she had grown drowsy and had thought that as soon as she got to the house she would take a nap. But now that she was here in her own room, lying on her own bed, she could not sleep.

On the other side of the door that separated their two rooms she could hear Mr. Reardon walking back and forth. She fancied that every time he came abreast of the door his steps grew slower. She felt sure that he would not open the door without knocking but there was nothing to keep his body from brushing against it as he turned. It was a thin door; the rickety old-fashioned latch would give at the slightest pressure. If she looked away for even a second it might fly open.

At any moment he might be standing there, gazing at her.

She lay on her back, staring at the white, paneled door, listening to the regular footfalls until her neck ached and her eyelids began to burn. She passed her hands wearily over her eyes, then sat up quietly in bed. The footfalls had ceased. Perhaps he was reading, or even lying down, as she was. She waited a few minutes. There were no sounds from the other side of the door. She got up and tiptoed out of the room and down the stairs to the first floor of the ell.

The door to her father's and mother's room was ajar. Her father lay in bed, smoking and reading the newspaper. A glass half full of whiskey stood on the table beside him. He was lifting it to his lips as Lucy came in.

She paused in the doorway. "Daddy, can I lie down by you?" she asked.

"Sure," he said and pushed the discarded sheets of newspaper aside to make room for her. "Been a rattling day, hasn't it?" he asked.

Lucy climbed up on the bed and stretched herself out beside him. "It sure has," she said with a sigh.

He reached over and patted her on the stomach. "They'll be gone tomorrow," he said.

She turned on her side and thrust her left hand under the cool pillow. The room was quiet except for their breaths and the rustle the newspaper leaves made as he turned them. You could hear Jenny's footsteps out in the kitchen. An aroma of vanilla floated in to mingle with the smells of whiskey and tobacco. Lucy wondered what they were having for dinner and as she wondered felt her lids drooping and knew that she would go to sleep now.

She awoke, feeling that there was some change in the room and did not know what it was until she saw her mother standing before the dresser. She was wearing a long dress, the green one that had no back, and her silver necklace, and had just finished spraying her neck and arms with cologne.

"I wouldn't want to do it again," she said.

He laughed. "I tried to keep you from stopping."

"I didn't think," she said, "or rather, all I was thinking about was that they'd be gone tomorrow. I felt like I wanted to do anything they wanted while they were here. And *she* wanted to stop, too. At least she wanted to stop as soon as she realized that Kev would be going in the other car."

He folded the newspaper and laid it on the cover between him and Lucy. "She doesn't encourage Tubby," he said. "You've got to hand her that."

"Not overtly. But she's not the way she was when she came. You must have noticed *that*."

"What do you mean?" he asked, frowning.

She turned around. "That's what's having such an effect on *him*. You must have noticed."

"What do you mean?" he asked again.

"You remember how she was when she first came—sort of dreamy and preoccupied? But with herself. Now she comes out of her daze every now and then—long enough to pay some attention to him. That's what's driving him nuts."

"Do you think she does it deliberately?"

She shrugged her shoulders. "They're always cunning, aren't they?"

But he was not listening to her. He stared at the footboard that had a thing that looked like a dragon's head carved on it. "Poor fellow," he said. "It's hard to watch him."

"Well, why don't you do something? It looks like you *could* do something. After all, he's your best friend."

"That doesn't give me a right to interfere in his private affairs. Why doesn't Kev do something. Hell, she's *his* wife."

She came a step nearer the bed then stopped. "It's harder for him than you realize," she said. "The complications . . ."

"There are always complications," he said, "but after all, if the fellow wants to hold on to his wife . . ."

"It isn't a question of *keeping* her. . . ."

"That's what you think. Let me tell you now, Tubby's a mighty attractive fellow."

She stared at him before she answered. "Kev told me something else the other night," she said. "He didn't say *not* to tell it. I suppose I'd have told you then if you hadn't been so mean."

"I'm not being mean now," he said and smiled.

"No, but you wouldn't believe me now any more than you would then."

"I don't disbelieve in Kev's visions," he said, "but they are Kev's visions, not mine."

She turned away and took a lipstick from the top drawer of the dresser and leaning forward rouged her lips, then compressed them till they were nothing but a straight line. "I'm not going to tell you," she said. "But I *could* if I wanted to. I mean it wouldn't be dishonorable. I knew it without his telling me."

"Knew what, for God's sake?"

"Cousin Sybilla Morris," she said, "used to sit on the front porch and rock. . . . There was always a little cold place around her."

He had been half raised on his elbow but now he slid back on his pillow. "Merry Point occultism!" he said.

"That's right," she said.

There was a knock. Jenny thrust her head in through the half open door. "There ain't any cream for the car'mel pudding," she said.

"No *cream*?" Mama said.

"No'm. Ne'er a drop."

"Take the top off the night's milk, then," Mama said. "That's plenty rich enough for these Yankees."

"Ain't no night's milk. Mr. MacDonough, he ain't milked today. Morning or evening."

"You mean he hasn't milked *all* day?" Mama said. "That poor cow! . . . *Steve!*"

But Daddy was already swinging his feet to the floor. "It's the meeting," he said. "Got him all upset."

"It does look like he could milk. That's all they do for their rent. It does look like he could at least do that. And Mike is big enough to milk if he can't. . . . Jenny, how soon will supper be ready?"

"Hit's ready now."

"Well, hold it a minute," Daddy said and went out the door.

Lucy sat up. "Mama, have I got time to take a bath?"

Mama started. "I thought you were asleep."

"I was. . . . Have I got time to take a bath?"

"Yes, if you hurry," Mama said. "What do you want to wear? Your yellow dress?"

"No," Lucy said, "my blue," and had slid from the bed and was at the door when Mama told her to go on and take her bath, that she would go upstairs and get her dress for her.

She came back in a few minutes with Lucy's clean underwear and the blue dimity dress. She laid the clothes down on the bed instead of giving them to Lucy. "How would you like to have your dinner in bed?" she asked. "We could all come in here and have our drinks with you and then you could eat here in bed."

"I wouldn't like that," Lucy said. "Mama, there isn't anything the matter with me."

Mama laughed and bent down to hug her. "I reckon not,"

she said, "but you know you did hit that ground mighty hard. Well, go on and take your bath."

When Lucy had finished bathing and dressing she went into the dining room. It was empty. She heard voices and laughter on the gallery and went out there. The old deal table from the milk room stood at one end of the gallery, covered with a white cloth, with a big bowl of zinnias in the middle of it. The tray that they mixed the drinks on was sitting on the feed box. They were all sitting around the table drinking. As Lucy walked out Jenny came and stood in the doorway.

"All right, Jenny," Mama said, "let's go ahead without him." She looked down the hill where you could see the lanterns already glowing through the leaves of the brush arbor. "Down there talking Holy Roller theology!" she said. "I bet he's forgotten all about the milk."

Uncle Tubby looked at her. His eyes were shining. "He may not even be there," he said. "The Spirit may have taken a-holt of him and wafted him to regions far beyond the ken of the likes of us. Personally, I am convinced that such is the case. You must remember that he is a man of no ordinary talents. Consider the case of the prophet Elijah. There was another one, too, but I never could remember his name. . . ." Lucy sat down in the vacant chair beside him. She smelled the whiskey on his breath as he laid his arm along the back of the chair and leaned over her. "How do you feel?" he asked in a low voice.

"I feel all right," Lucy told him.

Jenny brought the big platter full of cold beef and set it before Mama and Mama helped them all to slices of beef. Jenny brought baked potatoes for everybody and a slice of beef for Lucy that was browner than the rest and set a big bowl of salad on the table and everybody helped themselves from that.

When Jenny brought the hot rolls Uncle Tubby turned around to look up at her. "Jenny," he said, "I've got to leave you."

Jenny was so surprised that she jumped. "Sir?" she said. "Yes sir? We shore do hate to see you go."

Mama stopped talking to Mr. Reardon about digging up bones in Greece. "Tomorrow?" she said. "Do you have to go tomorrow, too, Tubby?"

He nodded. "There's a man in New York I've got to see. Name of Johnson. I've got so I hate the fellow."

Mrs. Reardon had seemed to be listening to what Mr. Reardon was telling Mama but now she turned her head and looked at Uncle Tubby a second before she looked off over the river. The water was dark blue but there were so many stars reflected in it that it looked as if it had been sprinkled with silver powder, or as if the same stars that shone yellow when you looked up overhead had turned to silver when they fell into the water. A little way down the hill the lights from the brush arbor shone yellow, too, like stars come to earth.

Lucy stared at the river and thought of Undine. All the time they had been sitting here the water had been flowing around the hill, as it flowed past at all times, night or day. Daddy said that the Cumberland River flowed into the Ohio. He had seen the place at Cairo, Illinois, where the Ohio and the Mississippi ran side by side, the water in one river yellow, the water in one river blue, until they flowed together into the sea. All water flowed into the sea before it was through. This water that flowed past them now, laden with stars, was on its way to the sea. Undine's father was a mighty prince of the sea. Where had Undine gone when she vanished over the side of the boat? To live with her father in a crystal palace at the bottom of the sea? Or had she stayed in the forest, with her uncle, Kühleborn? . . . She would have had to stay in the forest, to be near the fountain—the fountain in the courtyard that she herself had had sealed with a stone slab.

Father Heilman, the priest who had married Undine and the Knight Huldbrand, had stayed on in the forest, too, in a hut that he had made for himself out of moss and brushwood. The knight's squire, riding past, had asked him what he was doing there since he refused to give his benediction to the knight's marriage to the false Bertalda. "It may be that I shall be needed for some other ceremony," he said. "There is little difference between wedding and weeping." The next day they took the stone off the fountain and a white pillar of water soared high into the air and took the form of a pale woman veiled in white. The knight, standing in meditation before a mirror, in his chamber, heard a light tapping on the door and thought that that was the way Undine used to tap on the door. "It is nothing but fancy. I must enter my bridal bed." . . . "Yes, you must, but a cold one!" And the door opened and the white figure came slowly toward him. . . . "I have wept him to death," she told the servants who met her in the ante-chamber and glided through the midst of the terror-stricken retainers to disappear into the fountain that was now her home.

Jenny was nudging her. "Lucy, ain't you going to eat your car'mel pudding?"

"I don't want it," Lucy said.

Mama looked up. "What's the matter with you? Aren't you hungry?"

"I was," Lucy said, "but I'm not any more. My goodness, Mama! You want to make a hog out of me?"

Uncle Tubby came out of the house, carrying a bottle of wine. "Sally, do you mind if I open this?"

Mama started. "Heavens, no. I always forget about wine; Steve doesn't like it. What is it?"

"It is a bottle of *Chateauneuf du Pape*," he said. "I was rooting around in that enclosure where you keep your recalcitrant slaves and I found this little wee bottle of *Chateauneuf du Pape* and it seemed to me that we ought to toast the day and the hour."

"What *is* the day of the month?" Mama asked.

"August eighth."

"The eighth of August!" Mama said. "My God! . . . Jenny," she called, "Jenny! I didn't know that this was the eighth of August. Honest!"

Jenny came and stood in the doorway. She smiled. "That's all right," she said, "I didn't have nowhere to go, except in to the movies with Mr. Stamper."

"Leave the dishes," Mama said. "Jenny, just leave every dish. Will you, please?"

"I'm nigh about through 'em," Jenny said.

Uncle Tubby had poured everybody a glass of wine. "We will drink to the emancipation of all of us," he said. "Can't tell when it'll be, but it's bound to come." He held his glass up and made them all touch glasses with him. "And to the day and the hour," he said, "for when shall we four meet again, in thunder, lightning and in rain . . . ? Hell, how do they go about making a night as beautiful as this?" And he walked to the end of the gallery and stood looking out.

"It is extraordinary, isn't it?" Mama said. "All the years we've known each other, this is the first week we've all been together in one place."

"That's what they mean by 'Never the time and the place and the loved one all together,' " Uncle Tubby said. When he found that the others wouldn't have another glass of wine he poured himself one and sat down with his chair tilted back against a pillar. A branch of the trumpet vine cast its shadow across his head and shoulders. Lucy thought that he had moved his chair over there so he could watch Mrs. Reardon who had pushed her chair back into the shadows, too, but she could not be sure. The black branch fell straight across his face; his eyes were black holes in what might have been a skull; only the glass that he twirled in his hand gleamed in the light from the window.

"Here comes Steve!" Mama said.

Daddy walked on to the gallery, carrying a bucket of milk in each hand. Jenny took the buckets from him. He sat down in the place they had kept for him.

"Well?" Mama said as she helped him to beef.

He laughed. "He'd milked, all right. But he got preoccupied with theological problems right afterwards and he couldn't remember what he'd done with the milk. But the preacher reconstructed the crime, play by play: Brother Peachtree. He's quite a fellow. We went back to the place they'd been walking and he said, 'Brother Terence, you was standing thar and I was standing hyar and you said you been a-wondering what become of Adam all the time Christ was walking hyar on this earth and I told you he was laying up in Abraham's bosom but you said, No, he had to stay whar he was till Christ got up thar himself. . . ."

"I be damn!" Uncle Tubby said.

"Oh, they're having a feast of reason and a flow of soul down thar. The preacher's good, but I don't believe he's any better theologian than Terence. . . . More of an extrovert. He was the one dived into the fence corner and found the bucket, right where they'd dropped it when they began to consider the Harrowing of Hell."

"Full of flies, I reckon," Mama said.

"I didn't notice. . . . Say, you know that preacher's a Turtle Ponder."

"He looks too young to be a Turtle Ponder," Mama said.

"Well, second generation, of course, but he comes of a line of martyrs. Arnold Watkins was his great-uncle. He's tremendously excited to be here on this place. For him it's like a visit to St. Mary Major. He and MacDonough went over to Arnold's grave this afternoon and stayed a long time."

"Where is it?" Mr. Reardon asked.

"Over there in the woods. They buried him there at the foot of a big rock, so he wouldn't be so likely to get plowed up."

Uncle Tubby got up and poured everybody another glass of wine. "You've been holding out on me," he said, "I never heard of Turtle Ponders till this minute."

"It's a case of the mission outstripping the mother church," Daddy said. "Arnold got his revelation about snake handling here on this place, and he died here of a snake-bite. But his son moved to East Tennessee. Place near Cleveland called Turtle Pond. He introduced snake handling into that neck of the woods. They call 'em 'Turtle Ponders' for that reason. . . ."

"Not giving the proper credit to Benfolly," Mama said.

". . . I don't know whether the son was stronger in the faith than his father, or more adept. At any rate, he was a power in the church and handled snakes right up to the end—that is, until the legislature made it unlawful to possess venomous reptiles. This fellow, Peachtree, remembers being held up as a kid to see him pick up a rattler and coil it about his neck. His wife went right along with him. Used to drape them on top of her head and dance."

Mama shuddered. "I *hope* the MacDonoughs don't take up handling," she said, "but they couldn't get the snakes, could they, Steve? There aren't any rattlesnakes around here, are there?"

"They've been found over in Stewart county, and in North

Todd, too, I think. It's too low for 'em here by the river."

The legs of Uncle Tubby's chair hit the brick floor with a thud. "Look at that!" he cried.

They all looked up, in time to see the star fall.

"It's the Perseids," Daddy said. "They start shooting this time of year."

"Wait!" Mama said. "There'll be another in a minute."

They sat with their faces upturned, studying the heavens. The stars were so thick that the sky seemed crowded. And yet each individual star seemed larger than it had been the other night and shone with a softer luster. As they watched, another star fell from its place and sliding downwards dissolved into golden dust.

"The Perseids," Mama said. "We ought to have had a party."

"How do you have a Perseid party?" Mrs. Reardon asked.

"Last year about twenty of us wrapped up in blankets and lay out here on top of the hill and watched 'em. With a bottle, of course. It was Jim Eglinton's idea. . . . Remember, Steve? When Evelyn was in Atlanta."

"Before I had had the pleasure of meeting her," Daddy said.

"I can't imagine Evelyn at a Perseid party," Uncle Tubby said. "Yes, I can, too. Why, she'd be *good* at a Perseid party!"

"If you lie on your back and look at the stars long enough it's as if they were coming right down on you," Mama said. "Then when one falls it's really terrific. You feel as if you'd helped to bring it down."

"Let's try it," Uncle Tubby said.

"I'm going down the hill," Daddy said. "I promised the brethren I'd look in on the meeting. There are going to be big doings tonight. They're going to try to pray Clarence Shaw's son on to his feet."

"The one that had polio?" Mama asked.

"He's down there now. On an iron cot. . . . Any of you all coming?"

Uncle Tubby held his hand up. "There they go now," he said. From below the chorus swelled suddenly and as suddenly subsided, except for one voice that, soaring, seemed to hang above the hill long after the others had died away.

"That tenor is Claude Lancaster. It's unearthly, isn't it?" Mama said and shivered.

"Are you cold, Sally?" Uncle Tubby asked. "Want me to get you a coat?"

"I'm not cold," Mama said. "At least if I am, I'm enjoying it."

"What about you, Isabel?" he asked. "Are you all right?"

"I'm all right," she answered from the shadows. "It's the same voice we heard that first night, isn't it?"

"Yes," he said, "that first night."

Daddy stood up. "I'd better be getting down there. Anybody else coming?"

"I'd like to," Mrs. Reardon said. "Isabel?"

She did not answer for a minute, then she said, "I haven't packed."

He went toward her. "It's our last night," he said. "Can't you pack when you get back? I'll help you."

She stepped a little way out from the shadow of the trumpet vine and paused. She looked at the others and smiled. "I'd be too sleepy then," she said.

"Tubby?" Daddy said.

He was staring at her and did not seem to hear.

"Tubby?" Daddy said again.

"Sure," he said.

Mama came out from the kitchen where she had been talking to Jenny. "I don't think I'll go," she said.

"Why?" Daddy asked.

"Jenny's going to the movies."

"Well, Isabel isn't going," Daddy said, "Lucy can stay with her."

"Oh. . . ." Mama said.

"Why can't *I* go to the meeting, Mama?" Lucy asked. "You *said* I could go to the meeting. Long time ago you said. . . ."

"Hell's bells!" Daddy said. "Let her go. It'll do her good to see some real religion. I'm thinking about joining up, myself."

Mama sighed. "How I'm ever going to raise this child!" she said.

Uncle Tubby had gone over to stand beside Mrs. Reardon. "I bet you don't pack," he said. "I bet you don't even go upstairs."

She looked up at him and laughed. "Oh, yes, I will," she said. "I'm going upstairs right now."

But she was still standing there in her white dress in the moonlight when somebody opened the little gate and they started down the path between the old shoes and rusted tin pans and broken bottles, past the MacDonough house, where only a single lamp burned, on down the hill to the brush arbor.

You could hear them a long time before you got there: all the people, saying the same thing. Lucy knew what it was: "Jesus, Jesus, Jesus, *Jesus, Jesus. . . .*" There were a lot of young boys standing outside the arbor. They moved aside as the people from the big house came down the path. Daddy went first, Lucy behind him, holding on to Mama's hand. They pushed through the leaves and were inside the arbor.

People were sitting on the benches and other people standing around the old, dead hickory tree whose peeled trunk shone like silver in the light. Some of them moved back and forth as they stood, almost as if they were dancing, and held their hands high in the air. Some of them were bending over, but moving from side to side. Through their swaying bodies you could see something white and yellow. One long lean man was bending lower than the others. He was hollering so loud that the back of his neck showed scarlet over his white collar: "Jesus, Jesus, Jesus, Jesus, JESUS, *JESUS*!"

A man turned around. It was Mr. MacDonough. His eyes glowed. He laughed like a child and touched the lean, red-necked man on the arm. The red-necked man straightened up. He looked at them hard out of round blue eyes, then took a handkerchief out of his pocket and wiped the sweat from his face. "Hallelujah!" he yelled. "Praise the Lamb!"

Mr. MacDonough, still smiling, touched Daddy on the arm, too, then turned to all the people. "This here is Mr. Steve Lewis," he said. "As good a man as you'll find in this country. And this here's his wife, Miss Sarah Lewis. Her price is above rubies. And this here. . . ." He stooped and laid his hand lightly on the top of Lucy's head. "This here is little Lucy Lewis." He paused, blinking. "Them others are folks that I don't know the name of. Been visiting them from New York City. But all of them are our precious visitors. And Jesus' visitors. All of 'em come down here to see Jesus, to meet Him face to face."

"Amen," an old man said and got up from his seat on the front bench and moved to a bench behind it. Mr. MacDonough made a sign to Daddy to sit down but Daddy shook his head and they found seats farther in the back. It was a short bench and there was not room for all of them. Mama and Daddy and Mr. Reardon sat on one seat. Uncle Tubby had to take a seat behind them.

Daddy was whispering to Mama: "I thought he was going to give me the Kiss of Peace there for a minute."

"Shut up!" Mama said. "Don't you see everybody's looking at you?"

Lucy looked around her. There were more people there than she had thought. You could not see them for the leaves. It was like being in the woods. Over all the people's heads, high or low, hung leaves. Some of the leaves were already withering but most of them were still fresh and green. Everywhere light was beaming softly through the green leaves; lanterns were hung on forked poles at the end of almost every aisle.

They were sitting on the men's side of the church, but she supposed that didn't make any difference, as none of them were Saved or Sanctified. But the man sitting in front of them had turned around when they sat down. His hair was dark with grease or dirt, except for the one wide, light streak that ran straight back from his forehead. His cold eyes had slid past her face to fasten on some object behind her. Claude Lancaster. He had not been able to go home when he came out of the pen. His wife said that she was afraid he would shoot the children and his mother had got to think more of the children than she did of him and she wouldn't let him come around the place. The MacDonoughs were the only people who would take him in. He had lived with them now for two months, but sometimes he went over to Stewart county and stayed a while—to see his girl, Ruby said.

She became aware that somebody's eyes were fixed on her face. She looked at the seat across the aisle. Ruby sat with the old baby in her arms. Mrs. MacDonough sat next to her, holding the new baby. In the space between her and Mary Magdalene Lura Belle and David were stretched out sound asleep. Ruby's russet-colored eyes met Lucy's. There was a brighter sparkle in them than Lucy had ever seen before. She grinned, then resolutely turned her face toward the front. "She's proud of what they're doing," Lucy thought. "She's glad I'm going to get to see it," and she, too, looked toward the platform that was built around the tree.

The people had sat down. There was nothing on the platform now except a stand with a Bible on it and a white iron cot that had a boy lying on it, propped up against pillows. His hair was as yellow as David's, but his face was lined and shrunken like an old man's. His eyes were closed. He had on a white shirt, with gold cuff links. You could not see the rest of his body; a quilt made of blue and pink and yellow patches covered the cot.

The preacher stepped up on the platform beside the boy. Under his thatch of stiff black hair his deep-set eyes glinted blue. He took his handkerchief out again and wiped the sweat from his neck and hands. "Our visitors come too late for the sermon," he said, "but they're in time for the testimony. And testimony showeth forth the fruit of the Spirit. . . . Brethren . . . Sisters. . . ."

An old woman got up: Mrs. Agnew, who lived up the road. She picked turnip greens and sold them in town on shares. In summer she had permission to pick all the blackberries she wanted on the place. Her hair was as white as cotton, but her face was the color of the dirt under your feet and darkly wrinkled. She had on a white dress that looked a little like the ones Mammy wore in the summer time and she was so bent over that she could hardly look the preacher in the face.

She said: "I love the Lord. He has been my husband, my keeper, for lo, these many years. I thank Him for going with me over the high-ways and by-ways. I want to go back with Him when He comes. For He's soon to come, though no man knoweth the day nor the hour."

She sat down. The preacher said: "Amen, Sister. . . . He's soon to come. . . ." He suddenly sprang to the edge of the platform, shouting, his face as red as a rooster's comb: "Jesus don't come to make you believe in Him. You got to believe in Him before He'll come. . . ."

"Good God!" Daddy said to Mr. Reardon, "he's quoting St. Augustine!"

"Shut up!" Mama whispered.

There was a rustle on the opposite seat. Ruby was standing up, holding the child in her arms. She gave Lucy a sidelong glance, then she looked at the preacher. "I want to thank Him for keeping me saved all day," she said in a high, thin voice. "And all week, too. And the week before that. I ain't had a mean thought now in three weeks. I want to thank Him for keeping me pure in heart."

The preacher nodded. "Amen," he said. "Of such is the Kingdom of Heaven." His eyes roamed over the faces. His gaze brightened suddenly. "Brother Terence," he said, "you got a message for us?"

Mr. MacDonough had gone around to a seat on the side of the arbor but now he rose and stepped lightly out in front to where the boy lay on his cot. The boy's head was bent, his eyes fixed on his hands that were folded in his lap. Sweat glistened on his sunken temples. As Mr. MacDonough passed, the boy raised his head with a sickly flash of his blue eyes. Mr. MacDonough stopped and looked down at him. "Poor brother," he said, laying his hand on the boy's shoulder, and walked over and laid the same hand on the trunk of the dead tree before he faced the congregation.

He stood and looked at them a moment. His eyes shone. He

said: "A man's friends are not always those of his own household. I've been sitting here thinking about this tree. It don't look like much. Been dead a long time, we say. But it ain't dead to me. To me it's already shining in its glorified body. This tree is the best friend I've got in this world, the best friend I e'er had in this world. . . ."

"Amen," the preacher said and stepped over to the other side of the platform.

Mr. MacDonough turned again and ran his hand over the trunk of the tree. It was so old and so dry that it looked like bone, bone that might have been washed up out of some ocean. Mr. MacDonough smiled as he touched it. "This here's a scaly bark hickory," he said. "The bark has done dropped off hit long ago. But in the old days them big hickories was all over this river bottom. Must have been a pretty sight then. But when I was born—over yonder on Mr. Adam Ezell's place—there wasn't e'er one of them trees left, except this old fellow. Hit was in March, along about the time that the hickory buds swell, so big and so full of sap that you think it's flowers opening out, but it turns into leaves, green leaves, with little tossels to 'em. I come under this tree, I passed under the lowest branches, with a tow sack full of potatoes on my back. We had done run out and a neighbor was carrying us till ours come in. They told me to get back home in a hurry, which was why I was taking the short cut across the fields. But I war'n't hurrying myself. I was studying up some devilment I was going to do that night with Ellis Moseley lived up the road from us then. It's twenty years ago and I can't remember what it was we aimed to do that night. All I remember is it war'n't for the glory of God. Then I passed under one of the branches of this tree—hit was a big tree then and spread its branches far and wide and the fowls of the air come and sat in them. I passed under one of the low-swinging boughs and something touched me on the shoulder and I looked up, same as you turn around when a friend comes up behind you and lays his hand on your shoulder and says 'Terence' . . . 'Terence!' it says and I jumped and turned around. But there war'n't nobody there. 'Terence!' it says again and I looked up and there over my head was a million leaves. A million leaves and besides each leaf a tossel raining its golden powder on the ground, and standing there, under that tree, a shirt-tail boy that hadn't been up to nothing but mischief all his life, *I saw how it was. . . .*"

He stepped down off the platform. His red, knuckly hands were stretched out in front of them. His eyes gleamed. *"I saw how it was!"* he repeated. "Hit war'n't leaves and tossels. Hit was *God*. God, raining down on the ground! I stood there till the sack dropped off my back and I didn't even know it was gone. . . . Twenty years ago this March, but it's like I never moved out from under this tree. . . ."

A woman sitting in front of Mrs. MacDonough cried out suddenly: *"Like he never moved!"* Her head tilted sharply backwards. Her gaping mouth hurled words at the leafy ceiling. "God!" she cried. *"God!* Raining down on the ground!" and leaped from her seat and ran, half crouching, up the aisle, then whirled, to face the congregation before her body whirled again, like a tree whipped by a storm, and she bent over the boy, her hands weaving to and fro before his face. "*Jesus Jesus Jesus!* Heal him. YOU CAN DO IT!"

The boy kept his face set toward hers. His yellow lashes glistened; he winked each time her hands approached him. Then his lips distended. He made a wry mouth and trembling all over, shut his eyes and turned his face up to the ceiling.

The preacher stepped down off the platform. "That's the kind of faith you got to have!" he shouted. "That's the kind of faith you got to have if you're going to move mountains!"

There was a commotion in the seat in front of them. Claude Lancaster had risen and stood, tall and lean in his dark Sunday suit, before he slipped past two or three people sitting on the same bench and went quietly out the side way.

Two or three more women moved up the aisle. Men were stumbling up, too. You could not see the boy now, for the figures bending over him. Some of them swayed from side to side, tossing their arms. Others stood up straight, their hands raised high. The fingers of all of them clawed the air.

"They're bringing it down," Daddy whispered. "I' God, they're bringing it down!"

"Do you think it would be all right if I stood up?" Mama whispered, "I can't see."

He did not answer. He had turned his head and was looking up the middle aisle.

Claude Lancaster was walking slowly between the leafy boughs, holding a box in his hands: a wooden box, shaped like a rabbit trap that had a hole in the front of it and another hole in the side. He carried it held out before him, level with his chest. His pale eyes stared straight before him as he went.

Lights flared in the preacher's sunken eyes. He turned his head and looked at Mr. MacDonough. Mr. MacDonough slowly turned his head, too; his dark eyes swept all the faces before they came to rest on Claude's face. "Set her down there, Claude," he said.

Claude Lancaster continued to stand, holding the box out before him.

Mr. MacDonough stepped down off the platform to stand beside him. "Set it down," he said gently. "You brought it, didn't you? Are you feared to set it down?"

Claude Lancaster stooped and lowered the box until it rested on the ground at the foot of the platform, then walked over and sat down in a place that somebody made for him on the front bench.

The preacher jumped down off the platform. Crouching before the people, he threshed the air with his arms. "These signs!" he shouted. "These signs shall follow them that believe. . . . In my name. . . . In my name they shall cast out devils. They shall speak with tongues. . . ."

Across the aisle Mrs. MacDonough suddenly groaned and turned her face up to the ceiling. Lucy turned around and looked behind her. Uncle Tubby was not there.

"They shall move mountains!" the preacher shouted. "They shall take up serpents!"

Mr. MacDonough was walking slowly toward the box. He paused in front of it and raised his arms high above his head. "In His name!" he cried and his lean body swung backward and his foot went out and struck the box so sound a blow that it was moved a little from its place.

Everything got still. He drew his foot back and kicked the box again. This time you could hear the whirr from inside.

Mama's arm was suddenly around Lucy's shoulders. She was jerking Lucy's head in to hide it against her breast, Lucy struggled, tasting wet cloth, choking. "Let me go!" she sobbed, "Mama, let me go!" and broke from her mother's embrace and stood up.

Mama was staring at Daddy. "It *was* a rattlesnake, wasn't it?" she whispered.

He nodded his head.

"Then *do* something!" she cried. "You've got to do something!"

"I've got to get you and Lucy out of here first," he said and set his hand on Lucy's shoulder so hard it hurt. Mama got on the other side of her. They were pushing through the crowd to the side entrance. One old woman kept blocking the way.

Her hair was all torn about her face. In the black hole of her mouth her teeth gleamed yellow. She was whimpering like a dog.

Daddy pushed the old woman aside. A branch tore at Lucy's cheek. She turned her head to look back. Mrs. MacDonough was there, on one side of Mr. MacDonough, the preacher on the other. His arms were laid across their shoulders, the hands dangling limply. His head was thrown backwards. His eyes were closed, his cheeks sunk in. His mouth, a little open, showed teeth that were no larger than a child's. From the platform above the boy leaned forward, doll-like, over his pink and blue and yellow quilt, to stare down at them.

The air outside was fresh. Daddy stumbled over a bottle and cursed. Mama swung on to his arm. "Hurry," she said, "oh, please hurry!"

There were steps on the path. Mr. Reardon came up beside them.

"Where's Tubby?" Mama said.

Nobody answered her. They passed the hen house and came to the gate. Daddy let go of Lucy's arm to open it. Mama ran through ahead of them and stopped halfway to the porch. "Jim Eglinton," she said. "Permanganate of potash, isn't it?"

"He'll know," Daddy said and strode up on to the brick porch. They followed him through the kitchen and into the little hall where the telephone was. He fixed his eyes on Mama's face as he rang the bell. "They may not let him do anything after he gets here," he said. "You realize that, don't you?"

Mama snatched the receiver out of his hand. "Let me do it," she cried.

Daddy stood aside. She gave the operator a number. When she got it she took a deep breath and began talking very fast, smiling all the time:

"Sheriff Beauchamp?"

. . . .

"Mister Will, this is Miss Sally Fayerlee's granddaughter. . . ."

. . . .

"She's fine. How are you all?"

. . . .

"Oh, that's too bad. . . . Mister Will, we're having a little trouble out on our place. . . ."

. . . .

"One of our men. An awfully good man."

. . . .

"He's been bitten by a rattlesnake. . . ."

. . . .

"Yes, but he didn't do it. It was brought here by Claude Lancaster."

. . . .

"Yes. Hasn't been out of the pen six months. . . ."

. . . .

"Well, you know how they are. I thought if you sent two or three men. . . ."

. . . .

"Yes, I'm going to call him. But I thought I'd call you first."

. . . .

"Oh, thank you so much!"

. . . .

"Yes, we will. You come to see us."

She laid the receiver back on the hook and put her face down on her clasped hands. Her shoulders were shaking. Lucy began to cry. Her father took her in his arms. "It's going to be all right," he said. "We're going to get Dr. Eglinton out here to cure Mr. MacDonough."

Mama came over and put her arms around Lucy too. "Don't cry," she said. "Darling, *don't* cry!"

Daddy had taken up the receiver again. Mr. Reardon laid his hand on Mama's arm. "Come out on the porch," he said. "You can't do anything else now until the doctor comes."

They went out on the gallery. Mama sank down in the long chair and drew Lucy down beside her. "It's going to be all right," she said. "There is something they give. I think it is permanganate of potash. It acts instantly. Jim Eglinton will know all about that. He is a doctor. Doctors know all about that kind of thing. . . ." She turned her head to stare off over the lawn. Out on the lawn, a little way from where they sat, was a heap of something that had not been there when they sat here an hour ago.

"What is that?" Mama asked. "What *is* that thing out there?"

Mr. Reardon got up and walked over and stood for a second looking down at it before he came back. "It's blankets," he said.

"Blankets?" Mama said. "Oh . . . blankets?"

Daddy was coming through the door. "He's got the stuff and says he can be out here in six minutes. I told him the officers would probably get here before he did."

There was a scream, like some great creature that nobody had ever seen, wailing in the night. Mama jumped up and clapped her hands to both sides of her head.

"It's the siren," Daddy said and ran around the corner of the house. Mama and Mr. Reardon and Lucy followed him. Three pairs of eyes, large enough to be in a giant's head, were moving steadily up the driveway. The motorcycles were abreast as they came to a stop under the willow tree. One by one the machines fell to the ground as the big men flung themselves off them. They said: "Which way, Mr. Lewis?"

"Down the hill," Daddy said and ran after them toward the gate.

Mama started after them, then stopped. Daddy turned back from the gate. "Come on," he cried. "There might be something you can do."

"I'll take care of the doctor," Mr. Reardon said. He came over to Lucy and took her arm in his warm, hard grip. "I'll take care of Lucy, too," he said.

The doctor's lights were already glowing at the foot of the drive. They walked down to meet him. "It's this way," Mr. Reardon said and showed him the way through the little gate. He went through the gate, stooping, his bag swinging from his right hand. Once or twice dark figures stepped off the path to make way for him. They stood and watched until they saw him stoop to go under the boughs, then walked back toward the house. As they went they could still hear all the voices, but now that they had turned their backs on them they did not sound so loud. The moonlight was as bright as day.

They went in the front way. He stopped in the hall. "I have to go upstairs," he said. "You come with me."

They went up the stairs to the third floor. There was a light burning in his wife's room. The covers of the bed had not been turned down. The closet door was half open. He went over and looked inside and came back to stand beside the bed. He put his hand out and touched the night table. "There was a clock," he said, "a round, traveling clock. . . ."

"I saw it," Lucy said.

He started. He walked over to the dresser and stood with his back turned looking down at its smooth surface. He picked up a squat white jar and unscrewed the lid and held the empty jar in his hand before he threw it into the wastebasket and turned around.

"Let's go downstairs," he said.

They walked down the stairs. He went into the parlor and turned the lights on and turned the lights on in the hall, too. Then he went out on the gallery. Lucy followed him. He sat down. She sat down, too. They sat silent. From the slope below came a confused din of voices. Lanterns had begun to move over the field.

"I think he'll be all right," he said. "The doctor got there in time."

She did not answer.

"Yes," he said abstractedly. "I think he'll be all right." Suddenly he gave his shoulders a shake. "I've got to go in the house a minute," he said.

She stared at him in silence. He stared back at her. "You're not afraid to stay here by yourself?" he asked.

Slowly she shook her head.

He went into the house. She watched him mounting the stairs. Halfway up he paused, then turned off up the short flight of stairs that led to the ell. He was going to Uncle Tubby's room. But there was nobody in that room, either. He knew that but he had to go and stand in that empty room before he could say that they were really gone.

She slid from her chair and walked through the hall. The lamp had not been turned on in her bedroom but the gold letters gleamed in the shaft of light that fell in through the open door. She took the box from its hiding place behind the book and opened the box and took the object she sought out of it and threw the box down on the bed. She went back to the gallery. She was sitting, perched on the edge of the chair, her thin legs dangling, when he returned. As he came through the door, she extended her hand with the crucifix flat upon it.

He did not seem to see the shining thing. He walked past

her and, going over to the end of the gallery, stood with his back turned to her while he gripped the banisters with both hands.

She got up and went toward him, still holding the crucifix out. "Here," she said.

He started and faced her, staring. Slowly he took the crucifix from her. He held it up before him. It had never looked so beautiful to her as at that moment. In the hands and the feet, the rubies, gleaming darkly, rounded like drops of blood that might spill to the floor. Light shone from the eyes; a paler light on the white brow under the clotted curls. He turned it to and fro in his hand, as if trying to see how much light it would give, before his fingers suddenly closed upon it and he thrust it into his pocket. He was bending toward her.

She said: "Jenny. . . ."

"Jenny. . . .?" he said.

"She didn't take it."

His eyes came back from a distance to meet hers. "Where did you find it then?"

"I didn't *find* it," she said.

His own features were suddenly contorted, as if with anger. He said roughly: "You . . . I never thought . . ." and would have said more, but the child was crying and there were voices outside and steps in the hall. He put his arm about Lucy's shoulders and drew her forward to face her father and mother.

"What's the matter with her?" Sarah asked.

"Nothing. She's all right."

"But she's behaved so strangely. All week."

"She's all right," he said. "Is the man going to live?"

"Yes," Sarah said. "Jim got to him in time."

She sank down in the hammock. Her husband sat down on a chair beside it. "They didn't make any trouble," he said. "Even the preacher was willing for him to have it. But it was a good thing we had the Law there, just the same." He leaned over to take his wife's hand. "Honey, that was quite a stroke, telephoning the sheriff."

But she was sitting bolt upright in the hammock, staring down over the railing. "Those blankets!" she said. A sharper note came into her voice. "They were lying out there to watch the stars, weren't they?"

Reardon did not answer. She got up out of the hammock and went toward him. "They're gone?" she asked.

"Yes," he said.

She turned to her husband. "Tubby and Isabel have eloped."

"That's obvious," he said.

"You wouldn't believe me!" she said.

He was looking at Reardon. "Kev, how long has this been going on?" he asked.

"It started at St. Tropez," Reardon said. "Those three months that she was out of the hospital."

"Do you mean she had just got out of the hospital when he came down there?" Sarah asked.

He nodded.

"But what made them let her out?"

"It was my fault. She begged so hard. But I wouldn't have taken her out if I had known he was coming. It was understood that we were not to have any company. . . . She invited Jim Ferrebee, too, but he wouldn't come. But Tubby came. Then after he came she seemed so much better. And I liked having him there, too. I thought it was all right."

"Did she go back to the hospital after he left?"

"Yes. She was at St. Giles nine months after that."

"And you made them let her come over here with you?"

"I hated to come without her. And I didn't think we'd run into him."

"She telegraphed him to meet her here," Stephen Lewis said.

"I know it."

"Did you ever *tell* him she was mad?" Sarah Lewis asked.

"I tried to, once. . . ."

"He wouldn't believe you?"

He laughed. "I don't believe it, myself—sometimes."

"Do they think she can be cured?" Stephen Lewis asked.

Reardon shook his head. "We didn't find out soon enough."

"They think she is incurable?" Lewis persisted.

"They don't anticipate any radical change in her condition for some years. That's why they let me take her out of the hospital every now and then."

"I suppose so," Lewis said absently. He stared at his daughter. He lifted her chin and looked into her face.

He walked to the railing and looked down on the moon-drenched lawn. He raised his eyes to the sky. There was a rustle behind him. A slight form pressed up against his. He put his arms around the child's shoulders and drew her closer while his eyes ranged the heavens. There was his own sign, Scorpio: "The House of Death—unless a man be re-born." His friend had always been full of curious lore. . . . A Perseid fell, trailing its golden dust, and then another: little meteors that had been falling through space for God knows how many years. But the other stars that shone so high and cold would fall, too, like rotten fruit—when the heavens were rolled up like a scroll and the earth reeled to and fro like a drunkard and men called upon the mountains to fall upon them and hide them from the wrath to come. This very hill upon which he stood would shake. The river which lapped it so gently might turn and, raging against it, tear it from its green base and hurl it toward the sea. But there would be no sea!

He passed his hand over his brow. His eyes went to the house below where a single lamp glowed murkily. There a man still lay at the point of death. He told himself that it would have been no great matter if that man had died tonight, for all men, it appeared to him now, for the first time, die on the same day: the day on which their appointed task is finished. If that man had made his last journey tonight he would not have gone alone, but companioned by a larger presence, as the friend standing behind him had been companioned when he, too, lay at the point of death, in a strange country and in a desert. But all countries, he told himself wearily, are strange and all countries desert. He thought of another man, the friend of his youth, who only a few minutes ago had left his house without farewell. He had considered him the most gifted of all his intimates. Always when he thought of that friend a light had seemed to play about his head. He saw him now standing at the edge of a desert that he must cross: if he turned and looked back his face would be featureless, his eye sockets blank. Stephen Lewis thought of days, of years that they had spent together. He saw that those days, those years had been moving toward this moment and he wondered what moment was being prepared for him and for his wife and his child, and he groaned, so loud that the woman and the child stared at him, wondering, too.